Unseen Carnage

By

Joe B. Parr

Also by Joe B Parr

The Victim
Stolen Innocence

For the real Jessica Hunter and her parents, Alan and Deb.

Chapter 1

The gun in his hand was still warm, his feet stood in a pool of blood that had expanded outward from under the body. His face reflected in its smooth surface, distorted, almost unrecognizable.

Oh God...

His nose filled with the copper scent. The room swirled and shadows danced as his mind consumed the scene around him. His pulse pounded in his ears as he looked down at the man he hated, the vacant eyes, the open mouth, the gaping wound in the middle of the chest.

For a moment, he was calm as he thought about the carnage this man had inflicted.

You got what you deserved, bastard.

The satisfied smile evaporated as the sound of sirens growing louder jerked his head up. He froze in place and stared at the inside of the front door willing the sound to fade. Tires breaking hard on the pavement dashed those hopes. His heart rate jumped and his chest tightened. As if some revelation was hidden just out of sight, he looked frantically around the room. He found none, only metal shelves crowded with industrial parts, boxes and junk.

Car doors slammed, footsteps and voices filled the air outside. He saw shadows stretch across the dust covered blinds.

What do I do? They won't understand. I have to get out!

He breathed so hard that when he looked at the gun in his hand, his eyes could barely focus. On autopilot, his hand shoved it in the pocket of his hoodie. He turned and ran for the back door. Barely able to control his movements, his muscles twitched as he stumbled over a step and banged into a shelf. Junk flew in all directions and metal crashed to the ground, tripping him down the short hall.

The banging on the front door was drowned out by the slamming of the back door against the wall as he opened it. The muggy night air hit him in the face, sweat instantly appeared on his forehead. He stopped, leaned against the open door, looked back toward the body and the front door. He sucked in several breaths, the gulps so thick with humidity, he almost choked.

When the front door exploded off its hinges, it was as if a starter pistol had been fired.

"Fort Worth Police!"

The balls of his feet dug into the concrete and for a moment it was High School again and he was back on the synthetic rubber track, his only mission to outrun everyone around him. The back door slammed behind him and the sounds of the shouting from inside faded. His feet churned down the sidewalk, hammering like pistons. The back door crashed open and voices barked at him.

"Fort Worth Police! Stop where you are!"

He ducked into an alley on his left, and pressed his back against the wall, the bricks scratching through his sweat soaked T-shirt. He tried to listen over his gasping breathe. His chest heaved. . More shouting, more footsteps.

"Do you see him? Where'd he go?"

What now?

The voices continued to get louder. They'd find him if he didn't move. He took off down the dark alley trying to get away from his pursuers, stumbling over debris. His momentary advantage lost with his clumsiness. They were getting closer, relentless in their hunt.

"I hear him. This way."

Scratching, clawing, weaving his way through the obstacles, he raced toward the open end of the alley. Lights switched on around him and dogs barked as the neighborhood woke around him. He had to get away.

Can't stop. They won't understand.

The opening was just ahead. When he bolted past the corner, the world lit up. Bright red and blue lights flashing from everywhere. Tires screeched as a blinding white light hit him. He blinked and stumbled, disoriented.

"Police! Freeze!"

He shielded his eyes with one hand as the world spun around him. His body tried to move in all directions at once but seemed glued to the pavement.

"Let me see your hands! Now!"

The gun! Oh God!

His hand reached into his pocket, gripped the metal. He pushed his hands forward toward the voice, tried to yell. Two muzzle flashes, two deafening explosions. His body jerked backwards. The gun dropped from his hand and he stumbled, his legs numb and wobbly.

No. You don't understand.

The sounds of shoes slapping the pavement, shouting and the rumble of an engine enveloped him. He was on his back but couldn't feel the ground. The moon was directly above him. Full and bright. He hadn't noticed that earlier. A policeman stood over him now, shaking his head. He watched his lips move, but he couldn't understand the words. The chaos faded as the world went quiet. Then it went dark.

*　　*　　*　　*

Looking out from the dark alley, everything moved in slow motion. The gun in his hand silhouetted against the brightly lit street and smoke rose from the barrel after the two shots he'd fired. His hand, steady to that point, trembled slightly. The smell of cordite mixed with the heavy air filled his eyes and nose. In spite of the ringing in his ears, he could hear the labored breathing of the officer standing just behind his left shoulder. They hadn't run far but the adrenaline of the chase had amped them both up. He felt his own pulse now as his feet seemed to be stuck in place and his arm locked outward, the tremble becoming more pronounced.

I told him to stop. Why did he pull his gun?

The body lay in a heap in the middle of the road, awash in the spotlight from the police cruiser. No sound or movement, just a pile of rumpled laundry. A patrolman rushed over, holstered his weapon and stood over the lump, shook his head. The officer's lips moved as he motioned toward him.

Fort Worth Police Detective Jake Hunter had just shot a man. From the lack of movement and the reaction of the officer, the shot was apparently fatal.

Oh God. I didn't want to do that. He left me no choice.

"Detective?" The voice from over his shoulder made him to blink. "Your weapon."

As the officer tentatively clasped his shoulder, he realized he was still holding the gun out in firing position, his knuckles white on the handle. "Sorry." It was more of a mumble than a statement as he lowered his hand. He slid the Glock 17 back into the holster.

The world jumped back to full speed and the sound of the scene crashed through his ears. The officer standing over the body spoke into his radio and motioned for Hunter to step over. People seemed to appear from thin air, three more officers, a small crowd of onlookers. None of them had been there seconds earlier.

Or had they?

Hunter stepped over to the body on the ground hoping that his observations based on lack of movement were wrong. They weren't. He thought back on the only other time he'd shot a suspect. He barely winged the man and it seemed to have pissed him off more than hurt him. This was different. This guy would never be pissed off again.

Why did this have to happen? There was no reason for him to do that.

"Are you okay?" The officer searched Hunter's face.

He nodded robotically. "Yeah, fine. I just need a moment."

"You had no choice, Detective." The officer pointed back toward a parked patrol car. "My partner and I had just pulled up. We heard you identify yourself. He drew his weapon before we were set."

Hunter looked at the officer and realized how young he looked. The patrolman's eyes were wide, pupils dilated. A combination of fear and adrenaline.

He barely looks old enough to shave.

"Yeah." Hunter nodded absently. A paramedic brushed past him and knelt beside the body, but instead of working frantically, seemed to only go through the motions. There was no life left to save.

When he looked over the paramedic's shoulder, he stared down at the face of a young black man. Clean shaven and smooth, it was the look of a fraternity boy, not a street thug. He wore a plain white T shirt and a light weight charcoal hoodie. The picture didn't seem to make sense. He didn't look like a murderer, but beside him on the pavement lay a 9mm semi-automatic handgun.

Hunter's throat constricted and he closed his eyes. His body grew heavy with the realization of what he'd done.

Why did you do it?

Chapter 2

Hunter pulled up to the side of the small wood frame house and heard the radio call.

Officer down.

His mind raced as he jumped from his SUV and climbed the four steps to the front porch in two long strides. The first thing he saw when he topped the stairs was the huge hole in the flimsy front door. Ragged and splintered. What was left of the screen was pushed out and mangled, shards of glass littered the ground. He looked down at the figure lying on the concrete and froze.

Frank. Oh God.

A patrolman kneeling beside Frank had his head down, not moving. Hunter shoved him out of the way, dropped to his knees and grabbed his partner's hand but felt no response. He grabbed his shoulder and shook him. A gurgle rose from Frank's limp body. Hunter recoiled, his vision expanded to take in more of the scene. Blood was everywhere. Frank's shirt was shredded and soaked. What was left of his chest looked more like red stew than a person.

Hunter surveyed Frank's face. "Frank. Talk to me Frank!"

There was no response. Hunter's vision tunneled as he pulled back, his mind fogging over.

"Cowboy?" Detective Billy Sanders' voice sounded distant. "Cowboy, you okay?"

Hunter's mind snapped back to the moment, the muggy night air wrapped around him like a blanket. The warm asphalt dug into his knee as he looked down at the young man sprawled on the ground in front of him. He shook his head to chase away the memory.

"Cowboy." Sanders' hand touched his shoulder. "Why don't you step over to the wagon with me? Let the techs do their job here."

Hunter nodded blankly, the numbness saturated his lean, six-foot two-inch frame as he walked with Billy. The movement and chaos of the scene blurred around him as he sat on the bumper of the mobile ICU truck. Someone wrapped a blanket around his shoulders, and he looked up to a concerned expression on Billy's brown face.

"I'm fine." Hunter swiped a hand through his close cropped hair that was mostly brown but showing enough gray so that no one would confuse him for a rookie. "Stop staring at me like that. You look like my mother."

"You don't look fine. You're pale." Sanders halfheartedly laughed. "More than usual."

"It's the moonlight reflecting off your bald head." Hunter tried to downplay his condition. "Besides, what are you doing here anyway? Shouldn't you be home by now?" He pulled the blanket closer around his shoulders as a shiver spasmed down his body, in spite of the early summer temperature.

"It's shaved, not bald. Big difference." Sanders joined him on the bumper, his broad shoulders crowding the space. "I was almost home when I got the call that my partner had been in a shooting. That was a bit of a surprise since you too were supposed to be home."

The two sat for a moment, not speaking, just watching the choreographed movements of the crime scene. They'd been partners for nine months. Billy had only been a detective for those same nine months. Sanders broke the silence. "The patrolman said you'd been kneeling beside the body for thirty minutes. What happened?"

Hunter replayed the night in his head before answering. "He drew his weapon. I fired." He cocked his head and stared at nothing in particular. "It happened so fast. I had no choice."

"I know that part. The uniforms saw the whole thing." Sanders put his strong hand on Hunter's shoulder. "I meant, why were you even here? You left the Monticello Park scene over an hour ago. I thought you were going home."

"I was." Hunter shook his head. "I took University to

Northside Drive and was going to hit I-35 North. I had the scanner on for background noise." He shrugged. "Old habit, I guess." He paused, exhaled heavily. "When I crossed Jacksboro Highway, there was a call saying someone had heard shots." He hung his head. "Jesus, I should have just kept going."

Sanders kept his hand on Hunter's shoulder. He stayed quiet but his eyebrows knitted together in concern.

"The scene was a few blocks north of my location, a building at the corner of West Central and Clinton. I pulled up at the same time the uniforms got there." He paused as if reliving the scene in his head. "We looked in the window, saw a figure and some movement and made the call to breach the door."

Hunter took a deep breath, let it out slowly. "As we entered through the front, the back door was just closing from someone blowing out of it in a hurry. I shouted for one of the patrolmen to stay with the body and chased after the guy. The other patrolmen and I pursued on foot out the back." He continued to stare off into space like he was watching the scene on a movie screen. "It was dark and we lost the guy for a moment, but then he must've tripped on something. We heard a crash between the buildings, and followed him as he thrashed down the alley."

Sanders nodded. "That was when he drew his weapon."

"Yeah. He came out of the alley, and another unit hit him with their spots, and he froze." Hunter gave a helpless shrug. "I raised my weapon, and identified myself." He blinked rapidly. "There was no place for him to go. He was caught. It was over. I thought he was going to raise his hands. Hell, I started to relax." Hunter stopped.

"What happened?"

Hunter noticed his hands shaking and grabbed the edge of the bumper so that Sanders wouldn't see. "His hands were supposed to go up. But instead he reaches for his pocket and a gun comes out." He inhaled and exhaled again. "It scared the shit out of me. I heard two shots before I even realized it was my gun." His voice went hoarse. "I killed him. I killed the kid."

"He wasn't a kid. He was a suspect fleeing the scene of a

murder. Hell, he pointed a gun at you."

Both detectives looked up as a CSI tech approached. He handed Sanders a clear evidence bag with a wallet inside. "Thought you might want this."

Sanders nodded and set the bag down by his hip, away from Hunter. "Thanks."

Hunter turned and his eyes bore into Billy. "What was his name?"

Sanders' shoulders deflated. He shook his head and picked up the bag. The wallet flipped open with a display window for the driver's license. "Brandon Jenkins. Nineteen years old."

Hunter dropped his head. He closed his eyes and swallowed hard. After a moment, the Medical Examiner walked up with his two assistants. Dr. Benjamin Grimes was an older gentleman with unruly gray hair, a slight paunch and wearing a tweed jacket in spite of the heat. He looked more like a university professor than someone you'd see at a crime scene.

He stepped over and spoke in a tone far too refined to match his having grown up in Waco, TX. "How are you, Cowboy? I understand you had a close call this evening."

Hunter jutted his chin toward where the technicians had begun to process the body. "Considering the alternative, Doc, I think I'm doing just fine."

The concern in Doc's eyes didn't diminish. "According to the patrolman, the suspect didn't give you much of a choice."

"No, he didn't."

Doc patted him on the shoulder and looked at Sanders. "Take good care of him Billy."

Sanders nodded as Doc ambled back toward the scene.

Hunter and Sanders fell into an uncomfortable silence. Both men were lost in thought and neither seemed to notice the young patrolman until he spoke. "Detective Hunter, sir, my partner and I saw the whole thing. You did the right thing."

His sharp voice penetrated Hunter's thoughts. "Thanks." Hunter's voice was a raspy whisper.

"If it makes you feel better, we caught it all on the dashcam."

He thumbed over his shoulder toward his car. "The video shows the whole thing clear as day."

Hunter didn't move, but Sanders' head snapped up and his eyes widened as they followed the patrolman's direction. "Can we see it?"

His stomach lurched and Hunter gritted his teeth to calm his reaction. *The last thing I want to see right now is a video of me gunning down a kid.*

"Sure." The patrolman's head bobbed. "We can pull it up right in the car." He turned to walk toward his car and motioned for them to follow.

Hunter started to shake his head but felt Sanders tugging on his arm before he could protest. Sanders' voice was firm. "Come on. You need to see this so you can know you didn't have a choice." He didn't have the strength to argue.

The patrolman sat in the driver's seat with the door open and angled the mounted laptop display up so they could see. Sanders leaned in for a closer view but Hunter held back, preferring to watch from a distance. The officer punched a couple of keys. "The video starts when I slammed it into park."

As the scene started, it took a moment for the movement of the car to subside so that the picture stopped shaking. When it did, it was as if someone had staged a movie. A young, athletic, black man ran into the frame and stopped abruptly, shielding his eyes against the bright spotlights from the patrol car. There was background noise and lots of yelling but Hunter could hear his own voice clearly over the din. "Freeze, Police. Let me see your hands now!"

Hunter's heart raced as he watched the image of the young man turn to his voice. For a split second, he froze in his tracks. Then the man jerked his arm down toward his pocket. When Hunter saw the man begin this move, he fought the urge to walk away. Instead he turned his head so he didn't have to watch. He closed his eyes when he heard the shots.

Sanders watched the scene intently. "See Cowboy, you had no choice." He turned to see Hunter looking down, his face once again flushed and his eyes moist. He reached out and touched his shoulder. "Jake, you had to do it."

Hunter nodded his head but didn't speak. He leaned with his back against the car and closed his eyes.

"Detective Hunter?" A voice that sounded like a pack a day jolted him. His eyes opened to see a badge being displayed. "I'm Detective Curt Benson with Internal Affairs. We need to talk."

Chapter 3

He knew what it was like to kill a suspect in the line of duty. He also knew what it was like to almost be killed. Sanders may have been the younger of the detectives, but this was one area in which he was the most experienced.

The crime scene activity continued around him as he stood in the street a few yards behind the mobile ICU truck. He stretched his muscular running back frame before he removed a handkerchief from his pocket and wiped his forehead. Watching Hunter and Benson, from Internal Affairs, walk away toward an unmarked cruiser, he thought about how difficult the next few weeks would be for Hunter.

He shook his head. *Hang in there Cowboy.*

"Billy, where is he?" The normally melodic tone to Stacy Morgan's voice was tinged with urgency. He turned to see her vibrant green eyes wide with fear.

"He's with the IAD detective." He nodded in the direction of the car.

Her frantic eyes followed, searching in the dark street. "Is he okay?"

Billy nodded. "He says he's fine. But I know better. He's pretty shook up." He looked at his watch, noted it was now almost eleven, then pointed back toward the building. "Come on. It's getting late. We've got work to do."

He took a couple of steps and paused until she finally broke her stare and followed. She paused again when she saw the ME tech working over the body still lying in the road.

Her voice was hesitant. "Is that…"

"Yeah." Sanders held out the evidence bag with the wallet and driver's license.

Stacy looked at the license. Her hand moved to her throat. "Oh God, he was just a kid."

"It was a good shoot. The guy pulled a gun." He touched her elbow to move her toward the building. "Our focus needs to be inside for now. We know what happened out here. The IAD guys and Doc's team will take care of this scene for now. When they're through, they'll let us know."

They backtracked the path of Hunter's chase, walking carefully through the junk filled alley. The overly sweet smell of rotting garbage assaulted their nostrils and made them pick up their pace as they stepped around a dumpster.

*   *   *   *

Hunter stared out the window of the unmarked cruiser and answered variations of the same questions. "As I said, when we came through the front door, we caught a glimpse of someone leaving out the back door and we followed."

"And you didn't see who it was at that time?"

"No. All I saw was the back of someone in a hoodie."

"So you can't be sure the person you shot was the same person you saw leaving the building, can you?"

"We were right on his tail as he ran out into the parking area. We lost him momentarily, but then heard noises from the alley and gave chase." Hunter paused, leaned forward and ran his hand through his hair. His heart rate ticked up as he relived the chase. "We caught up to him when he cleared the alley and ran out into the street."

"And that was when you shot him?" Bensons' voice cut through Hunter.

"That was when I identified myself. He drew his weapon, leaving me no alternative but to discharge my weapon" He turned and glared at Benson, his voice growing louder. "You've seen the video. What was I supposed to do?"

Detective Benson returned his glare. He was a large, unattractive man whose facial skin seemed too tight for its frame. His close-cropped, copper hair matched the dark freckles across the bridge of his nose. "Detective Hunter, I'm just doing my job. Please don't take it personally."

Hunter started to speak, but pursed his lips and looked out the windshield. He was thankful for the air conditioning on his face as he wiped the excess sweat off the back of his neck.

The conversation continued for the next thirty minutes. Hunter's mind replaying the scene multiple times. Each time he wondered if there was anything he could have done differently. Each time the answer was the same.

Benson closed his notebook. "I think we're done for now. I'll write up the report in the morning, but I see no reason to pursue the matter further." He paused. "I will need your weapon to be processed for ballistics, and you'll be on desk duty until I get the report signed off."

Hunter's vision blurred around the edges. *Turn over my weapon? Desk duty?* He blinked away the shock. "What about this scene? Billy needs…"

Benson cut him off, his stale breath polluting the small space. "Detective, your partner can handle this scene. It's late. Go home and get some rest. If you need a ride, I can arrange it."

Hunter shook his head listlessly. His voice was a mumble. "That won't be necessary."

There was an uncomfortable silence. Benson stared at him, then gestured toward his gun. Hunter nodded and slowly unclipped his holster. His stomach twisted as he handed it over.

Benson dropped the holstered gun into an evidence bag. "Thank you, Detective. I know it's Friday night, but I'm guessing that your lieutenant will want this wrapped up as quickly as possible. So please make yourself available so I can reach you in the morning."

Hunter stared out the windshield. "You've got my number."

Benson pointed to the passenger door. Hunter stepped out and stood in the night. As the car pulled away, his hand rubbed against his naked hip where he normally felt his Glock.

*   *   *   *

Stacy's team was in full swing when they entered through the back door Hunter had bolted out of earlier. One CSI tech took pictures while a second dusted for prints. Stacy joined them as Sanders perused the overall crime scene.

Doc was on one knee examining the body of a heavily tattooed white male that had clearly lived a hard life. He frowned, scanned through his notes, looked at the body on the ground and shook his head.

Billy stepped over. "What is it, Doc?"

"Something doesn't make sense."

Sanders watched but didn't speak.

Doc stood with some effort. "Cowboy arrived on the scene approximately 9:30pm, right?"

"That's what he said. Time stamped footage from the dashcam is 9:35. Why?" Sanders cocked his head.

"And the 911 call had come in only a few minutes before saying that someone had been shot, right?"

Sanders nodded. "Yes. Doc, what's the issue?"

Doc adjusted his wire rimmed glasses and took another look at his notes. "That scenario would lead one to believe that Hunter and the patrolmen arrived moments after this man was shot, found the perpetrator standing over the body, gave chase and responded with deadly force when he pulled his gun."

He looked up at Sanders and continued. "The problem with that theory is this man's been dead too long."

Sanders looked down at the body. "Are you saying the guy Cowboy shot didn't kill this guy?"

Doc shrugged. "I'm saying that if he did, he stood and admired his work for quite a long time before the authorities arrived."

The statement took a moment for Sanders to absorb. "Stacy." He signaled for her to step over. "Can you have one of your techs do a preliminary GSR test on the hands of both bodies before they get transferred?"

"Sure. Do you have a particular concern?"

"I just want to make sure that one or both of them have fired weapons." He nodded toward Doc, who had stepped back over to the body and was finishing up his notes. "Looks like a discrepancy in time of death."

"I'll do it myself." She started to turn away.

Sanders held out his hand. "Stace. Don't take this wrong, but since Cowboy was involved in that shooting, I'd prefer for you to have one of your team process anything related to that scene."

She started to object, but he gave her a look that clearly communicated that in Hunter's absence, he was in charge. "Yeah. No problem."

Chapter 4

"Catch the ME techs before they transfer the bodies. I want GSR tests on both victims before they leave the scene. I also want all personal effects bagged and brought to Detective Sanders." Stacy dispatched her CSI tech with a wave.

She looked at her watch, noted it was almost midnight and realized that she'd now been on scene for over an hour and still hadn't seen Hunter.

The conversation with IAD is taking forever.

With Sanders busy debriefing the two patrolman who'd breached the door with Hunter, Stacy stepped out the back door to look for Cowboy. She slipped off her gloves and shoved them in her back pocket.

The IAD detective's car has been at the end of the alley. But an engine crank pulled her attention to the front of the building instead., As she stepped around the corner of the building, Hunter's SUV backed out of its parking spot and squealed away.

Stacy reached into her pocket for her phone as she watched his tail lights move down the street. The smell of burned rubber hung in the air as she pulled out her phone and called him. The phone rang twice before it went to voice mail. He'd rejected the call. Not just didn't answer, but out right rejected it.

Oh, Cowboy, don't try to deal with this alone.

Her chest tightened as she clicked off without leaving a message. The night seemed darker and the humidity in the air felt more oppressive as she stood alone staring at the empty parking spot.

Taking a deep breath, she turned and walked back to the

door. The chaos of the scene had calmed as the CSI and ME techs wrapped up their tasks. The ME team lifted the body of the first victim onto a gurney. She regained her focus and called over to one of her team members. "Did we get everything we needed from that one?"

The tech held up a handful of evidence bags. "GSR results and personal effects."

She pointed to the table she'd been using to collect evidence. "Set it over there. Billy and I will review it in a minute." When she looked around and didn't see her other tech, she got impatient. "Can you go find out what's taking so long for the other body?"

The tech nodded and headed out the back door.

"Detective Sanders." Stacy motioned for Billy to come over. He held up one finger so he could wrap up his conversation with one of the patrolmen.

When he stepped over, she was looking at the results of the gunshot residue test performed on the body found in the building. "What have we got?"

She glanced down through the write up from her tech. "Whatever happened, this guy didn't get a chance to fight back. GSR tests are negative. He didn't fire a weapon tonight."

"Hmm." Sanders nodded slowly, turned and took in the crime scene once again. He turned back to Stacy. "You got a look at the guy, right? Did he strike you as the type who wouldn't be armed on a Friday night?"

"Not a chance."

"Didn't think so." Sanders took out a handkerchief and wipe the sweat from his forehead. "He also doesn't look like the type who would be easily disarmed and shot with his own gun."

"Certainly not by that baby faced looking kid out in the street." Stacy winced as she realized how harsh that sounded and the implications for Hunter.

Sanders frowned. "Yeah."

He jutted his chin toward the baggie of personal effects. "Anything of interest?"

"Let's see." Stacy dumped the small number of items onto the table. "We've got a wallet on a chain." She opened it, pulled out the license. "Michael Logan. How much you wanna bet, his buddies called him Mickey or Mick?"

Sanders smiled but didn't comment.

Stacy continued. "Nothing else in the wallet but some cash. About fifty bucks." She reached up spread the other items out. "We've got a pocket knife, a pack of gum and a keychain with a house or apartment key and one that looks like a motorcycle key."

Without waiting for a comment, Stacy waved to one of her team members. "Roy, do a sweep of the parking areas around the building to see if you can find a motorcycle missing a rider."

Roy gave a quick nod and headed for the door.

Sanders nodded toward the table. "Any cell phone?"

"Nope."

"Who walks around without a cell phone these days?"

Stacy arched an eyebrow. "It's hard to make a living, legal or otherwise, these days without one."

"Yes it is. Hmm, no gun and no cell phone. Looks like he traveled pretty light." Sanders twisted his mouth. "We'll run a full history on him in the morning. That should be some fun reading."

Stacy smiled and started to comment, but was distracted by two techs walking through the back door, one holding a similar set of evidence from Brandon Jenkins.

"It's about time." She snatched the items from the tech and dismissed him with a glare. Grabbing the GSR report first, she quickly scanned it as Sanders looked over her shoulder. Her hand reflexively moved to her throat, the words blurred on the page. Without saying a word, she let her hand with the form in it, drop to the table.

Sanders finished reading and his body seemed to deflate. He leaned his head back and rubbed his eyes with both hands. After a moment, he broke the silence. "Doesn't matter." His voice was hoarse.

"It will to Cowboy." Stacy blinked away the water forming in her eyes.

"I know. But at the end of the day, whether Brandon Jenkins

shot Michael Logan or not is irrelevant. He pulled a gun on a cop and the cop did exactly what he was trained to do." He turned to look directly at Stacy. "He defended himself. That's all there is to it."

Stacy shook her head slowly. "You and I know that, but wait until the media gets ahold of it." She turned back to the table. "I can already see the headlines – Innocent black teenager gunned down by white detective."

Sanders started to rebut her comment, but pointed to the table instead. "What else was in his wallet?"

With her gloved hand, she reached for the wallet. This time taking each item out individually. "We've got a driver's license as noted before, a Fort Worth Library card, a student ID for Tarrant County College and eight dollars in cash."

"Not what you'd expect in a street thug's wallet." Sanders voice sounded as dejected as his body language implied. "What else?"

She opened the plastic bag and dumped it onto the table. "Cell phone." She punched the button and the phone lit up flashing a picture of an F-35 fighter jet streaking across a clear blue sky. Stacy showed it to Sanders. "Go figure."

Sanders shrugged. "We'll get a warrant and have the tech guys hack in to see who he was talking to tonight."

Stacy picked through an assortment of items, half a bag of M&M's, an ink pen, some coins and a waded up store receipt. She unfolded and scanned the receipt. "It's the receipt for the candy and it puts him four blocks away from the scene at 8:45pm."

"Based on Doc's preliminary time of death, that's about ten minutes after the murder." Sanders stared at the items on the table and seemed to let that thought sink in. "Well, I think we know who didn't kill Michael Logan."

Chapter 5

The alarm clock's red digital lights glowed, taunting Hunter in the early morning darkness. The air conditioner humming teamed with the mechanical breeze of the ceiling fan to make him feel like he was in an artificial wind storm. Both worked overtime to combat the heat, but a light sheen of sweat still covered him.

Attempting sleep had been useless. Every time he closed his eyes, the scene replayed in his head. Young Brandon Jenkin's face stared up at him.

Panther had uncharacteristically planted himself beside Hunter on the bed, keeping watch. The oversized black cat seemed to know he was needed. Hunter reached over and stroked Panther's back, eliciting the rattling purr. The cat blinked and nuzzled his hand.

"I know buddy. I'm keeping you awake. Sorry about that. Rough night."

Hunter had pulled into his driveway shortly after midnight, not really remembering the drive home. For the first time in years, he'd turned his cell phone off, dropped it on the table and unplugged the home phone on his way through the kitchen. He didn't want to speak to anyone.

The hot shower and the three Tylenol PM helped with the aches of a long day, but nothing more. He'd shot a kid. No medicine in the world could take that away. He could logic it and rationalize it however he wanted, but it didn't change things. Sometime in the middle of the night, a Police Officer had knocked on a mother's door to inform her that she'd never see her son smile again, and the only way she'd ever hold him again would be in her dreams.

Hunter knew that devastation. He'd lived it on both sides. He'd delivered that news to far too many parents over the last decade as a homicide detective. He hated those conversations. Almost as bad as being abruptly widowed or losing a partner in the line of duty. His chest ached and his gut tightened.

While he understood the pain, he had never been responsible for creating the pain. If the last few hours were any indication, this was going to be a long, difficult road.

He noticed that the first signs of the sunrise warmed the blinds. With a quick glance at the clock, he noted it was almost six. Giving up on sleep, he gave Panther a few moments of well-deserved attention before pushing the covers away and wobbling to the bathroom.

After starting the brew process for his morning coffee, he stood in the kitchen and stared at his dead phone. His normal morning regimen stalled by an unfamiliar anxiety. It was before seven am on a Saturday morning and he was fully dressed and ready for work. He twitched and fidgeted as he listened to the coffee maker and contemplated the fact that he officially had no place to go. A quiver radiated through his stomach.

The first sip of coffee jolted him out of his paralysis. He sat down at the kitchen table, tapped his phone to life and noted that he had two text messages and a voicemail.

I may be sidelined, but the team is busy.

He punched up the first of the texts. From Stacy at 1:45am.

Jake, I'm guessing by you not picking up earlier that you want to be alone. Please call me when you get this. Don't care what time. Stace.

A pressure rose in his chest and up through his throat. He leaned forward in the chair, chewed on the inside of his cheek before moving on to the second text. From Sanders just a few minutes later than Stacy's.

Cowboy, just leaving the scene. Hope you're getting some sleep. Need to talk in the morning. Some interesting twists. Will be in the office by

9. Hang in buddy.

Hunter reread his text three times.

Interesting twists? Wonder what the hell that means.

Without spending more time contemplating it, he switched over to retrieve the voicemail. From Lieutenant Sprabary. He raised a brow. Based on the time stamp, he must have called just minutes after Hunter had turned off his phone. He hit the speaker phone.

Hunter, Sprabary here. Just got the message about the incident this evening. Was on the road and not paying attention to my cell. Sorry about that. We need to connect first thing in the morning. I'll be in the office. I want to get the IAD stuff processed ASAP so you can get refocused. Um... Come see me.

The line clicked off without a goodbye. Hunter smiled at the all business nature of Sprabary's message mixed with the awkward concern in his voice.

Panther interrupted his thoughts by rubbing against his shins. Hunter smiled and patted his head.

Looks like I've got someplace to go this morning after all.

*   *   *   *

Not having his Glock 17 clipped to his belt as he walked into the stations' back door made Hunter feel conspicuous, almost naked. Even with the lighter Saturday morning staffing, he kept his head down and went straight to Sprabary's office. He had no desire to make small talk with anyone.

Although Sprabary hadn't said a specific time, Hunter knew him well enough to know that he'd be in his office early as if it was any other day of the week. He wasn't surprised to see him at his desk reading through reports.

Sprabary was slightly older than Hunter with a strong jaw and chiseled features. He was in his mid-forties and his sometimes overly formal nature did little to hide the fact that he cared about his team members deeply.

When Hunter knocked on the doorframe, Sprabary motioned for him to enter. As Hunter sat down, Sprabary looked at his watch. "It's 8:15. Did you decide to sleep in today because it's Saturday or because you're officially on desk duty?"

Hunter started to respond, but when he looked up, noticed the sarcastic look on Sprabary's face and just shrugged.

The smirk faded as the lieutenant dropped the report on his desk. "I'm glad you got my message. I was driving back from Houston late last night and after the day I'd had, I didn't really want to talk so I wasn't paying any attention to my phone."

Hunter looked at him as if he didn't understand.

"I was down there for Desiree's trial. You remember the change of venue issue."

"I forgot." Hunter nodded but averted his eyes. He thought about the former Police Dispatcher who had been a mole for the Eastcide Kings. She'd been a trusted member of Sprabary's team until he had to arrest her. "How'd it go?"

"Every bit as bad as you could imagine." Sprabary absently shook his head. "She was foolish not to take the plea deal. Guilty on all charges."

"Damn." Hunter looked down and shook his head. "Poor kids."

There was a long pause before Sprabary continued. "Yeah. Anyway, I didn't realize there had been an incident until I got home." He leaned forward. "How are you doing?"

Hunter fidgeted in his chair, not used to his boss displaying concern about his welfare. "Better shape than the other guy."

"That you are." Sprabary let the silence hang for a moment. "I've already read the reports. I spoke to Benson and I've seen the video. It was a good shoot. You did what you had to do, but you already know that, right?"

Hunter nodded as he stared down at his folded hands. "That's the consensus."

"Still sucks ."

"Yep."

"Look Jake, if you need some time, just le—"

"That's the last thing I need right now." Hunter cut him off. "What I need is to get back to work, figure out why Brandon Jenkins killed Michael Logan." He ran his hand through his hair. "Then maybe I can make some sense out of all this and be able to get some sleep."

Sprabary nodded. "Benson will be in later this morning. He'll get the paperwork taken care of and get you off the desk." He paused. "From a procedural standpoint, Sanders has to be listed as the lead on the Logan murder."

Hunter sat up straight and stared across the desk, but Sprabary stopped him with a wave of his hand. "Don't go there. Technically, I should give it to Reyes and Parker, but Sanders is already running with it. Besides, you and Sanders caught two new cases last night. I need you to run point on the Monticello Park scene."

He didn't like it, but Hunter knew there was no point in further argument. "I'm fine with Sanders leading the Logan investigation Lieutenant if there's no other choice, but I really need to focus on the Logan case. Can't we give the Monticello Park murder to Reyes and Parker?"

Sprabary pursed his lips. "No. You caught it. I need you to lead it, but..." He paused. "What I will do is have Reyes be your arms and legs on it. Get with him and catch him up." He eyed Hunter. "As for the lead on the Logan case, this will be good for Sanders."

"Thanks Lieutenant. Speaking of Sanders..." Hunter stood. "I need to get with him, so if that's all..." He thumbed toward the door.

"Before you go." Sprabary grabbed a note pad and scribbled a name and number down. "Department policy requires all officers involved in a fatal shooting to have a few sessions with a department psychiatrist. Call this guy on Monday. Get in to see him ASAP."

Hunter frowned, but took the paper. He shoved it in his

pocket. Sprabary nodded toward the door. "Tell Sanders I want regular reports. We need to close this case before it gets a chance to blossom into a media circus."

Chapter 6

Hunter glanced at his watch as he bounded up the stairs to the second floor. Almost 9:00 AM. While conversations with Sprabary weren't always uplifting, he was glad they connected. It felt good to talk and think about something other than Brandon Jenkins, even if it was for a short time. It was also good to know that the lieutenant was pushing to get him back on the case quickly.

He thought for a moment about being second to Sanders on a case. *The student takes over for the teacher.*

He smiled. *It'll be strange, but at least it won't be for long. The case is pretty straight forward. We caught him at the scene with a gun in his hand. All we have to do is catalog the evidence and complete the paperwork.*

Before he went to the conference room, he called Jimmy Reyes to enlist his help. Sprabary had beaten him to the punch. Reyes didn't bother saying hello when he answered. "So Cowboy, I hear you're looking for me. On a Saturday morning no less." Years of police work had thinned and grayed what used to be a full head of dark hair on Reyes. It had done similar damage to the rest of him. Despite the mileage, he still had a great attitude and sense of humor. "Word is, I get to be your boy on a case."

"I just need a little help so I can focus on the Logan thing that blew up last night."

Reyes' face went solemn. "How are you doing? I hear you did what you had to do."

"I'm fine." Hunter waved him off. "I could use your help though."

"Give me the scoop."

"The start of the investigation is pretty straight forward. The victim is James Tyler. Single gunshot wound to the head. Found him in Monticello Park about 6 p.m. yesterday. Witness heard the gunshot and saw a guy wearing a hoodie running off into the woods."

"Did they get a look at him?"

"Nope, only saw him from behind and at a distance. Doubt their statement will do us much good." Hunter stood in the hall outside the conference room and held the phone to his ear. "I'll email you everything I've got. You can reach out to Stacy since her team worked the scene."

"I'll call her today. It's either that or yardwork and you know I hate yardwork."

"Thanks Jimmy."

Hunter hung up, stepped around the corner and into the conference room. As he'd expected, Sanders was already there. He was wearing designer jeans and a khaki vest over a crisp white shirt. Fashionably casual for a Saturday and not showing the wear from a late night.

Must be nice to be young.

Sanders was writing on the whiteboard. At the sound of Hunter dropping his laptop on the table, he turned and looked at him like a mother to a sick child. Hunter frowned. "Don't give me that look. I'm fine."

"Good morning to you, too."

Hunter ignored the sarcasm, leaned back against the table with his arms folded across his chest and nodded to the whiteboard. "That's an awful lot of information for a Saturday morning on an open and shut case."

Sanders scanned the whiteboard and rubbed his forehead. There was a long pause before he turned back at Hunter. The look on his face sent a ripple through Hunter, his stomach did a back flip.

"Cowboy, uh…" Sanders groped for words. "I'm not so sure about the open and shut part."

Hunter pushed away from the table and stepped toward the board. "You mean..." Hunter's throat constricted, cutting off his airflow. "You mean Brandon Jenkins didn't shoot the guy in the building?"

Sanders cleared his throat. "The guy in the building was Michael Logan and from everything we could see last night, no, Brandon Jenkins didn't kill him."

Sanders words hit Hunter's ears as if through a tunnel, distorted and distant. Hunter's eyes lost focus on the board and he felt his hand reach down to grip the table.

A moment later, Sanders' voice tore through the haze. "Cowboy? You alright?"

Hunter found himself sitting on the edge of the table and felt like his knees might buckle. He pulled out the nearest chair and slid into it. "I'm fine." His own voice sounded strange to his ears. "Let me get out my notepad. I think you need to run down what you've got."

After a moment of rummaging in his bag, Hunter looked up to see Sanders with that same look of concern. This time he didn't complain. He pointed to the board. "Start talking."

Sanders exhaled heavily. "Doc noticed the first discrepancy when he checked on time of death. Michael Logan had been dead for at least an hour, maybe more, before you kicked in the door."

"Okay." Hunter scrambled through his thoughts. "So, our boy admired his work for a while. I've seen stranger things."

"Like I said, that was the first discrepancy." Sanders turned back toward the whiteboard and pointed to two bullet points. "We performed GSR tests on both bodies. Neither had fired a weapon. On top of that, Brandon Jenkins had half a bag of M&M's in his pocket along with a crumpled up receipt. He was at a store several blocks away when Logan was shot."

Hunter stood and stared at the words on the board. His mind raced but to no particular destination, just random thoughts and images jumbled together. After a moment, he broke off his trance and cleared his throat. "So, what you're saying is that I killed an innocent kid."

"You shot a suspect in self-defense. He pointed a gun at you Cowboy. Don't forget that."

"I won't forget." Hunter stepped away from the board and sat down, rubbing his face with his hands. "Not any of it."

"Look... Cowboy." Sanders dropped the marker in the tray. "I've been where you are. It sucks. You're right. You won't forget." He stepped forward, struggled to do something with his hands, finally shoved them in his pockets. "I don't have any magic words to make it better, but I am here if you need to talk."

"This is different." Hunter hadn't looked up. "The guys you shot were bad dudes who were actively trying to kill us. They deserved what they got."

"Jenkins had a gun..."

"I know. I know. He had a gun. Okay. I get that. " Hunter looked up at Sanders, pain radiated from his face, his eyes glassy. "But I'm sure you pulled a history on him this morning and I'll bet it was clean as a whistle, right?"

"No, it wasn't."

Hunter stared at him.

"He had a felony charge of possession over an ounce."

"And?"

Sanders frowned. "That was it."

"That's all?" Hunter's voice rose, his tone incredulous. "You're kidding me. His lone offense was smoking weed?" He snorted. "Yeah, I took a killer off the streets, didn't I?"

The two men went silent. Hunter leaned forward with his elbows on his knees and shook his head.

Sanders broke the silence, his voice curt. "Would it have been better if he'd taken you off the streets?"

Hunter folded his arms hard across his chest and clinched his jaw.

"I'm sorry." Sanders shook his head, his voice softer. "Look, we'll have more information this afternoon. Why don't we get back together then?"

"All right." His voice was complete resignation. Hunter looked at his watch. "I need to see Benson with IAD. Where are you headed?"

"I'm going to visit the Jenkins family."

Hunter's head popped up and he started to speak, but Sanders cut him off. "No, the lieutenant specifically said you can't go with me."

Chapter 7

The light blue siding, covered front porch and white shutters of Brandon Jenkins' house made Sanders' stomach flip over. Not the expected home image of a cold blooded murderer and would be cop killer. It looked warm and welcoming with the front lawn freshly cut and tiered with two rock retaining walls.

Carter Riverside is the furthest northeast neighborhood still within Fort Worth city limits. Most of the homes date back several decades. Much of the community teetered on the edge, with some of the homes fighting the decline, while others giving up entirely into condemnation.

As he maneuvered around the cars parked along both sides of Marigold Avenue, he observed a small group of people standing near the front steps, their expressions somber. This reminded him that Detective Benson had notified the family late last night and he would now be walking into a large family wake. The thought made him reconsider, but he knew there was no such thing as a good time to speak with a grieving family.

When he found an open spot, he parked and sat for a moment. He had been in Homicide for less than nine months, two of which had been spent rehabbing after getting shot in the shoulder. Although he'd accompanied Hunter during next of kin notifications, his experience with suffering relatives was limited. He'd certainly never had to interview the relatives of someone shot by his partner.

He took a deep breath.

This is going to suck.

On the walk from his car, he passed well over a dozen cars,

all of which he assumed belonged to visitors of the Jenkins's. He was somewhat surprised that they all seemed to be fairly new, and then he chastised himself for stereotyping. After all, from everything he'd dug up, the real Brandon Jenkins seemed to be someone very different than the suspect who murdered someone then pulled a gun on a cop.

As he walked slowly up the sidewalk toward the home, all conversation stopped and the somberness in the faces was replaced with suspicion. Billy might have fit in ethnically, but he was clearly an outsider at a time when outsiders weren't welcome.

He nodded and stepped to the door, but before he could knock a sharp voice stopped him. "Can I help you?"

A lean, athletic woman in her early twenties glared at Sanders when he turned to face her. Her eyes burned through him.

"I'm here to see Mrs. Jenkins." He discreetly displayed his badge. "I'm Detect—"

"You killed my brother and now you want to talk to my mom?" Her voice had gone up in both pitch and volume. She stepped toward him with her finger poking the air, but was restrained by her companion. "You've got no right—"

"Ma'am, I'm sorry for your—"

"How dare you."

She stepped forward, but her companion wedged his way in front and blocked her. "Audie, stop it. This man didn't shoot Brandon. He's just doing his job."

Sweat beaded up on Sanders' forehead as his heart rate climbed. Dealing with relatives was Hunter's area. Billy was much more comfortable busting heads than soothing feathers. Feeling awkward, but seeing his opportunity, he turned toward the door and knocked.

Audie huffed, extracted herself from the man's grip and stomped to the opposite end of the porch. She continued her tirade as much to herself as to Sanders. "I see how it is. They send a black cop over to appease the family. Like that's gonna make it all better."

The man calmed her down and turned to Sanders with a look that was less than apologetic. He motioned to the door. "I'll show you inside." He nodded back over his shoulder toward Audie. "She might not be the only one with that kind of reaction."

Before he had a chance to comment, the man opened the front door and stepped over the threshold. Sanders followed him into a small entry hall with a crowded sitting area off to the left. As had happened on the front porch, his presence quieted the room and drew the attention of every pair of eyes. His stomach flipped and he felt short of breath as he absorbed the anger of the room.

"This way."

Sanders hadn't realized he'd stopped walking until the man touched his elbow and directed him forward. When they stepped through and into the family room, Sanders identified Mrs. Jenkins immediately.

Like her daughter, she was lean. And for her age, fit. Unlike her daughter, she had a presence about her. A strength and resolve that kept the raw emotion in check, but still conveyed the agony she was experiencing.

Even though she wasn't as old as Sanders had expected, she was clearly the matriarch of the family with a select group of relatives attending to her. When she looked up at him, he felt his 220 pound frame shrink and every ounce of his resolve evaporate.

"Momma, this is a detective." His escort's tone was deferential as he positioned himself in between Sanders and Mrs. Jenkins. "He asked to speak to you, but if you're not up to it…"

His voice trailed off as she dismissed him with a wave and once again, stared up at Sanders.

Billy fought to regain his composure and cleared his throat. "Mrs. Jenkins, I'm Detective Billy Sanders of the Fort Worth Police." As he spoke, he showed her his badge. "I'm very sorry for your loss." His eyes scanned the defiant faces of the group that had packed more closely around her. "Is there someplace private we can speak?"

She paused and studied him as if deciding just how much she

would make him endure. She gestured dismissively to the group. "Why don't y'all get some coffee while I speak with the detective."

It took another, more emphatic wave of her hand for the group to dissipate. All but one. Much like her, the man had a presence about him. His shoulders, while not large, were pulled back straight and his jawline was square. He looked as though he was used to getting his way. "If you don't mind Valerie, I'd like to stay."

She gave a barely perceptible nod and pointed to a chair. Her words were soft but very articulate with no hint of an accent. "Please have a seat detective."

Chapter 8

The man and Mrs. Jenkins stared at Billy with an intense mixture of grief and anger. Billy sat down to her left in a dining room chair that had been brought into the family room to accommodate the extra guests. The gentleman remained standing just behind her right shoulder, even though his knee was inches from an empty chair. Mrs. Jenkins noticed his posture. "If you're going to stay, please be polite enough to introduce yourself to the detective." This was not a request.

"I'm Maxwell Arnett, Valerie's brother."

When he didn't elaborate further, Mrs. Jenkins continued on his behalf. "Maxwell is a Professor of Economics at the University of Texas at Arlington. Brandon's mentor."

Sanders nodded. "Nice to meet you, Professor."

Mr. Arnett nodded with little change in his demeanor.

Turning back to Mrs. Jenkins, Sanders cleared his throat and repeated his condolences before continuing. "Ma'am, we're trying to piece together the events of last evening so we can determine what happened."

"A white cop shot down another young black man in the streets. Does that clarify what happened for you?" Although his voice wasn't raised, his jaw was tight and the level of Arnett's rage was clear.

"Maxwell, please." Mrs. Jenkins shot him a look.

Billy followed the exchange with his eyes but didn't interject. He was caught off guard that they already knew it was a white cop. As is standard in officer involved shootings, Hunter's name had not been released to anyone outside the investigating team. Was he just playing the odds to see if Sanders' reaction would confirm his suspicion.

He tried not to react and let the silence linger for a moment as he collected his thoughts. "As I was saying, if you don't mind, I have a few questions that I hope you can help me with."

She nodded.

"Why was Brandon at the warehouse last night?"

Her eyes narrowed. "My son is…" She paused, took a breath. "Was a responsible young man. I didn't feel the need to monitor his every movement. He left with a friend around seven." Her face and voice both softened. "That's the last time I saw him."

"Do you know his friend?"

"Yes, Darren Hollis. He's a good kid. They grew up together."

Sanders took down Darren's contact information and spent the next several minutes asking background questions and confirming what all his research had shown, Brandon was not the type of kid to be involved with a drug dealing scum like Logan.

Billy paused before the next line of questioning. "Does the name Michael Logan mean anything to you?"

Mrs. Jenkins' brow furrowed. "No." When Billy paused to make a note, her look transformed to understanding. "Is he the man Brandon supposedly shot?"

Billy stopped writing, looked up at her. "He's the man who was shot at the scene last night. Although we are looking at all possibilities, it doesn't appear that Brandon shot him. That's why I'm here, trying to determine who did."

Throughout the process, Arnett had fidgeted, squirmed and seemed about ready to burst at the seams. Every time he had started to interject, Mrs. Jenkins had shut him down with a look or gesture. This time, he wouldn't be denied. "So what you're saying is that Brandon was shot for no reason. He wasn't even the shooter."

"Mr. Arnett, we're very early in the invest—"

"My son was innocent?" Mrs. Jenkins' voice was barely a whisper.

Sanders watched as the previously strong, composed expression was now hollow and gray. It was as if she could somehow accept her son's death if he had done something wrong. That acceptance was shattered at the realization that he was innocent. That is, if you don't count pulling a gun on a cop.

Sanders tried to respond as he watched her seem to shrink in front of him, but words failed.

Maxwell's hands gripped the back of the chair he stood behind. "It's just another black man the system has taken off the streets." His comment seemed to be more to himself than Billy. His agitation grew. "War of drugs, my ass! It's a war on the black community. Always has been since day one." He towered over Sanders, his eyes burning. "How do you sleep at night? You work for them. As a black man, don't you see it? The 'justice system' has been systematically killing and incarcerating black men at an epidemic pace since the end of slavery.

"First there were the Ku Klux Klan, Jim Crow laws and lynching. When the Civil Rights movement finally overcame those obstacles enough to reduce their effectiveness, they just shifted gears and ushered in the era of Mass Incarceration."

Sanders shifted in his seat, opened his mouth to say something but was cut off again as Arnett continued.

"Did you know that one out of every three black men in America is either in jail or on probation? In inner cities, that rate soars to one out of every two. How is that possible? Are you really trying to tell me that one out of every two black men is a dangerous criminal?"

"Mr. Arnett, I'm here to—"

"Oh, here it comes. Let me guess. You're just doing your job, right? Wake up Detective. Educate yourself. There's a bigger picture out there you're missing."

"Enough." Her voice had regained some of its strength, but

was still hoarse. "I won't have politics and conspiracy theories intrude today." She turned to Sanders. "Detective, I'm not feeling well. Can we continue this at another time?"

"Certainly." He handed her his card. "Again, I'm sorry for your loss."

He stood and shook her hand. She nodded silently.

Arnett straightened up and gestured to the front of the house. "Don't perpetuate the cycle Detective. I'll show you out."

Chapter 9

"Earth to Cowboy." Stacy reached across the table and gently touched his forearm.

Hunter's fork absently picked at his enchiladas as they sat in a booth at The Mexican Inn Café, one of their regular lunch stops. His usual ravenous appetite had vanished.

She could tell his mind was a million miles away down a dark tunnel. "Hey, where are you?"

"Huh? Oh, sorry." Hunter waved it off and adjusted in his chair to be more present. "Didn't sleep much."

She searched his face and raised an eyebrow.

He cleared his throat. "Just a lot on my mind."

Her eyes smiled as they searched his and she squeezed his arm. "I know. Is there anything I can do to help?"

He shook his head. "Time's the only thing that's going to help. What I'd really like to do is get this case solved. The sooner we can close the books on this thing the better."

After another long pause, Stacy tried again. "How did the conversation go with IAD this morning?"

Hunter straightened and exhaled as if he were trying to wake from a nap. "Fine."

He sounded like a teenager. One word responses scratched at her brain. But Stacy played the role of the parent to perfection and glared at him to let him know she expected a little more information.

As he fidgeted, the waitress picked up their half-eaten meals and dropped off the check. When she left, he continued. "Officially, I'm cleared. The video evidence was pretty overwhelming." He paused and looked down at his plate. "But now I'm required to see a shrink to make sure I can get past any lingering effects of the trauma." He made a face indicating that might be only slightly better than a caning.

"I feel sorry for that poor psychiatrist." She smiled at Hunter's faux outrage and for a few brief seconds they were back to their normal ease. When the moment passed, Stacy continued. "When is your first session?"

"Monday."

She arched her eyebrows in surprise. "They're not fooling around, are they?"

He shook his head. "Nope. That was the condition for me getting off desk duty. I've got to be actively in counseling." He leaned back and looked around the restaurant, watching the handful of Saturday lunch patrons. Avoiding her eye contact.

Only fifteen hours since the shooting, and Hunter was clearly beating himself up inside. Stacy expected the trauma to have some impact. But her heart caved in watching Hunter struggle to even talk to her. To even look at her..

"You should take the afternoon off, maybe drive out to your folks' place." The sentence tumbled out before she realized she was talking.

His jaw set and his eyes narrow as they snapped forward to glare at her.

"I mean... All I'm saying is—"

"What?" The sharpness of his tone made her jump. "That I can't handle my job? That I shouldn't be on the case?"

"Cowboy, please." She reached across the table, but he pulled away. "You know that's not what I meant. It's just that it would be understandable if you needed a day to decompress."

"I don't need to decompress. I need to solve this case." He pushed back in his chair and tossed his napkin on the table. "Are you ready?"

Her mouth fell open slightly.

He was up and headed to the cashier before she could reply. She grabbed a last drink of tea before she scurried to catch up with him.

Stacy had to almost jog to keep up with his long strides across the steamy parking lot. She normally would have given him some playful grief for not opening her door, but decided it might be wise to let it slide this time and crawled up into the SUV as he cranked the engine.

Sweat immediately popped on her forehead when she closed the door. It was like stepping into a sauna. She started to reach for the air conditioner controls but Hunter beat her to it and almost twisted the knob off turning it to high.

"So, what have you found from what you've processed this morning?" Hunter was all business now as he jerked the vehicle out of the parking lot and south onto Henderson.

"I didn't bring my notes, but I can give you some highlights." She paused to see if his mood was calming. He just glared at the road.

"The only fingerprints on the gun belonged to Brandon Jenkins. There weren't even any other partials. It was clear the gun had been wiped clean before he touched it." She waited to let that sink in.

Stacy watched as Hunter's shoulders loosened slightly. *Maybe he was right. The best therapy for him is to bury himself in the case.*

"That's interesting." Hunter turned south on 8th Avenue, instead of north.

Stacey frowned. *Where is he going?*

As if answering her unspoken question, Hunter nodded forward. "Sanders asked me to meet him at the morgue to see if Doc found anything. I'll drop you at the lab." He squinted into the afternoon sun. "You were saying?"

"The cartridges were wiped clean, too. No prints. Whoever loaded the gun was probably wearing gloves."

Hunter nodded. "Sounds to me like it was no accident that

the shooter left the gun behind." His mood continued to soften as he processed the information, turned east on W. Allen and made the slow journey through all the traffic lights toward I-35.

A sly grin spread across his face.

Stacy caught it out of the corner of her eye. "What's that look for?"

"I guess Billy's first case as Lead Investigator isn't going to be such a slam dunk after all." The grin grew into wide smile.

She cut her eyes toward him. "Cowboy, you are evil." Her hand reached over and stroked his shoulder. "But I am glad to see you smile again."

When he looked over at her, his smile remained but the pain in his eyes was unmistakable.

Chapter 10

"So what does all of this have to do with what happened last night?" Billy shrugged, trying not to let his impatience show.

Professor Arnett had not only walked him to the door, he had walked him all the way to his car. Along the way, he had passionately lectured Billy on what he referred to as Mass Incarceration.

Billy had listened politely, occasionally being alarmed, but mostly skeptical as the professor told him that the United States had the highest rate of incarceration in the world. He told him that from 1972 to 2012, the number of inmates in U.S. prisons increased from 300,000 to over 2.3M. That's over a 765% increase during a time when the country's population grew less that 50%.

The professor made it clear that the driving force of mass incarceration was America's War on Drugs and that the group most impacted were minorities, specifically black men. He indicated that over 30% of black men across the country are either currently in jail, on probation or on parole. In the inner cities, that percentage soars to over 50%.

"The point I'm trying to make is that Brandon is just another victim of a racist system."

Billy scrunched his face. "Brandon wasn't arrested. He was shot when he pulled a gun on a cop." He folded his arms across his chest. "I don't see the correlation."

"It's not just about what happened last night." He shook his head as he gathered his thoughts. "Last night was just the final act in a long chain of events. Brandon shouldn't have even been there last night." He paused and his voice softened. "Hell, he shouldn't have even been in Fort Worth." He looked at Sanders. "I assume you did a background check on Brandon?"

Sanders nodded and leaned back against his car, feeling the warm metal through his shirt.

"Then you know that he was on probation for possession. He was busted while riding in a car with some friends. It was bullshit but he took a plea."

"Not exactly the first time I've heard that." Sanders shrugged. "Why didn't he fight it?"

"Detective, look around you." He gestured toward the neighborhood. "This is Riverside, not University Park. My sister is a very capable woman and has done well, but she's a single mom. Spending thousands of dollars on attorneys just doesn't happen here.."

"Okay, but I still don't see the connection."

"I'm getting there." Professor Arnett held up his hands to ask for patience. "What you probably don't know is that Brandon was a superb student, top of his class. He had already been accepted into the Pre Law program at Rice University." The memory seemed to hit him hard as he paused.

His voice was strained when he started again. "As a final step in the admission process, Rice did a cursory background check. When they did, they saw the conviction and revoked their acceptance. He had no alternative but to enroll at TCC." His eyes blinked. "Classes started last week. He shouldn't have even been here. He should've been in Houston starting college at one of the best universities in the country."

Sanders dropped his head so that his chin almost touched his chest and his eyes closed for a moment. He thought about Hunter, how devastated he seemed last night.

If Cowboy hears this, it'll crush him.

"Sorry." The professor's voice pulled him from his thoughts.

Sanders looked up and gave a half-hearted wave. "No

worries."

"I didn't mean to…" He shook his head. "I just get passionate about what's happening to an entire generation of black men. I've seen it happen to so many young men, my students, the kids from the neighborhood. It's an epidemic."

"I'm sorry for your loss." Sanders had regained his composure, his cop face. "I have no doubt that Brandon had some challenges to overcome, but last night wasn't about what happened six months ago and it wasn't about not getting into Rice. It was about pulling a gun on a cop."

Professor Arnett stiffened and pulled back, his eyes narrowing. "Yes. Well. Please keep us informed about the progress of the investigation."

"I will." Sanders reached for the handle, opened the car door and stepped in.

"Detective."

Sanders looked back over his shoulder.

"Think about what I said."

Billy closed the door and hit the ignition. He reached over and cranked up the air conditioner and watched in his rearview mirror as the professor strolled up the sidewalk toward the Jenkins' home.

What was that all about? Talk about oversharing.

He sat for several minutes. He couldn't help replaying the professors' words over in his head as his mind drifted back to his early childhood. So many of the kids from that neighborhood had eventually spent time in the Texas prison system. So many others ultimately wound up in the Tarrant County morgue.

Chapter 11

The stale, industrial smell of antiseptic infiltrated the morgue's lobby, adding to Sanders unsettled stomach. Combined with knowing what happened behind those closed doors, all the slicing and dicing, creepy didn't even begin to cover it. Even as he stood in the lobby waiting for Hunter, he could still smell it. He shook his shoulders as if he were shaking off cobwebs, walked over to the window, looked out to see Hunter pull up.

Stacy was with him, but their goodbye seemed less cozy than usual as she headed toward the the forensics lab and Hunter strode toward Sanders.

When Hunter pushed through, he barely slowed down as he moved across the lobby. "Have you spoken with Doc?"

Sanders followed. "I just got here a couple of minutes ago. I thought I'd wait for you before I went searching for him." He had to hurry to catch up. "Hey, everything okay, Cowboy?"

Hunter shot him a glance, frowned and kept walking.

"Trouble in paradise?" He thumbed over his shoulder toward the parking lot.

"Everything's fine. Let's find Doc."

Sanders acknowledged Hunters' answer by nodding but wasn't convinced. Before he had a chance to ask any more questions, Hunter had already signed in at the desk, flashed his badge and was pushing through the door leading to the autopsy area.

Hunter led the way down the hall, stopping first at Doc's office, just to confirm he wasn't there and then moving further into the building to the row of autopsy rooms.

They found Doc working in Autopsy Two and stepped through the door. The smell of formaldehyde mixed with decay overpowered Sanders' senses. He covered his nose. Even Cowboy flinched slightly and scrunched his face.

"Oh, come now, after all these years, you still haven't gotten used to my aftershave?" Doc cocked an eyebrow at Hunter and grinned.

"I think you put it on a little heavy today." Hunter waved his hand in front of his face as he nodded toward a body on the table.

"I assume you're here regarding Mr. Logan and Mr. Tyler. I made Logan a priority considering..." He looked at Hunter and then pointed to the table. A body was splayed open with most of the internal organs removed and stacked in various spots on an adjoining table. "I'll get to Mr. Tyler before end of day." He shrugged. "Saturday mornings around here are kind of like rush hour."

"Logan is the priority. Looks like you've been busy. Learn anything interesting?"

Doc picked up his clipboard and put on his reading glasses. "Not a lot. No surprise on the cause of death, single GSW to the chest. I retrieved the bullet and have it bagged for ballistics." He slid his index finger down the page and mumbled to himself before flipping to the second page.

He widened his eyes and nodded. "Here's something of note. The full tox screen won't be back for a couple of days, but I ran some preliminary tests. Alcohol and THC. No surprise there. It was Friday night, after all." He smiled at his comment but was met with flat looks from both detectives.

"I won't know the levels until the lab completes their process. He also has MDMA residue on his hands." He looked up to see both detectives staring back at him blankly. "That's the chemical compound for Ecstasy."

Sanders cocked his head. "What's the significance?"

Doc shrugged. "Maybe none, but the amount of residue was

significant which means he'd handled a lot of it and very recently." He looked at Sanders over his glasses. "I don't recall the CSI team finding any on him, do you?"

"Not that I know of. I'll check with Stacy."

Doc nodded. "Good. I'd also asked her to test his clothes for it as well. Maybe he was a dealer and this was a sale gone bad."

Sanders scribbled in his pad.

"Last thing, I narrowed time of death." Doc once again referenced his notes. "He departed this world sometime between eight and nine at night."

Sanders stopped writing and looked at Hunter. He leaned against the wall staring at the ground. It was a long moment before he looked back at Doc. "So we're sure this guy was dead long before the 911 call was placed."

"Minimum of thirty minutes. Most likely closer to an hour. No doubt."

The hum from florescent lights increased to a deafening buzz. Both detectives absorbed the possible ramifications of that revelation. Cowboy looked like he was about to throw up.

The double doors swung open, and a gurney pushed through. A tall, morose looking man in a white lab coat piloted the cart and stopped abruptly when he saw the men.

When he saw the Doc, his mood changed from gloomy to flustered. "Doctor Grimes, I'm so sorry. I thought you were... The schedule said..." He quickly looked at his clipboard and stabbed at it with his finger. "I was supposed to deliver Brandon Jenkins to you at two o'clock." He looked at his watch. "It's two."

Doc waved his hands to indicate it was no big deal and then pointed to the far wall. "Wheel him over against the wall. I'll get to him shortly."

Brandon Jenkins?

Sanders' heartrate jumped. He turned quickly to Hunter. Cowboy had turned pale, his knuckles white as he grabbed the edge of a countertop.

"Cowboy, let's get some fresh air."

Hunter stared, glassy eyed at the sheet draping the body on the gurney. His jaw was clenched so tightly that it vibrated.

He grabbed Hunter's arm. "Cowboy, let's go.."

Hunter didn't respond. It was as if his feet were locked in place. His hands were rigid and his eyes were like lasers burning a hole in the sheet.

The realization of what had just happened launched Doc into action. "Get that gurney out of here. Now!"

His assistant flashed wide, panicked eyes at him. "What? But you just said —"

"Forget what I said. Move him to Autopsy One. I'll process him in there."

"But—"

"Do it now, damn it." Doc's voice roared and the assistant nearly tore the doors off their hinges getting the gurney out of the room.

The chaos transformed to complete silence in a matter of seconds and the three men once again stood without speaking. Hunter continued to stare at the spot where the gurney had been, his face had now gone from pale to flushed with a sheen of sweat. Sanders gripped his elbow to steady him, his eyes locked only on Hunter.

Doc watched both of them, his mouth agape. Finally, he spoke, his voice just a murmur. "Sorry, Cowboy."

Chapter 12

Seeing Brandon Jenkins' body had sent him reeling. He was barely able to remain standing. All he wanted to do was run for the door. And the worst part of it were the pitiful looks from Sanders and Doc. He had told Billy that they'd regroup back at the station and he stumbled out of the room as fast as he could.

Hunter now stood in the conference room trying to remember the drive from the morgue. He'd been on autopilot, trusting his muscle memory to pilot his SUV down the well-worn path.

He took a couple of deep breaths, closed his eyes and focused on slowing his heart rate. After his mind had cleared, he began to think about the case and the questions began to pop. Why the lag between the actual shooting and the 911 call? Why was Brandon there at all? What was his connection to Logan? Where was Logan's gun? Where was his stash?

Sanders bounded through the door. He stopped, put down his bag and looked warily at Hunter.

Hunter ignored the look, picked up a marker and walked to the whiteboard. "Don't ask. I'm fine."

"Okay. Whatever you say Cowboy." Sanders pursed his lips. "Before you get going too far on the notes, I've got an update."

Hunter furrowed his brow, glanced at Billy sideways but didn't say anything.

"I got a call from Sprabary on my drive over..."

"Spraybary?" Hunter's voice was curt and his glance had turned into a glare.

"I am the lead on the case, Cowboy." Sanders paused. "He

was just following protocol."

Hunter chewed on his lip and nodded his head. "Go on."

Refusing to react to Hunter's sarcastic tone, Sanders continued. "He got a call from a Lieutenant over in Narcotics. Apparently he has some information to pass on regarding Michael Logan."

When Billy didn't continue, Hunter shrugged. "So, what did he say?"

"Don't know. He wouldn't tell him. Said he wanted to talk to us in person." He looked at his watch. "In fact, my guess is he'll be here sometime this afternoon. I let Sprabary know we were headed back here and he said he'd let the guy know."

Hunter arched an eyebrow. "That's interesting. What's the guy's name?"

"Trevor Carlson. Ever heard of him?"

"The name's familiar. Don't remember ever meeting him. Strange that he wouldn't tell Sprabary anything."

Sanders shrugged. "Who knows? Guess we'll find out when he gets here." He pointed to the whiteboard. "In the meantime…"

They spent the next thirty minutes documenting what they knew, possible leads and what questions were still wide open. The two detectives fell into a familiar rhythm and Hunter's anxiety dissipated somewhat. He stretched as the tension in his shoulders eased.

A knock on the door stopped their conversation and both turned to see a man who looked like a CEO about to address a Board of Directors meeting. He was a couple of inches shorter than Hunter with a severe expression and close cropped dark hair. There were just enough hints of gray to give off an older vibe. In spite of it being Saturday, he was dressed in a full suit and tie with buttoned down white shirt.

Hunter deduced this was Carlson and had to suppress a grin.

"I guess all lieutenants are cut from the same mold. This guy could be Sprabary's cousin."

"Are you Sanders and Hunter?" His voice matched the CEO motif as well, deep and elegant.

Billy nodded. "I'm Sanders. Are you Lieutenant Carlson?"

"I am. I understand someone popped one of my favorite scumbags."

"I assume you're referring to Michael Logan?"

"Yeah. Saved the taxpayers some money, but might have really fucked up one of my operations."

Hunter pointed at him. "Ah. Now I get the secrecy."

Carlson looked at Hunter. "And you are?"

"Sorry." He stepped forward, his hand extended. "I'm Detective Jake Hunter."

As they shook hands, Carlson eyed both of the men. "Were you the two guys involved with that human trafficking thing a few months ago?"

They nodded.

"Nice work." He gestured to the table and everyone sat. "Doubt this one will get you on CNN, but who knows."

"How can we help you, Lieutenant?" Sanders had his notepad ready.

"I'll cut to the chase so we can all get some of our weekend back. I've had a guy deep under for over a year now. He's embedded in Logan's operation." He paused. "Up to now, it hasn't bourn much fruit, but we were hopeful that was about to change."

"Who is it?" Sanders jotted notes.

"Can't tell you that."

Hunter leaned back. "Can we meet with him?"

"No. When I say he's deep under, I mean he's way deep and any contact will put him and the operation at risk. I'm one of his only contacts and we only communicate through coded messages on burner phones."

Sanders turned out his hands. "Then how does this help us?"

"Because I think I can tell you why this piece of dirt got shot." He paused to make sure he had their attention. "Over the last two weeks, we've had three separate cases of tainted Ecstasy. Two resulted in fatalities. One is still in the hospital fighting for her life."

Both detectives nodded.

"Word on the street was that the tainted stuff had come from Logan. My guy was trying to determine if it was something Logan did or if it was further up the food chain." He tapped his finger on the table. "My point being that you've got a whole bunch of very upset friends and relatives. It was common knowledge that Logan was the supplier and any one of them could have been upset enough to take him out."

Sanders leaned back in his chair and scratched his smooth scalp. "How does Brandon Jenkins play into that scenario?"

Carlson shrugged. "Not sure. Never heard the name. But I'd check into his circle of family and friends and see if one of the victim's names pops up."

"We can do that." Sanders jotted down a note. "I was at his house this morning and no one said anything about it, but that's not surprising. They weren't exactly a welcoming committee. I'm kind of surprised that they spoke to me at all."

Hunter looked at Carlson. "What else can you tell us about Logan and his operation?"

Carlson spent the next thirty minutes giving them a rundown. He told them that Logan was fairly low on the food chain and that his guy had been more focused on Logan's boss. The boss, Dalton Foster, ran a multilayered narcotics distribution organization that dealt in everything from pot to coke. His guy had been part of the organization for over a year and still had almost nothing on Foster. "Seems like every time we thought we had him, he was one step ahead of us."

After Carlson left, Sanders and Hunter sat in silence and absorbed the new information.

Sanders finally spoke up. "Could it be as simple as a distraught relative or friend of one of the overdose victims?"

"Might be." Hunter nodded. "But how do you explain

Jenkins being there?"

"Maybe he was actually going there to kill Logan after all."

Hunter was shaking his head before Sanders finished the sentence. "Doesn't add up." He leaned forward and ticked off points with his fingers. "He showed up well after Logan was dead. It looks like the gun he had was one he found at the scene. The 911 call was made after he arrived."

"It was almost like someone wanted him to be caught at the scene."

Hunter leaned back, interlocked his fingers behind his head. "Sounds messed up to me. I'm just glad I'm not the Lead Detective on this one."

Chapter 13

Hunter didn't even bother to look at the display on his phone when it buzzed Sunday morning. There wasn't anyone he wanted to talk to at the moment, and based on the dozens of calls he'd already let go to voicemail over the weekend, it was either Kipton from the Star Telegram again or one of the pests from the local TV stations.

He didn't need or want to talk with any of them. The stories, sound bites and headlines were already in heavy circulation. A white cop had shot a black teenager. There was nothing he could say to any of them that would tamp down the fury, even the truth.

The calls had started yesterday evening long after he and Sanders wrapped up their discussions for the weekend. It didn't seem to make sense spending all weekend chasing non-leads. After all, Brandon Jenkins' death wasn't a mystery and Michael Logan wasn't getting any deader. And until now, the press wasn't involved.

Hunter rubbed his eyes. He had assumed that Friday night would have been the worst but he was wrong. It felt like he hadn't slept at all last night either. Every time his head hit the pillow, Brandon Jenkins' face played on the movie screen in his mind. After a few wasted hours, he just gave up and flipped channels all night.

"What?" Hunter looked through his fingers to see Panther sitting in the middle of the breakfast table staring at him as if he didn't know what he was seeing. "I know I look like shit. You don't have to remind me."

Panther eased up on his paws, stretched and sauntered over to head butt Hunter. He sniffed at his face and gave him a look that suggested *take a shower.*

Hunter leaned back in his chair. "Yeah, well. You don't smell so great either." He pushed away from the table, stood and began to aimlessly pace again, as he had since the middle of the night.

This would have been a great day to have worn that Fitbit thing that Stacy gave me for my birthday.

He smiled at the thought and then wondered if he even remembered where he'd put it.

Stacy... I need to give her a call.

He looked at his watch. It was ten a.m.. This had to be the most unproductive Sunday morning he could remember. All he'd done is drink coffee and pet the cat.

Maybe this is what normal people do on Sunday mornings.

His phone buzzed again. This time curiosity got the better of him so he picked up the phone and looked at the display. Stacy. He stared at it. A second buzz. His chest felt heavy.

Pick up the phone. She just wants to help.

This is my issue, not hers. I shot that kid. I need to deal with it.

A third buzz. His finger hovered over the green button.

A fourth buzz. He felt his throat tighten as he set the phone down on the table, stood and walked toward the master bedroom. A shower sounded like a better alternative.

The water was hot, almost scalding, but Hunter let it wash over his scalp, down his neck and onto his aching shoulders. His mind kept churning, but it was all rehash. He and Sanders had gone over every aspect of the case for another couple of hours after Carlson had left. Nothing had piqued their interests.

Brandon being there still didn't make any sense. Why the 911 call came in when it did was strange. And why would a guy like Logan, who had to have been packing, not even get a chance to struggle, much less get off a shot?

Hunter leaned his head back and the jets of water beat on his closed eyelids and splashed into his nose. No matter how hard the water hit, it didn't seem to make a dent in the fog that had enveloped his mind.

As the force of the water drowned out the outside world, he drifted back to Friday night. Running through the alley, sidestepping boxes and pallets. Smelling the dumpster. Seeing the shadow of the figure running in front of him. Watching that shadow morph as the spotlights hit it. The figure stopped. Hunter yelled. The figure stood still. But then...

Hunter's eyes flashed open at a sound in the room. He pushed back from the jets with such force that his back slammed against the tile on the back wall of the shower. One hand shot up to wipe his face while the other slashed across the shower door glass to create a clear swath in the condensation.

His heart was pounding as he squinted.

"Stacy?" He steadied himself against the shower wall. "Jesus, you scared the shit out of me."

She cocked one eyebrow. "Good. Then I guess we're even. I've been leaving you messages since yesterday afternoon. For all I knew, you were dead on the side of the road." There was no smile to indicate she was trying to be funny.

She opened the shower door and turned off the water. After a quick approving glance up and down, she smiled. "Now get yourself dried off and take me to brunch."

Chapter 14

As Hunter pulled into the station lot on Monday morning, he almost ran over Reyes. Jimmy gave him a 'what's up with that' gesture and waited for Hunter to get out of his SUV.

"You trying to kill me Cowboy?" Reyes tried to sound serious, but he couldn't suppress the grin.

"Sorry about that. My mind was elsewhere." Hunter didn't reflect Jimmy's good mood.

"No worries. I wanted to catch up with you anyway. Made some progress on the Tyler case."

Hunter had been so preoccupied with the Logan murder, it took him a moment to register that there was another case he was supposed to be leading. "Oh yeah. Find anything interesting?" He gestured for them to step inside the door to get out of the morning sun.

"Not too much. As you indicated, single gunshot to the head. Doc managed to get the autopsy in late on Saturday. Nothing particularly noteworthy. It was a 9mm slug. It was in good enough condition to run ballistics so I retrieved it from Doc. I'll get it processed ASAP."

"Sounds good. Let me know when you hear something."

"Will do. Other than that, just followed up with Stacy's team. No DNA or fingerprint evidence worth processing."

"Okay." Hunter noticed a thoughtful expression on Reyes' face. "Is there something else?"

"Yeah. The gunshot was at fairly close range and I thought it was interesting that the CSI team didn't find the cartridge. Stacy said they hit the whole area with a metal detector and didn't find anything."

Hunter tilted his head. "You think the shooter policed his brass?"

"Looks like it."

"That usually indicates someone who knows what they're doing. Was this Tyler guy anyone special?"

Reyes shrugged. "Haven't done a complete work up on him yet, but he looks like your typical sleaze ball. He doesn't look like the type someone would waste good talent on."

Hunter leaned against the wall, the tile felt cool through his shirt. "Let me know if you think we're looking at something out of the ordinary. Did you find anything else?"

"I was able to confirm your eyewitness with a shot from a security camera. Unfortunately, the shot was from about as far away as the witness. It was grainy and didn't show a face."

"Typical."

They both started walking down the hall. Reyes frowned. "You know, I heard some statistics the other day about how often the average person in a major city is caught on camera every day. In the U.S., it's around seventy five times. In the U.K., it's closer to three hundred."

Hunter glanced at him but didn't respond.

"I'm just saying that you'd think with all that surveillance, you and I'd be obsolete."

Hunter arched an eyebrow. "Apparently, getting caught on camera and getting caught on a good camera at a good angle are very different."

Chapter 15

Before meeting up with Sanders in the conference room, Hunter took a detour downstairs to the IT department. It took a few minutes to navigate through the maze of cubicles and the stacks of boxes laying in the aisles, but he finally found his destination.

Sean Jackson's tattoos and body piercings gave him the look of someone law enforcement would typically throw in handcuffs. But Hunter was glad this guy was on their side. In the world of IT security, where it's hard to tell the hackers from the good guys, Sean fit in perfectly.

Hunter rapped on the metal frame of his cubicle loud enough to get his attention through the headphones. Sean looked up and smiled. "Hey Detective. Been a while. How are things?"

The corner of Hunter's mouth ticked up. "Things are fine, but I need a favor."

"Name it."

"I need a copy of some dashcam footage from Friday night."

Sean nodded. "Easy enough." He leaned forward and tapped some keys. "You got a case number?"

Hunter gave him the number for the Michael Logan case, but when Sean typed it in, he frowned. "Don't show any footage logged against that number."

"I'm not sure it'd necessarily be logged against the case. Can I give you the patrol unit number, date and time?"

"That'll work."

Hunter gave him the information and he went back through the same process. This time his look was more puzzled. "Dude, this says it's logged against an Internal Affairs case. I'm not sure—"

"Consider it a personal favor. I just want a copy."

Sean's face twitched and he blinked several times. "All right. But you didn't get it from me."

After Sean burned the video to a USB thumb drive, Hunter thanked him and headed back upstairs to the conference room.

"Don't take this wrong Cowboy, but you look like shit." Sanders grinned as he watched Hunter drop his bag onto the conference room table. He was standing in front of a whiteboard already full of notes.

"Good morning to you, too." Hunter's voice was more animal growl than human. His hair was spikier than usual and there were dark circles under his eyes. He dropped into a chair, rubbed his face and unpacked his bag.

"Tough weekend?"

"You might say that."

"Want to talk about it?"

"No."

Hunter plugged in his laptop, hit the start button and looked up at the whiteboard, finally noticing all the notes. He glanced at his watch wondering if it was later than he thought. "Looks like you've been busy. Did you work yesterday?"

"Not exactly. I just had a lot swirling around in my head so I got here early this morning to get it on the board."

A smile broke across Hunter's face and he sat up a little straighter in his chair. "Now isn't that a switch. You're in early getting stuff moving while I get to walk in at nine. I may get used to you taking the lead on cases."

"Yeah, well. Nothing's moving yet, but I do think I've at least got a plan started." Sanders turned to the board. "Carlson told us there were three victims of the tainted Ecstasy, two were fatalities and one was in the hospital. I was able to track down the names and many of the details." He paused and stared at the board.

"And?"

"Sorry. It's just that all three seemed like pretty good kids with a lot going for them." He sighed and shook his head.

Hunter nodded and stared off into space.

Brandon Jenkins was a pretty good kid with a lot going for him also.

"Anyway." Sanders continued, jolting Hunter back. "I've got the three files and I thought we'd try to at least hit the immediate family members this morning. From there we can expand out to friends."

"Okay, so who's first?"

Sanders tossed a file onto the table. The picture of an early twenties Hispanic woman looked up at Hunter. She had big brown eyes and long dark hair. For a moment, his mind flashed to the picture of Jimmy's daughter on his desk.

"She's in the hospital." Sanders twirled the marker between his fingers as he spoke. "My hope is that we can eliminate her family and friends pretty quickly since most of them have been spending every waking hour at the hospital. Chances of them stepping out to plan and execute a murder are pretty slim."

"I like your thinking. Always good to thin the herd early."

Sanders looked at his watch. "She's at North Hills Hospital in North Richland Hills. If we get going now, we can be there by 9:30."

"Let's roll." Hunter closed the file and packed up all the stuff he'd just removed.

*   *   *   *

The heat seemed to radiate up through the floorboards of Hunter's Explorer as they made their way northeast on Airport Freeway and then north on Loop 820. As he exited on Glenview Drive and headed west, Hunter nodded toward the file in Sanders' hand. "What's the rundown?"

Sanders opened the file and flipped through some pages. "Martina Ruiz, 21, student at Tarrant County College. She was brought in last Thursday night, unresponsive. They had to bring her back twice and she's been fighting for her life since."

After a right hand turn on Booth Calloway, Hunter turned into the parking lot of North Hills Hospital. "Student at TCC?"

"Yeah, already on it. Trying to find out if she had any connections to Brandon Jenkins."

"Any details on where she got the stuff?"

"Nothing specific. Since it appeared to be an accidental overdose at the time and there was no connection to anything else, the information in the file is pretty basic. We'll have to see if we can get more from the family."

Hunter gestured toward the front of the building as he got out. "I'll follow your lead." He smiled.

The intensive care unit on the third floor was packed. They checked in with the duty nurse. She directed them to a group of people in the waiting room, all of whom looked worn out.

"Mr. and Mrs. Ruiz?" Sanders flashed his badge to a Hispanic couple who looked to be in their mid-fifties. They were surrounded by family members, including two young men in their mid to late twenties.

When they nodded, he introduced himself and Hunter and gestured to the two men. "Are these your sons?"

"Yes." Mr. Ruiz pointed to the older son and then the younger. "This is Hector and that's Manuel."

Sanders jotted down the names and continued. "May we ask you a few questions?"

They nodded and Sanders quickly rattled off the basic information that he had regarding Martina's situation.

"Yes, that's correct." Mr. Ruiz gripped his wife's hand. "We've been here since Thursday night." He looked down and his voice got soft. "She hasn't regained consciousness yet."

Sanders nodded. "Do you have any idea where she got the Ecstasy?"

The couple looked at each other with some confusion and then Mr. Ruiz answered. "We told the officer on Thursday night that a friend gave it to her." He paused. "Look, he's a good kid. So is Martina. They didn't know this stuff was bad."

"Mr. Ruiz, I'm going to need his name. We need to find out where the drugs came from."

Both heads were nodding before Sanders finished his sentence. "We told the officer that as well. It was from a guy named Mickey Logan. We were hoping that you were here to tell us you'd arrested him."

Sanders didn't respond to their statement, he just jotted down some notes and continued. He looked specifically at Mr. Ruiz. "Do you or…" He pointed to Hector and Manuel. "Any of your family know Mr. Logan?"

Mr. Ruiz' face scrunched up. "Of course not. None of my children hang out with scum like him."

"Can you tell me where you were on Friday night?"

He looked straight at Billy. "As I said, we've been here since Thursday."

"And your sons?"

"They were here as well. What does this have to do with catching Mickey Logan? Why does it matter where we were?"

Sanders shifted in his chair. "Michael Logan was murdered on Friday night, Mr. Ruiz. We just needed to confirm that you and your sons weren't involved."

Mr. Ruiz slowly pushed himself up from his chair, his face turning pink, then red. His voice started low and slow, but rose in volume and speed as he spoke. "My daughter is fighting for her life twenty feet from us and you have the gall to come in here and accuse me and my sons of murder?"

Mrs. Ruiz began to mutter under her breath in Spanish. Hector and Manuel got to their feet.

"Mr. Ruiz, I—" Sanders didn't get the words out.

"Get out!"

Both sons stepped forward. Sanders and Hunter reflexively stood and found themselves nose to nose. Before things got out of hand, Sanders stepped backwards to diffuse the situation. "Mr. Ruiz, I—"

"You heard my father. Get out of here." The oldest son started poking the air with his finger. "This is typical. When a chica is dying, no one cares enough to even write down what we told them, but when some scumbag turns up dead, you're here accusing us. We have nothing more to say to you."

Sanders looked past the brothers while Hunter kept them at bay. "Mr. and Mrs. Ruiz, my apologies." Before he finished, Mr. Ruiz and his sons had already turned away and Hunter motioned him onto the elevator.

When the doors closed, everything went silent for a moment and Sanders stared at the doors with his mouth agape.

"That went well." Hunter tried to hide his smirk. "For future reference, you might want to start off with asking them how their daughter is doing. Might soften them up a bit."

Sanders looked at him in disbelief, started to comment but stopped and exhaled deeply.

By the time they made it to the SUV, Hunter was in almost full belly laugh. The scowl on Sanders' face continued to grow as he crawled into the passenger side and slammed the door. "You could have spoken up anywhere along the way, you know."

Hunter shook his head. "Oh no. No need. You had it under control." He turned the ignition and grinned over at Sanders. "Look on the bright side. There's no need to ask how they're doing at our next stop."

Sanders looked at Hunter in disbelief. "That is wrong on so many levels."

*   *   *   *

"Okay, give me the details on this one."

Hunter had finally relented and regained his composure after having teased Sanders as they made their way back over to the Carter

Riverside area.

While they moved west on Belknap, Sanders seemed relieved as he opened the folder. "Tyson Hancock, black male, 18 years old. He was a senior at Amon Carter-Riverside High School. Lost his Mom to cancer a few years ago." He flip through a couple of pages. "No history of trouble with the law. On paper, looks like a pretty good kid." He shook his head. "What a waste."

"Aren't they all?"

His head nodded absently as he pointed out the windshield. "Take Yucca Street. The house isn't too far from the Jenkins' house."

Hunter's jaw tightened as he followed the directions. He hadn't been with Sanders when he visited the Jenkins. He had purposely not looked up the address. He didn't want to know.

Noting his reaction, Sanders winced. "Sorry, Cowboy."

"Don't be." His voice was terse. "We can't investigate this case without talking about Brandon Jenkins or his family. I just need to deal with it."

Sanders looked over at him. "That's not going to be easy Cowboy. If you need to talk about it, I'm here man."

A pained grin spread across Hunter's face. "That's what the shrink is for, isn't it? I get to go see him later this morning."

"Yeah, well. Having been there, done that, I got news for you. Don't expect miracles. I can guarantee you that shrink has never been in your shoes."

Hunter stared out of the windshield and changed the subject. "Where are we headed?"

Sanders guided them on a winding path through a neighborhood just north of Yucca and west of Beach Street. They ultimately came to a house on Carnation Drive.

The Hancock home was small, but sat on a larger plot of land than most of the tiny frame houses around it. It was brick, and separated from the street by an ornate brick fence with wrought iron gates. The yard had a couple of large Oak trees and minimal grass but the landscaped shrubbery across the front of the house indicated someone cared about the upkeep of the home. Two late model cars were parked on the concrete drive off to the left in front of a single carport.

"Looks like they're home." Sanders nodded to the cars.

"Try not to piss this group off, okay?"

Sanders shook his head as he stepped out of the passenger side and stepped up onto the sidewalk. The late morning heat stopped him in his tracks. "Jesus, it's hot."

Hunter shrugged and he followed Sanders through the gate, up the sidewalk and onto the front porch. There was audible movement from inside the house when Sanders punched the doorbell but it took several moments before the door opened.

"Can I help you?" The door inched open to reveal an outline of a man's face. Even in the shadowy lighting, it was clear he wasn't expecting company.

"Mr. Hancock?"

"Yes."

"I'm Detective Billy Sanders and this is Detective Jake Hunter. May we come in for a moment and talk with you about your son?"

Billy's question was met with a long silence. When he was about to state it again, the door slowly opened to reveal a man who, according to the file, was in is early fifties but the sunken cheeks and deeply etched lines made him appear much older. He was a big man who had the look of a broken down thoroughbred. His muscular shoulders slumped as he used the door handle for balance. His clothes were wrinkled, his eyes looked tired and he clearly hadn't shaved in several days.

Mr. Hancock halfheartedly gestured toward the couch as he shuffled to a chair, fell into it and looked at the two detectives. Now that he had adjusted to the room light, Hunter could see the man's eyes were bloodshot. There was the faint odor of liquor mixed with sweat and the staleness of the room.

He caught Sanders' glance and raised an eyebrow. Sanders

just frowned, sat down and jumped right in. "Mr. Hancock, I'm glad we caught you at home."

"Yeah, well, the last week has been rough. I haven't felt up to working."

"I understand. Sir, we're here investigating a number of things that might be related to your son's death. Can you tell us a little about Tyler and what happened?"

His slow mannerisms became glacial while he processed the question. When he spoke, his voice wasn't much more than a whisper. "He was a good boy. I don't know what happened." He shook his head and his eyes fixated on a spot on the floor. "This wasn't like him. I taught him better than that."

Over the next few minutes, Mr. Hancock struggled through telling the story of a high school athlete who had everything going for him. Good looks, good grades, a winning attitude and a real opportunity to take that next step in life.

He spoke of a young man with a close knit group of friends and provided Sanders with the names of his three closest buddies. "They were like brothers. They'd grown up together." He shook his head. "Boys that age shouldn't have to suffer this kind of loss. It's unnatural."

"I guess they took it hard?"

He nodded his head. He closed his eyes and his lip trembled slightly. "Yeah. They took it hard." His voice cracked. "Everyone's taken it hard."

"Have you seen them since the funeral?"

"No." He shook his head. "It's probably for the best. I haven't exactly been up for entertaining." He gestured around the room. "As you can see, I've been a little messed up."

Sanders paused for a moment and noted the pizza boxes, soda cans and beer bottles deposited on most of the surfaces in the room. "Mr. Hancock, have you seen anyone since the funeral?"

"I unplugged my phone and haven't answered the door until you knocked."

Sanders looked at Hunter. Hunter just rubbed his forehead and gestured for Billy to continue.

"Mr. Hancock, just a couple more questions. Did Tyson know Brandon Jenkins?"

He tilted his head slightly. "Is that Audie Jenkins' brother?"

"Yes, sir."

"I'm sure he did then. He and Audie were classmates. For a while, they dated a little. Don't think they ever got too serious." He paused and his face slacked. "I saw her last Thursday at Tyson's funeral. She was so upset, she could barely stand."

He continued to speak, and as he did, his voice modulated first between pride and then anguish, but grew louder and more angry as he went. "This shouldn't have happened. Are you here to find the bastard that did this to my son?"

Not taking the bait, Sanders continued. "Do you know where he got the Ecstasy?"

For the first time in the conversation, Mr. Hancock's former stature broke through as he sat up straighter and pushed back his massive shoulders. He glared at Sanders, his voice was strong and his speech was clear. "Detective, whoever gave that shit to him killed my son and took away my only reason to live. If I had any idea who did this, you'd have another crime to solve because I'd kill him with my bare hands."

Both Hunter and Sanders shifted in their seats as they absorbed the intensity of his stare. Billy started to ask another question but Hunter cleared his throat and quickly spoke up. "Mr. Hancock, we're sorry for your loss. As we know more, we'll try to keep you informed. Thanks for your time."

Walking back to Hunter's Explorer, both men squinted against the mid-morning sun and neither spoke. Once they climbed into the truck, Hunter cranked the ignition and let the air conditioner strain for a few moments. Neither detective was anxious to break the silence, but eventually Billy spoke. "Cowboy, why did you cut me off?"

"He's not our guy."

Sanders nodded. "I think you're right, but he's got no alibi and he clearly has enough rage to do it. I know it was going to be uncomfortable, but didn't we need to press him on where he was Friday?"

"Nope." Hunter slipped the SUV into gear and pulled away from the curb. "When he pointed out the trash in the room, I looked at the pizza boxes. I noticed the delivery ticket taped to one of them. It was delivered at 8:30 on Friday night. He was here when Michael Logan was shot."

A look of relief swept across Sanders' face. "Good. I really didn't want to push him any further. He's suffered enough."

Hunter looked at his watch as he turned onto Yucca and headed toward Beach. Sanders stared out the passenger side window and seemed to drift off into thought.

"You okay Billy?"

He continued watching the storefronts pass by in a blur. "Working murders is bad enough, but at least there's some logic. Someone gets pissed off at someone else and they react violently." He breathed in deeply and tapped his knuckles on the window. "Kids dying from party drugs is just senseless."

"Guess that's why there're so many cops fighting the war."

"Yeah, right." Sanders' voice dripped with sarcasm. "The war on drugs." He shook his head. "We're not only losing that war. We may actually be making it worse."

Chapter 16

God, as if this morning wasn't painful enough, now I have to go deal with some shrink who has no idea what I've been through.

Hunter turned and headed west on Airport Freeway.

Sanders shot him a questioning glance.

"I need to get back to the station for my session with the shrink. Besides, I think we've all suffered enough for one morning. We'll track down the third family after lunch."

Sanders shrugged. "I can go talk to them by myself."

"No." Hunter's voice was louder than he intended and Sanders looked surprised. "Sorry." He softened his tone. "I know you're the lead on this investigation Billy, but we don't split up." He stared out the window. "I won't let that happen again."

"Shit Cowboy. I wasn't thinking." He nodded his head. "No problem. I can do backgrounds on the names we collected from this morning."

The short drive from Beach Street to downtown was quiet. Hunter was lost in thought. He glanced over at Sanders who just looked tired. This case was taking a toll on both of them for different reasons.

Hunter dropped Sanders at the station and weaved his way across town to the corner of Commerce and Calhoun. He dropped down into the parking garage under what used to be one of the Bass Towers but is now called the D. R. Horton Tower, and found an open spot near the elevator.

He sat for a moment before he killed the engine. Stepping out, he let his mind drift as the sounds of the city echoed in the concrete space. *What is this guy going to tell me that will make killing an innocent kid okay?* He shook his head. *Nothing. Absolutely nothing.*

Self-consciousness didn't hit him until he opened the nondescript door and stepped into the small lobby. Even though there were no other patients, his stomach flipped when the receptionist opened the sliding glass window.

"Detective Hunter?"

He looked up and stumbled over his words. "Uh, yeah."

She smiled warmly and handed him a clipboard with some forms and a pen dangling from a beaded chain. "Doctor Murray is finishing up with another patient. This information will help him help you." She sounded almost like a TV commercial. "I'll call you when he's ready."

"Uh, okay. Sure."

He sat on a leather chair and began answering the questions. Before he was halfway finished, she stood, opened the door and motioned for him. She led him back to a plush office with an ornate desk, two large cushioned chairs and a couch with a number of throw pillows. Hunter couldn't help but smile at how it looked just like he would have expected.

"The doctor will be with you in a moment."

She closed the door and the silence enveloped him. Instead of sitting, he paced slowly and absorbed his surroundings. He looked around for a second door, but didn't see one. *I wonder what he did with the last patient.*

He noted the bookshelves, diplomas and a smattering of papers spread across the desk. This was a new world to Hunter. While he had taken a short leave of absence after Frank's death, he had steadfastly refused to see anyone about it. Long walks and several conversations with his Dad had managed to keep him off the ledge and still on the force.

This was different. For one thing, it was mandated. For another, while he felt some responsibility for what had happened to Frank, he knew that he hadn't pulled the trigger. This time he had.

His thoughts were interrupted when the door opened and a man dressed in faded blue jeans and an untucked yellow golf shirt entered the room carrying a folder. For a moment, the two men stood and appraised each other. They were about the same age with similar size and build.

"Not what you were expecting?" The man smiled and reached out his hand. "I'm Chapman Murray, you must be Detective Hunter. Please have a seat."

Hunter perused his options, decided on the couch and rearranged the pillows so that he could sit. "I'm not really sure what I was expecting. I've never been to a... uh..."

"Shrink?" Another broad smile. "I'm good with that term detective." He sat in one of the chairs, ran a hand through his thick, blond hair and opened the folder. "I understand you were involved in a 'line of duty' shooting. I'm sorry to hear that."

Hunter just nodded.

"Our meeting is mandatory and I'm guessing you'd rather not be here, right?"

Hunter shrugged but didn't say anything.

The doctor set the folder in his lap and looked over at Hunter, his smile gone. "Detective, let's get past the cliché tough-TV-cop thing. The sooner we have a real conversation about what happened and how it's impacted you, the sooner you can get on with your life and not have to slink into a shrink's office."

"Okay." Hunter twisted his fingers together uncomfortably. "I'm just not sure what you're going to tell me that's going to make shooting an innocent kid okay."

He nodded. "You're right. There's nothing I can say that will do that. It's really about how you reconcile it internally that's going to make the difference." He took out a notepad. "Why don't we start with what happened?"

Hunter spent the next twenty minutes going over the shooting. He tried to be as clinical as possible, but found he had to clear his throat at the key moments in the story. "I've never killed anyone before." He looked down at his hands and felt his throat constrict. "The fact that he was an innocent kid…" His voice trailed off and he clenched his jaw.

"I understand your father was in law enforcement also?"

Hunter cut his eyes toward the doctor, his head nodding almost imperceptibly.

"Have you spoken with him about what happened?"

"Isn't asking about my dad a little cliché?"

Murray smiled and nodded. "Touché, detective. Guess I stepped into that one." He leaned back. "I don't bring him up because I think all of your emotional issues lead back to your father. It's more practical than that. If he dealt with this in his career, maybe he could provide some guidance."

"Oh, yeah. He's had a little experience in this realm." He pursed his lips. "I just wanted to get my head wrapped around it a little more before I had that conversation."

"Now, that sounds like some father issues… But let's focus on one thing at a time."

They spent the rest of the hour talking about Hunter's history on the force, the officers in his department and even dipped into why he followed his father into law enforcement.

Dr. Murray set his notepad and pen down on the decorative table beside the chair. "Detective, it looks like our time is up for today."

Hunter looked up and then at the doctor and then quickly back at his watch.

"You see, detective, time really does fly when you're having fun." He smiled. "Since I know you'd like to get through with these sessions as quickly as possible, why don't we plan to connect again on Wednesday?"

They scheduled the appointment and Dr. Murray escorted Hunter out a back door off the hall. Hunter made his way to his SUV and let the air conditioner cool him down. The tension drained from his shoulders and he wasn't really sure why, but a part of him was looking forward to Wednesday.

Chapter 17

"Are you ready for another fun filled interview with a distraught family?" Hunter shook his head and sighed as he strode into the conference room.

Billy was hunched over his laptop clicking away. He looked up and cocked an weary eyebrow. "What exactly did that doctor prescribe for you? Whatever it is, I hope you're sharing."

"Ah yes. Sharing is caring, but unfortunately, he wasn't that kind of doctor. All he wanted to do was talk." Hunter looked at the board and the smile slid off his face. "What have you got on our next interview?"

Sanders got up, rolled his shoulders and walked to the whiteboard. "Juarita Chaler, 22 years old, worked as a cashier at the Best Buy over in Hurst near Northeast Mall."

"What kind of name is Juarita Chaler?"

"Not sure." Billy slid a folder to Hunter. "But check out her picture. She was drop dead gorgeous."

Hunter looked and the photo and whistled low. "Damn. What a shame."

"What? It wouldn't be a shame if she were ugly?" Sanders shot him a glance.

"Hey, you're the one that brought it up." Hunter stood up and nodded toward the door. "Let's roll. We can finish this conversation on the drive."

The afternoon sun was blazing, making it impossible for the Explorer's air conditioner to keep pace. Even in warm weather, Hunter always wore a jacket. It looked more professional, and for functional purposes helped conceal his Glock. Though, today was testing his will and he took it off for the drive over.

They headed east on Airport Freeway and when they crossed over the Trinity River, he thought back to the Madison Harper case.

Sanders must have done the same because as they crossed the bridge, his eyes drifted south. "Have you talked with Barkley recently?"

"Not in several weeks."

Billy glanced back over to Hunter. "You ought to give him a call." He let the sentence hang without bringing up the fact that Texas Ranger Colt Barkley had more than a little experience with on the job shootings.

Hunter gave Sanders an understanding look as he exited at Riverside Drive. "Maybe I'll do that. In the meantime, you want to give me some directions?"

At Sanders' guidance, Hunter took a left at the light and looped under the freeway to the access road. After a short block, he made a right onto N. Retta into a small neighborhood bracketed by the Freeway on the south and Belknap Drive to the north.

The houses were small, mostly clapboard with large, old oak and pecan trees providing shade and privacy. Midway down the block on the right side, they pulled to the curb.

Both men perused the house, almost hidden by foliage. They then took in the rest of the neighborhood. It was midafternoon and in the middle of August so any sign of life was hidden inside the walls of air conditioned homes.

Satisfied there were no surprises in store, Hunter killed the engine. "Let's get this over with."

The ring of the doorbell garnered no results so Hunter rapped on the door with his knuckles and finally heard the faint sounds of movement.

There was a hint of the daughter's beauty in the face of the woman who answered the door, but her eyes were tired and her overall appearance disheveled. When she spoke, her Caribbean heritage was clear. "Can I help you?"

Sanders flashed his badge and introduced himself and Hunter. "We have a few questions about your daughter. May we come in?"

Her hesitation seemed to stem more from slow processing than from defiance. After a moment, she stepped back and motioned them into the house without a word.

"Is your husband home?"

She nodded. "Charles, da police are here and need ta talk wid us." She pointed to the couch. "Please have a seat, officers."

The husband looked equally disheveled, but clearly did not share her lineage. More Midwest farmer than Islander with his pale skin and reddish blond hair. Introductions were made again, the detectives accepted her offer, sat and brought out their notepads.

Hunter looked at them, and despite the evidence of their grief, could see where Juarita inherited her exotic look. He surveyed the cozy sitting area, his eyes moving from one wall to the next. *Based on the family photos, she was their only child. No wonder they both look like they've been hit by a bus.*

"Mr. and Mrs. Chaler, thank you for your time." Sanders' voice pulled Hunter's attention back to the couple. "Can you tell us about the night of Juarita's overdose?"

There was a pause in response as if each were waiting on the other to answer. Mrs. Chaler's mouth opened to speak but her bottom lip trembled. She gently bit down on her fist to control her shaking. "It was dat boy."

Sanders sat up a straight, his eyes widening.

"Her boyfriend." Her shoulders heaved with a sob.

"He's scum." The husband's voice boomed. "I told her from day one he was no good." He leaned forward in his chair, agitated, staring at his hands.

"Charles." Mrs. Chaler frowned at him, turned and shook her head. "He weren't bad. He was just searching, tryin' ta find his way."

"Late twenties with no job, no education and nothing to do

all day except hover around her." He finally looked up, his eyes wide. "And yet he always seemed to have a wad of cash in his pocket. What does that tell you?"

"Can you give me his name?"

"Vance Harvey. He lives over off Yucca on North Sylvania street."

Sanders jotted down the address and listened until Mr. Chaler ran out of steam. "Was he with her when it happened?"

"No." Mr. Chaler frowned, his eyes retreating back to his hands.

"She was out wid a group of her girlfriends." She gave an I told you so look to her husband. "Vance just about went crazy when he found out."

"Have you been in touch with him since?"

She shook her head. "He came to da funeral, but was a mess. We haven't seen him since."

Hunter listened as the conversation unfolded through strained voices, much like the others. *She was a good kid... They never knew she did drugs... This must have been her first time... She had such a bright future...* He watched their hollow eyes, their wringing hands, their slumped shoulders. The pain seemed to have consumed every ounce of their energy. They were barely there.

He thought about the Jenkins family and how they were going through the same process. But their pain was because of his actions. His throat constricted and his chest felt like a car was parked on it.

"Cowboy?" Sanders' voice shook him from his thoughts. "Did you have any questions for the Chalers?"

"No." He regained his composure and looked at the couple. "We're sorry for your loss."

Mrs. Chaler's eyes met his and froze him in his place. "Will you catch da man who poisoned my baby?"

Hunter didn't have the heart to explain their real reason for being there. "We'll do everything we can ma'am."

Back in the truck, Hunter cranked the air conditioner, positioned one of the vents directly at his face and closed his eyes. It was only Monday, only three days since the shooting. He felt like he'd aged ten years.

As if reading his mind, Sanders broke the silence. "Monday afternoon and it's already been a long week."

"No shit." Hunter leaned his head back against the headrest and his phone buzzed. He saw it was Stacy, rubbed his forehead and punched decline. The pressure on his chest was back. He looked at his watch. It was shortly after four. "You hungry?"

"Always."

"Then today's your lucky day. I'm buying."

Chapter 18

The waiter handed menus to Hunter and Sanders. "What can I get you gentlemen this evening?"

Without hesitation, Hunter took the menu. "Cold beer."

"Any particular brand?"

"You got anything interesting?"

"Ah." A Cheshire Cat smile broke across the waiter's face. "Have you ever gone down the Rabbit Hole?"

Both Hunter and Sanders looked up at the waiter with questioning expressions.

"I see I have you intrigued." He cocked his head. "What do you get when you combine a couple of award winning home brew masters, Mike Modano of the Dallas Stars, a small building in Justin, TX and someone with an Alice in Wonderland fetish?"

Hunter set his menu down and leaned back. "All right, I'm game. What?"

"You get Rabbit Hole Brewing. They make some of the best locally brewed beers around. Their selection includes an IPA, a Brown Ale, a Saison Ale and my personal favorite, the Mike Modano 561 Kolsch."

Hunter smiled. "I have no idea what a Kolsch is, but if it's good enough for Mike Modano, it's good enough for me."

Sanders held up two fingers. "Make that two."

After a long day of interviews and white board discussions, Hunter and Sanders were beat. Looking for any excuse to avoid a deep meaningful conversation with Stacy, or even worse, time alone with his thoughts, Hunter had suggested they grab a bite at Frankie's

Sports Bar on Third Street.

The place was bustling, even for early on a Monday evening. The tables were filled with mostly small groups of young professionals from various downtown firms.

They had barely decided on food when the waiter was back with two frosty mugs. The detectives toasted each other, took their first sips and smiled their approvals to the waiter, who gave a mock bow before he took their food orders.

With the waiter gone, Sanders looked at Hunter. "Cowboy, I want to run something past you."

Hunter nodded.

"You remember on Saturday morning when I went to the Jenkins' home to talk with the family.

Another nod.

He recounted the conversation with Maxwell Arnett. He cited all of the incarceration statistics and the disparity based on race. Their food arrived as he finished.

Once the waiter had cleared out again, Sanders looked at Hunter, who already had both hands full of a cheeseburger moving toward his mouth. "Well, Cowboy, what do you think?"

"About what?"

"About everything Arnett said."

Hunter finished chewing his first bite The cheeseburger was great and complemented the cold beer. "Not sure. Sounds like he's done his research and has a bunch of statistics." He left it hanging there and went back to work on his dinner.

"So you don't believe him?"

This time Hunter put his fork and leaned forward on his elbows. "It's not that I don't believe him. I'm just having a hard time swallowing his implications."

"What do you mean?"

"His point seems to be that cops are all a bunch of racists going around arresting black guys for no reason."

Billy started to interject, but Hunter held up a hand to stop him and continued. "I've been on the force for over fifteen years. I can assure you that during that time, I have never arrested someone when I didn't honestly believe they were guilty of the crime. Furthermore, I can't think of a single cop I know who would say any differently. Have you ever arrested someone you didn't think was guilty?"

Billy shook his head. "No."

"Do you know anyone who has?"

"No, but I don't think that was his point. He wasn't saying we were arresting people for things they didn't do. He was saying that the laws were written in a way that disproportionally affect young, black men."

Hunter nodded. "Okay, so it's not the cops that are the racists, it's Congress." He smirked. "That makes me feel better. I didn't much like Congress anyway."

Sanders shook his head. "Never mind. I shouldn't have brought it up."

"Billy, do you know why most conspiracy theories turn out to be crap?"

Sanders shrugged.

"In order for a major conspiracy to actually happen, any major conspiracy, it requires a large group of people to somehow coalesce around an idea to a point that they are willing to do something really radical. Then, they have to all get together to plan and execute this radical event or series of events. And most importantly, after it's all done, they have to keep it a secret.

"That's as close to impossible as it comes. It's completely against human nature. If you believe fervently enough in something to act out radically, you believe too much in that something not to talk about it."

"So you don't believe the statistics?" Sanders tilted his head and shot Hunter a disappointed look.

"I don't doubt the statistics. Hell, I don't even doubt that they're linked to the war on drugs. I just have a hard time buying that anyone or any group could have had the foresight and ability to actually purposely make it happen."

Sanders' eyes grew intense. "But you do see the results?"

"The results are obvious. The world of criminal justice isn't fair. The guy on the bottom end of the scale gets the shaft. That's just reality." Hunter leaned back, picked up his fork. "And neither of us needed anyone to quote a bunch of statistics to know it."

Chapter 19

The temporary lightness he had felt after his hour with Dr. Murray was a distant memory by Tuesday morning. After a fourth night of restless sleep and disturbing dreams, the baggage under his eyes looked as if he'd been in a fight.

Hunter was on his third cup of coffee by the time he hit the conference room and found Sanders already at the whiteboard making notes. It was a little after eight. "You're making me look like a slacker." His forced levity was obvious.

Sanders glanced over his shoulder and furrowed his brow. "You look like shit... Again. You sure you should be here?"

"I already have a mother. Don't need another one." Hunter's voice was almost a growl. He paused. "Sorry. That came out a little harsh."

"No worries."

Hunter pointed to the whiteboard. "What's all this?"

"Random thoughts." Billy shrugged and tapped the left side of the board with the marker. "This side is a list of the names we collected yesterday from our family visits. I also added a few based on some phone calls. I spoke with three of Martina Ruiz' teachers at TCC and Juarita Chaler's manager at Best Buy." He nodded to the right. "That side is a list of questions that need answers."

Hunter's eyes were tired, forcing him to squint as he perused the notes. "Good start. Let's walk down the questions."

"Okay. First one. What was on Brandon's phone?" Sanders raised an eyebrow at Hunter seemingly expecting an answer.

"What?"

"I just assumed Stacy had told you once she had examined it."

Hunter fidgeted. "Haven't really spoken with her much since Friday night."

Sanders looked confused. "Um… Okay." An uncomfortable silence hung for a moment before he continued. "I can call her this morning to see what she's found."

"Why not just ask me?" As if on cue, Stacy's voice pierced the conference room. "How can I help you Billy?"

Both detectives spun toward the door to see her standing with a folder in her hand. Hunter's stomach dropped when he saw how her jaw was set and how, even though she was speaking to Sanders, her eyes were locked on him. "Hey, Stace."

"Good morning, Cowboy." The frost in her voice was like a December wind in a cemetery.

Billy stood at the whiteboard, mouth slightly agape, holding the marker and watching the exchange. "Um, why don't I go grab some coffee?"

"This won't take but a minute." Stacy was all business and she continued to speak to Billy but stare at Hunter. "I thought I'd drop off the information we got from Brandon Jenkins' phone."

She finally switched her focus to Sanders, stepped toward him and handed him the folder. "Most of it's pretty mundane, just a lot of texts from friends. Normal stuff. The smoking gun is a single text early Friday evening telling him to meet at the crime scene at 9:15 pm."

Billy's eyes lit up. "Holy crap. That's awesome." He opened the folder to look at the printouts inside.

"Don't get too excited. It was from a burner phone that was bought with cash and doesn't show to be turned on."

Sanders' shoulders slumped. "Shit. So much for the smoking gun."

"Hang on. Don't completely discount it." Hunter wagged his finger as he started to pace. "This tells us a couple of things. First, we now know why Brandon was there in the first place and second, we know that whoever wanted him there, timed it specifically so that he'd show up after the murder."

"So somebody was deliberately setting him up?"

"Looks that way. Hell of a coincidence otherwise." Hunter snuck a quick glance at Stacy only to see that her attitude toward him had not changed. He turned back to Billy. "It ties in with the timing of the 911 call and the lag between the time of the shooting and the call."

"Yeah, but why?"

Hunter shrugged. "Who knows? Could be a grudge or it could be that Brandon was just an easy target."

"Well, I'll leave it to the brain trust to figure that part out." Stacy's voice once again caught their attention. "I need to get back to the lab."

The tension in the room that had temporarily dissipated was back in full force. Billy fidgeted and played with the marker in his hand. Hunter stopped pacing and turned to look at Stacy but only made peripheral eye contact.

"I'll, uh, give you a call."

"So you're phone isn't broken after all?"

"Uh, no. I'm sor…"

"A call would be nice." She cut him off before turning to Billy. "We're still processing our collections from the scene. I'll keep you posted on anything else we find." With that, she spun on her heels and was out the door before either detective could respond.

The silence in the room seemed to suck all the oxygen out. Hunter just stared at the empty doorway while Billy rocked on his feet and glanced around the room. After a moment, he cleared his throat and looked over at Hunter. "Guess I don't need to ask if everything's okay with you and Stacy."

"Nope."

"Look, it's none of my business, but—"

"You're right. It isn't." Hunter's voice cracked like a whip and his shoulders immediately tensed. He just as quickly relaxed. "Sorry. It's been a tough weekend."

Sanders nodded. "I can imagine." He paused, dropped the marker into its holder. "You know she only wants to help."

"Yeah, well. Let's just say that asking for help isn't my strong suit."

"Really?" Sanders flashed a short smirk, but it slid off his face quickly. "Some unsolicited advice? Don't make a bad situation worse. Take it from me. You're going to need every ounce of help you can get over the next few weeks. She can be your best life preserver. Unlike most... significant others, she knows the job and understands the life. All you have to do is let her in."

Hunter pursed his lips and rubbed his forehead. "Didn't you say something about coffee? I think I could use some."

Chapter 20

"Oh Cowboy, I'm so glad you stopped in. I heard what happened on the news." Bernard looked paler than usual behind the counter at Starbucks. His jet black bangs crept over his eyebrows. "Are you okay?"

Hunter motioned his hands to quiet Bernard. "I'm fine."

"But weren't you involved in that sh—"

"Don't believe everything you see on TV." Hunter cut him off, looked uncomfortably over his shoulder to the crowded coffee shop. He continued, but lowered his voice hoping Bernard would follow suit. "This really isn't the time or place. Let's just leave it that I'm fine, okay?"

"Of course." Bernard waved his hand at Hunter. "What was I thinking? Can I get you and Billy your usual?"

"That would be great." Hunter looked at Billy and shook his head in disbelief.

The two detectives had decided to walk the few blocks to Starbucks so they could get out of the stuffy conference room and enjoy some real coffee while they planned their day. They had a list of names and addresses to chase down based on the conversations with the families from the day before.

Once Bernard delivered their coffees to the table and apologized once again for his indiscretion, they spent the next hour planning out the most efficient path to locating and interviewing each on the people on their list.

By late morning, Billy was in the passenger seat of Hunter's Explorer with a stack of folders in his lap. He opened the top one as

Hunter cruised down Airport Freeway toward the Riverside area. "Let's see. First on our list are Juarita's friends at Best Buy. We'll start there and work our way back to the TCC Northeast Campus to talk with Martina Ruiz' friend."

"Let's go shopping." Hunter accelerated and headed east.

They introduced themselves at the customer service kiosk in the front of the store and asked the employee to page the store manager. He was on his phone and giving instructions to another store employee simultaneously as his quick steps brought him to Sanders and Hunter. When Billy flashed his badge, his eyes widened. "I've got to go." He punched off his phone. "I'm Stan Walker." He slid his phone into his pocket and reached out his hand. "You must be Detective Sanders."

"I am, Mr. Walker." Sanders nodded toward Hunter. "This is Detective Hunter. Is there a private area where we can speak with the employees you mentioned on the phone last night?"

He spun around, motioned for them to follow and took off down the aisle. As they followed, they passed the Apple section and Hunter couldn't help but slow to peruse the latest gadgets. "This way, detectives. There's a small office near the receiving docks." He continued to speak as Hunter and Sanders hurried to catch up. "We were all stunned with the news about Juarita. She was the last person I would have ever guessed would die of an overdose."

"Technically, she died from a tainted substance." Hunter felt compelled to clarify even though he knew he shouldn't. "For all we know, this was the first time she'd ever tried the stuff."

Walker nodded as he pushed through the double doors and directed them to a small, standalone office cluttered with stacks of boxes on the floor and folders on the small desk. Sanders moved some clutter off one of the three chairs in the room and spoke to Walker. "Could you ask Jazmine Moore to come speak with us?"

"I'll send her back immediately." He turned and headed back through the double doors.

"Ah, the glamour of police work." Hunter grinned as he

pulled a tissue from a box and used it to wipe off the other two chairs before he sat. He started to make another comment but was distracted when he saw the double doors open. A lean brunette walked through, saw them and headed their direction. In spite of the standard issue khaki pants and Best Buy golf shirt, she was breathtaking. "Birds of a feather..."

"No kidding." Sanders nodded to her through the glass and motioned for her to come into the office.

"Please sit down, Ms. Moore. I'm Detective Sanders." Billy directed her to the third chair. "This is Detective Hunter. We need to ask you some questions about Juarita Chaler."

She blinked several times and her eyes glistened. "Sure, how can I help?"

Sanders began with some basic questions about her relationship with Juarita. Hunter took notes and observed. She played with her hands and her voice trembled often. She seemed genuinely upset about Juarita's death.

"We didn't really socialize much outside of work. I tried to get to know her better but she spent all of her time with that scumbag boyfriend."

Sanders flipped a few pages in his notebook. "You mean Vance Harvey?"

She nodded. "He was a little older. Seemed to have a lot of time on his hands because he would come by the store all the time. Almost like he was checking up on her."

"Did you know she took drugs?"

"No. In fact, I was shocked to hear she had died of an overdose."

Hunter started to correct her as he'd done with the store manager, but decided to let her continue.

"She never showed any signs of drug use while at work. She was always smiling, hap—" The words caught in her throat and her face contorted momentarily as she wiped a tear away. "I'm sorry." Her voice now raspy. "She was just a wonderful girl. None of this makes sense."

Billy calmed her down and continued with the questions, but other than confirming the Chaler's distrust of Vance Harvey, she wasn't able to provide anything useful.

After speaking with Jazmine, they had brief conversations with three other store employees. They knew even less and, as they were all males, their only interest in Juarita was that they all seemed to have barely hidden crushes on her.

"Not exactly earth shattering information." Sanders flipped his notebook closed. "What do you say we head over to TCC?"

"Works for me."

"I think I've found a new place to buy my electronics." Sanders grinned as Hunter circled under Airport Freeway on Bedford Euless Road and took a right on Strummer Drive.

"I'm going to have to report you as a pedophile."

"Pedophile? She's what, twenty three? I'm only thirty. That's not that big of a gap."

Hunter shook his head. "I clearly need to get you connected with some adult women."

"I think we hunt in different forests. Besides, I don't have time. You work me too hard."

"Don't blame me, partner. It's you who's the lead on this case and the one who beat me into the office this morning."

Sanders looked out of the passenger window as they turned right onto Highway 26. "This one's important."

Hunter nodded, the smile dropping out of his voice. "They all are."

Chapter 21

The detectives found the room and positioned themselves in the hall across from the door. Both had reviewed Kaylee Santiago's file, class schedule and photo. They knew they were looking for a fit 20 year old with blonde highlighted brown hair.

The short drive down Highway 26 to Tarrant County College had been quiet. Hunter parked on the Northwest corner of the campus near the Technology and Arts Building. After a short walk from the parking lot, it was a relief to be waiting in the cool air conditioned hall.

As the door opened and the herd of students flowed out, Hunter searched each face but had to do a double take when Kaylee walked right past him. The bright eyes in the photograph had dulled and the lean, muscular body was now thin and almost frail.

"Ms. Santiago?" He took two quick steps and tapped her on her shoulder.

She nearly jumped out of her shoes and she continued backing down the hallway as she turned to face him. "Who are you?"

"Kaylee, I'm Detective Hunter with the Fort Worth Police Department." He nodded toward Billy. "This is Detective Sanders. We need to speak with you a moment about Martina Ruiz."

Sanders stepped quickly past her as she continued to shuffle backwards. He slid behind her giving her no alternative but to stop. The herd of students flowed past them without a second glance.

"What do you want? I've already answered a bunch of questions. I can't be late for my next class."

Hunter tilted his head. "According to the Registrar, you don't have another class until tomorrow."

Her eyes cast downward as she hugged her notebook to her chest. "I meant work. I'll be late for work."

"We'll write you a note." Hunter had shifted to his take no prisoners tone. "Let's step around the corner to the break room and sit down for a moment."

Her head nodded but her eyes remained glued to the floor. Billy gently touched her elbow and guided her around the corner and into a plastic chair.

He took over from there. "Kaylee, we're not here to cause you any issues. We're just trying to get more information about Martina so that we can make sure something like that doesn't happen again."

She again nodded vigorously, but now her eyes were glued to the notebook she'd set on the table. The fingers on her left hand flicked at the spiral ring on the edge while her right hand was splayed flat on the table. Even pressing on the table couldn't hide the twitching.

Sanders started again with the basic questioning while Hunter observed. An ache grew in the pit of his stomach as he watched her. He'd seen it all before. He understood her suffering.

"Have you ever heard the name Mickey or Michael Logan?"

Her eyes blinked rapidly. "He was at the party. I didn't know him, but Martina did."

"Is that who she got the Ecstasy from?"

"I don't know but it wasn't long after they left that she started getting sick."

"They?"

"There was another guy with him." A shy smile almost broke across her face. "He was kind of cute in a messy sort of way."

"Did you know him?"

She shook her head. "He never said a word, just hung in the background. I asked Martina about him after they left. She said his name was Vance."

Hunter and Sanders exchanged glances. As Billy continued

with the questioning, Hunter's mind drifted. He could see the young woman Kaylee used to be but he knew that former person was lost and may never make it back.

"Can I go now?" Kaylee's voice pulled Hunter back to the moment. Sanders glanced at him to see if he had anything else to add.

Hunter reached into his pocket and pulled out his business card, flipped it over and wrote a number on the back. "Kaylee, you need to get your Oxy use under control." She started to object, but he held up a hand to stop her. "The number I wrote on the back is for Recovery Resource Council. They're not far from here. Call them. Get some help. My cell number is on the front. If I can help, let me know."

Her hand shook as she took the card and it was clearly a struggle for her to make eye contact with him. "Thank you."

Back in the truck, Hunter cranked the air conditioner as soon as the engine engaged. "Can I call an audible?"

Sanders nodded.

"Seems like the name Vance Harvey has popped up numerous times. I know he's on our list, but why don't we pull him up to the top?"

"Works for me. Let me grab his address."

Sanders gave Hunter the information as they took a left onto Highway 26 and headed southwest. A grin broke across his face. "Cowboy Hunter, playing the part of social worker. What's up with that?"

Hunter frowned.

"Seriously, though, how did you know she had an issue with Oxy? I could tell she was using something, but I wouldn't have known what."

"The nervousness, the tremors, the loss of weight. I've seen it before up close. My brother struggled with it for a long time."

"Brother?" Sanders looked at Hunter and raised an eyebrow. "You have a brother?"

Hunter's hand gripped the wheel as his jaw tensed. "Had." The word came out like sandpaper. "He wasn't able to beat his addiction. Ultimately it beat him."

"Jesus, Cowboy. Sorry."

"You didn't know." He paused and swallowed hard. He nodded toward the road. "Let's go find Vance Harvey."

Between the afternoon sun and the silence in the truck, the drive from Hurst back to the Riverside area was oppressive. When they drove through the Haltom City area near where they had recently been involved in a human trafficking case, Sanders commented on the case and tried to spark a conversation but all he got from Hunter were nods and one word answers. By the time they took a right on North Sylvania off of Yucca, Sanders had given up and let the silence have its victory.

Hunter pulled to the curb between Springdale and Selma in front of a set of two, tan, brick apartment buildings. He looked at the well maintained buildings and grounds and arched an eyebrow. "Not exactly The Ritz but nicer and way more conservative than I would've expected for a small time drug dealer."

Sanders deadpanned. "Maybe he lives with his mom."

Hunter snorted which made both men laugh and the tension of the drive disappeared. "What does this guy look like?"

"Like a throwback to the seventies." Sanders opened the folder and handed Hunter a photo of a white male in his twenties with long, curly dirty blond hair and a scraggly beard.

They sat for a moment and planned. Sanders noted that the parking was in the rear. "The front of the building is wide open, not a tree in sight. We should park around the corner and approach staying near the front of the building."

Hunter concurred, pulled away from the curb and circled the block coming up on Springdale street. He parked on the street near the stop sign and they moved north on the side walk. When they found apartment four, Hunter motioned for Sanders to step to the other side of the door.

Once in position, both men drew their weapons and Hunter banged on the door. "Harvey, this is the Police. Open up. We need to talk."

His order was met with silence. Both detectives stood perfectly still and listened. Hunter shook his head and then repeated the process garnering the same results. Silence.

"What kind of self-respecting drug dealer is out and about in the middle of the afternoon?" Hunter smiled. He reached down and tried the doorknob but it was locked.

"Really?" Sanders shook his head. "You know that 'oh look, the door just happens to be open' shit only works on TV."

Hunter shrugged his shoulders and grinned. "It was worth a try."

"Let me guess, the next thing you're gonna do is pretend to hear someone screaming for help so that you'll have a reason to kick in the door, right?"

"Nah, it's too damn hot to exert that much effort. Besides, I like my job too much to pull that kind of shit. We'll just come back later."

Both detectives holstered their guns and walked down the sidewalk toward Springdale street and the cool air conditioning of the Explorer. They moved south along the building staying in the shade wherever possible.

As they turned the corner towards the parking area, , they stopped in their tracks. A man in ragged jeans and sunglasses carrying a bag of groceries walked around the corner. He caught their eyes, dropped the bag and bolted back around the corner.

"Harvey, stop, Police." Hunter bellowed as his legs started churning. He managed to stay up with Sanders for about the first twenty feet, but as they rounded the corner Billy pulled away.

Now Sanders was yelling and he flew down the driveway. "Police. Stop!"

Harvey had a lead on them and stopped to try to get in his car but realized Sanders was gaining on him too fast. He headed for the sidewalk, instead. But he only managed a few steps before he was hit with the full force of Sanders' 200 pound frame and he went down in a heap.

"Get off me you son of a bitch." His face was smashed in the dirt but the anger in his voice was clear.

"Shut the hell up and stop moving before I break your arm." Sanders clamped the cuffs on as the man continued shouting obscenities.

By the time Hunter caught up, Sanders had him cuffed and half way through the Miranda Rights. Hunter leaned over with both hands on his knees, sucking in air with sweat pouring off his face.

He looked over as Sanders yanked Harvey off the ground with one arm, showing no signs of exertion. "Jesus, you're not even out of breath."

Sanders shrugged. "Told you I wasn't too old."

Chapter 22

"What's up with this guy?" Hunter stared through the glass with his arms crossed.

"No idea. He's barely moved a muscle in the last hour. Just sits there."

After their foot chase and take down of Vance Harvey, they had him transported via patrol car to the station, escorted him directly to an interrogation room and cuffed him to the table.

"Really?"

"Yeah. Want to know something even weirder?"

Hunter arched an eyebrow.

"According to the patrolmen, as soon as they pulled away from the curb, his whole demeanor changed. He went quiet and rode to the station like a kid being driven to a birthday party. When they escorted him from the car to the box, he even thanked them for their courtesy."

"What?" Hunter looked incredulous.

"No kidding." Sanders nodded to the one way observation glass. "He's had that Zen like peaceful look on his face ever since."

Hunter ran both hands along his belt and adjusted his pants. "I guess it's time to see if we can disturb his happy place. Mind if I take the first crack at him?"

"Go for it, Cowboy." Sanders snickered.

The slap of the folder down on the table echoed off the hard surfaces of the room. "It really pisses me off when I have to chase suspects. I don't like running for recreation and I sure as hell don't like to do it on the job." The chair legs screeched against the tile floor as Hunter pulled it out from the table. He flipped it around and straddled it as he sat across from Harvey. "Care to tell me why you ran from us before we even had a chance to say hello?"

Harvey didn't speak. His expression remained placid, but his eyes darted around the room. They first came to rest on the camera mounted on the wall and then on the microphone pointed toward him on the table.

"Yes, you're being recorded and filmed." Hunter smirked and continued in an overly professional voice. "For your own safety." He paused and opened the folder. "Now why don't we have a little chat before my level of pissed off gets beyond my control?"

With an almost imperceptible tilt of his head, Harvey looked Hunter directly in the eyes. "Would you please turn off the recording devices, detective?"

His piercing stare and the level of calm in his voice unnerved Hunter to the point that it took him a moment to respond. He cleared his throat, narrowed his glare at Harvey and attempted to regain the high ground in this battle of wills. "Well now Vance, that's not how things work around here. In this room, I'm the one who asks the questions and assuming you've got a brain in your head, you're the one who answers them." He slapped the folder shut and shoved it to the side. "Juarita Chaler."

Harvey remained silent but blinked in a quick burst. It was the first indication that the guy wasn't a robot.

"Oh? Did I strike a nerve?" Hunter reached into the folder, grabbed a photo of Juarita and slapped it down in front of Harvey. "What? Talking about your dead girlfriend upsets you?"

With a meditative look on his face, Harvey closed his eyes for a moment and took a slow breath. When he opened them, the unnatural calm had once again washed over his face and he looked directly at Hunter. "Things aren't always as they appear, detective. I'll ask again. Would you please turn off the recording devices?"

Hunter pushed back from the table, sat up straight and let out a quick laugh. He was trying not to let this guy rattle him. "You are hell bent on making this a very long day for both of us, aren't you?" He leveled his stare at Harvey and let his expression go blank. *Two can play this game.* "I'll tell you what. I've got two fatal overdoses, one more headed in that direction, and one murdered drug dealer. I'll be happy to turn off the recording devices just as soon as you're done answering my questions."

The two men looked directly at each other, neither moving for almost a minute. Finally, Hunter cocked his head to the right, set his jaw and stood up. "Maybe you need a little more time to think about things." He turned and moved toward the door.

"Detective." Harvey's voice was slightly louder but retained the eerie calm.

Hunter stopped at the door but didn't turn to look at him and didn't speak.

"If you will do as I ask, I assure you, I will provide you enlightenment that may help you to reconcile Brandon's death."

The words pierced Hunter like a knife between the shoulder blades. He had to squeeze the door handle to hide his reaction. His heart rate shot up and his breathing thinned.

He slowly pivoted toward the man sitting at the table. His eyes burned into him. "What the fuck?"

Harvey, his expression having never changed, made a slight gesture with his cuffed hands toward the microphone sitting on the table.

Hunter took two slow steps toward the table, picked up the microphone and spoke into it. "Turn off the camera."

Billy's voice crackled over the playback speakers. "Cowboy, you know I can't—"

"Turn off the God damn camera, Billy!"

Silence hung in the air for several seconds before Harvey's eyes tracked up to the camera. The red light switched off.

Hunter continued to focus on Harvey. He then took the cable plugged into the back of the microphone and yanked it out. With a flick, he casually tossed the microphone on the table.

"You've got thirty seconds to give me at least one good reason why I shouldn't take this opportunity to kick the living shit out of you."

In a slow, deliberate tone, Harvey spoke. "Five seven three one two." He paused and let the silence engulf the room.

Hunter's expression hardened. He could feel the color wash over his face. "Fifteen seconds."

"My name isn't Vance Harvey. It's Bonner Hopkins. That's my badge number. I'm with FWPD narcotics."

Chapter 23

For a moment, all Hunter could do was stare at the ragged man cuffed to the table. *Harvey... Hopkins... A cop...* As the words sank in, he blinked and clinched his jaw. He turned and took two steps toward the mirrored observation window. Although unnecessary because he knew Sanders was watching him, he rapped on the glass and motioned for Sanders to join him.

Within seconds Billy bulled through the door, eyes wide and shoulders back, looking at Hunter. "What's up, Cowboy?"

"We have a situation." Hunter nodded toward the prisoner. "Detective Billy Sanders, meet Detective Bonner Hopkins."

"What?" Sanders' eyes bounced between the two men. "You're kidding." He shook his head. "A situation? More like a disaster."

"You took the words right out of my mouth, detective." Hopkins held up his cuffed hands. "You mind?"

Sanders moved toward him to uncuff him but Hunter stopped him. "Wait a minute, Billy." He turned to Hopkins. "Not that I don't trust you, but before I take those cuffs off, I'm going to need to verify your story." Without breaking eye contact with Hopkins, Hunter spoke to Sanders. "Billy, take a picture of our friend here and run it up to Lieutenant Carlson and confirm he's his guy. Don't show it to anyone but Carlson. Don't mention any of this to anyone."

"You got it." A quick click later, Billy was out the door and headed upstairs.

Hunter sat down and leaned back in the uncomfortable

plastic chair. "While he's tracking down your boss, why don't you catch me up on your operation?"

Hopkins eyed him for a long moment, then slowly nodded his head. He took a deep breath. "I've been deep undercover for just over a year. Up until last Friday, my main contact had been Michael Logan but my long term target was Dalton Foster."

"You say that like it should mean something to me." Hunter opened his hands. "Let's pretend for a second that I'm a homicide detective who unfortunately stays too damn busy to be completely dialed in to the drug trade."

A grin spread across Hopkins' face. "Duly noted. Dalton Foster is one of the top five suppliers of narcotics in the Metroplex. His territory is the northern half of Tarrant County, mostly east of I-35. He's a wholesaler to the street sellers and gangs that don't have their own supply chain. He doesn't waste time with weed. He's all about small packages with big price tags."

The chains attached to his cuffs rattled as he started to get animated. "His distribution business includes importing cocaine and heroin. Domestically, he buys and sells every kind of pill you can imagine. Oxy, Valium, Ludes, whatever. In the last few years, he's even branched out into manufacturing meth and Ecstasy."

"How close are you to making a case?"

Hopkins shook his head, his hands droping to the table. "On Foster? Not very. He stays insulated with guys like Logan. We could've busted Logan anywhere along the way." He snorted a short laugh. "I guess someone else pulled the trigger before we got the chance."

Hunter nodded. "So, you don't know who killed Logan?"

"You mean Brandon Jenkins didn't? I assumed it was him. He's always been a bit of an anti-drug crusader and a pain in Logan's side, and with his buddy Tyson dying..." He stopped short. "But wait, wasn't he shot at the scene?"

Hunter's whole body stiffened and he had to pause to control his voice. "Yes, he was there and he was shot when he drew a weapon. We later determined that he did not shoot Logan."

There was a long pause as Hopkins stared at Hunter. He leaned back, blinked and shook his head. "You were the cop that... I'm sorry. What happened?"

"I'm not the one telling the story. You are." He motioned for him to continue. "How does Logan's death affect your situation?"

"Oddly enough, Logan getting whacked may actually help me. I figured that Foster would close ranks and shut me out, but instead he's actually pulled me in closer. Maybe not exactly a full promotion but he's connected me with several of Logan's customers and he's expecting me to start moving heavier volumes now." He looked up at Hunter. "Hell, for all I know, Foster was the one who plugged Logan. Maybe he was skimming too much."

Hunter pursed his lips, folded his arms across his chest and changed the direction of the conversation. "Tell me about Juarita."

Any hint of levity in Hopkins' expression drained. His voice sounded like it was being strained through hot coals. "She was a sweet kid who seemed to feel the need to live on the edge."

"Were you dating?"

"You might call it that." He looked down at his cuffed hands, his eyes blinking rapidly. "I was doing what I could to keep her from going over the cliff." His voice went to a whisper. "I wasn't successful."

"How does she fit in this mix?"

"I met her through Logan. He liked to throw parties and she was always there. I'm not sure how she got into that crowd but she didn't seem to fit. She had too much going for her."

Hunter nodded. "I've done very little undercover work but I seem to recall that rule number one is to not get personally involved."

Hopkins let out a laugh that sounded more like something bursting. "Yeah, I kind of blew that one."

"Do you know where she got the tainted Ecstasy?"

His jaw set and when he looked up at Hunter, his eyes were

lasers. "I didn't know she'd gotten it until it was too late. She'd never done Ecstasy before." He shook his head. "I know she enjoyed the party scene, but she'd never stepped over that line. She had to have gotten it from Logan. Logan was scum. He'd sell anything to anybody. He didn't care what happened."

The silence was deafening as the two men looked at each other. Hunter finally broke the silence. "Sounds to me like you might have had a reason to kill Logan."

Before Hopkins could answer, Sanders slammed back through the door. He stopped a few feet in, saw their facial expressions and looked from Hunter to Hopkins and back. "What did I miss?"

Hunter unfolded his arms and shrugged. "Detective Hopkins was just giving me a briefing on his undercover assignment. I'll catch you up later." He looked from Hopkins to Sanders. "What did Carlson say?"

"He's legit. FWPD. In fact, Carlson asked that I pass on a message." He turned to Hopkins. "He hasn't heard from you in almost a week and wants an update through the regular channels."

Hopkins nodded. "With everything that's happened, I haven't been in a position to report in." He looked to Hunter and rattled his wrists. "So, do I get these off now?"

Hunter stood for a long moment before he reached into his pocket and pulled out his key. "We're not done with our debrief but no need to keep those on."

After uncuffing Hopkins, the three continued to talk for another thirty minutes going into detail about Foster's operation and specifically the role that Logan played. They speculated on who might have killed Logan and why. Hopkins indicated that he'd thought the same as Hunter and Sanders, that it was likely a friend or family member of one of the victims.

When Hopkins made that suggestion, Hunter cocked an eyebrow. "No, Detective Hunter, it wasn't me. Not that the thought didn't cross my mind, but I haven't been under long enough to forget

I'm a cop."

Sanders chimed in. "Where were you Friday night?"

"I was at my apartment drinking my way through a bottle of tequila." He turned back to Hunter. "And no, I don't have anyone that can corroborate my alibi."

"No need at this time." Hunter stood and looked at Sanders. "If you don't have any more questions, we should probably cut him loose and get back to working the list."

A nervous look washed over Hopkins' face. "Wait a minute. You can't just release me."

Both Hunter and Sanders looked at him.

"I've got eyes on me at all times. That's why I ran when I saw you. I couldn't be seen willingly talking with cops. And I definitely can't be seen just strolling out of here as if I've been visiting with old friends."

Hunter shrugged. "Okay, what do you suggest?"

"Hit me."

"What?"

"Punch me in the face. I need to look like I've been roughed up by the cops. Otherwise, I'm going to have a lot of talking to do."

Hunter grinned and shook his head. "I'm not going to punch you in the face." He nodded to Sanders. "Talk to him." He started to turn and walk away.

"Him?" Hopkins smiled and pointed at Sanders. "Are you kidding me? He'd break my face. I'll take my chances with the skinny white guy."

Without a second's hesitation, Hunter spun with a balled up haymaker. He connected with Hopkins' jaw and sent the man slamming against the wall. Hopkins grunted, grabbed his jaw, and slid to the ground.

Hunter flexed his fingers and looked down at Hopkins. "Skinny white guy my ass."

Chapter 24

Hunter had been starring at his laptop for the last thirty minutes. The video sequence from the dashcam had played over and over. Each time, his stomach had twisted as he saw Brandon's hand reach for his pocket, the metal object come out, the two flashes and the jerking of his body as it fell.

His daze was finally interrupted when he heard the doorbell ring. He stepped around Panther in the entry hall and opened the door. Stacy stood on the front porch. His breath caught in his throat. She was holding an ice pack in one hand and a bottle of cabernet in the other. She held up the ice pack. "Billy suggested that I bring this by. He said you might need it." She then held up the bottle of wine. "Considering your mood lately, I thought this might help too."

He stood and stared at her but couldn't seem to get words to form.

"You're not really going to make me stand here and sweat, are you?"

With a slow grin, he stepped back and held the door open. "Sorry, I uh... I was expecting the pizza guy." He looked at her and his smile widened. "You're a significant upgrade."

"I should hope so." Stacy handed him the ice pack. "Here, put that on your hand." She looked down at his purple knuckles. "I'll open the wine since you're wounded."

After strolling a few steps down the hall, she turned back to Hunter and nodded toward his hand. "Is that what happens when a skinny white guy punches someone?"

"Very funny."

By the time the pizza guy had come and gone, Hunter finished up his second glass of wine. He brought the bottle with him, gently nudged Panther off the couch and they settled in with their plates and glasses. Panther stretched, gave them both a disdainful look and slinked off to the bedroom.

Looking at Stacy, he could feel the tightness in his chest slowly dissipate. She held up her glass, the forced smile sliding off her face. "So, Cowboy, how are you really doing?"

He averted his eyes and drained his glass. "I'm eating pizza and drinking wine with a beautiful woman. I'd say I'm doing pretty good."

She shook her head. "Nice try." She reached over, took the glass out of his hand and set it on the table. Her hand caressed his. "Don't think you can flatter your way out of this conversation. You've been avoiding me for four days. You look like you haven't slept in a month. And you just about broke your hand on a prisoner's jaw today." Her green eyes were glassy when she looked into his. "I want to help, but you've got to let me."

His throat tightened as he tried to swallow. He started to say something but hesitated and shook his head. When he finally spoke, his voice was strained. "Sorry, Stace, I'm just... This is something I..." He stopped, took a breath. "I don't know how to fix this and I don't know how you can help."

"Just talk to me. You'll feel better."

Looking down at the floor, Hunter felt as if there was a refrigerator sitting on his shoulders. He squeezed his eyes shut. "There's nothing to say." He looked up at her, his face gaunt. "I shot an innocent kid and there's nothing you or anybody else can say that's going to change that fact."

Stacy started to speak, but Hunter kept going.

"Brandon Jenkins will never graduate from college, never get married, never have kids. His mother won't get to see those things in his life." He blinked rapidly and looked down at the floor again. "I'm the one who took those things away from him and his family."

"If you hadn't reacted, it would be your family suffering."

He nodded but didn't look up. "Yeah, well, at least I've had forty years." His shoulders sank further. "He was just a kid."

Stacy leaned over, kissed the top of his head and wrapped her arms around his shoulders. They sat on the couch for several minutes in silence, just holding each other.

When the emotion had drained from both of them, Hunter reached for the bottle of wine only to find it empty. He tilted the bottle toward Stacy. "Looks like we could use a little more." He stood and walked around the couch.

Hunter rummaged around in a kitchen drawer until he found the cork screw. After he popped open the bottle, he stopped and looked around the corner at Stacy. "Oh, and by the way, technically, he wasn't a prisoner. He was a cop."

When her mouth gaped open, he smiled.

"I guess Billy didn't tell you the whole story."

She leaned back. "Sounds like you need to."

Over the next thirty minutes he told her about all the fingers being pointed at Vance Harvey, about finding him, chasing him down and arresting him. He explained Harvey's strange behavior and then finally that Harvey turned out to be Detective Bonner Hopkins.

"I guess that's a first." She smiled and held up her hands like she was reading a headline. "Cowboy Hunter arrests a cop."

He took a long sip of wine. "Well, technically it's not, but I certainly don't make it a habit."

Stacy furrowed her brow until her memory kicked in and she nodded. "Oh yeah, Desiree. I'd forgotten." She looked at the pain on Hunter's face. "I'm sorry. I didn't mean to dredge that up." She leaned forward, reached over and stroked his arm. "So much for my plan to cheer you up."

He placed his hand on hers and gritted a smile. "It's working better than you think."

When she turned her hand to grip his, he winced and she

pulled back. "Wait a minute. You never explained why you punched your prisoner or cop or whatever. What's up with that?"

Hunter's body language lightened as he leaned back to tell the story. "He insisted."

She squinted at him. "What?"

"He said that if he walked out of there unscathed, the guys watching him would suspect he'd cooperated with the police so he asked me to rough him up."

"And you just did?"

"No. Actually, I told him I wouldn't and suggested to Billy that he do it. Hopkins didn't like that idea. He seemed to think that if Billy hit him, he'd break his jaw or something. He said he'd prefer the skinny white guy do it." He smiled and saluted with his wine glass. "So this skinny white guy obliged."

Stacy shook her head and rolled her eyes. She put her wine glass down, took his face in both hands and pulled him to her. "Can this skinny white guy do something other than punch people?"

"He's certainly willing to try."

Chapter 25

Even with Stacy beside him, Hunter's sleep was restless and his dreams tormented as they had the four previous nights. On Wednesday morning, he was up, dressed and on his second cup of coffee when the sun brightened the edges around the shades.

Hunter's reflection in the oven's glass door revealed the bags under his eyes. So heavy, as if Hopkins had punched him instead of the opposite. He was so tired, he tightened his grip on his coffee cup to make sure he didn't accidentally drop it.

I've got to figure this out or I won't be able to function.

He looked at his watch. A little after six. Stacy was still asleep and it was too early to go into the station, so he paced. Not for his normal inspiration but out of nervous energy. Although he had the paper delivered every day, he rarely read it except on weekends. He decided to make an exception this morning and quietly stepped out into the front yard to retrieve it.

The street was like a panoramic oil painting, serene but still. Even in the middle of the week, at this time in the morning, no one was out. The only sounds were the muffled traffic from Western Center and the crunch of the grass under his shoes, brown and brittle from a long, dry summer. The heat already infiltrated his shirt as the sun cracked over the tops of trees and rooftops to the east. Normally, this moment would have been relaxing, even meditative. As he walked back up the sidewalk with the paper, all he felt was oppressed.

The running shower let him know that Stacy was up. He thought about joining her but even that possibility didn't lift his spirits. He opted for reading the paper at the kitchen table. He had to step around Panther in order to sit. When he did, the cat launched himself onto the table, sat directly in front of Hunter and stared at him.

*   *   *   *

If you never go to sleep, you don't have to worry about setting an alarm clock.

Mrs. Jenkins' mind hadn't stopped running as she stared into the darkness of her bedroom. She been staring since she turned off the light the night before. Seeing black men die young was something she'd experienced many times before. Seeing her son die at age twenty left a hole in her soul that would never heal.

There was a light knock on the door. "Mama. You awake?" Audie's voice was quiet, tentative.

"Yes baby. Come in."

Audie's face appeared around the edge of the door, her eyes red and puffy. She looked at her mother and her tears started to flow again. Mrs. Jenkins had watched Saturday and Sunday as Audie had spent most of her time throwing things and picking fights, acting mad at the world. But the last two days she hadn't been able to stop crying. It seemed the realization that her older brother was never coming home again had finally hit.

"How did you sleep Mama?" Mrs. Jenkins ignored her question. "Let's get some coffee."

The two hugged close and walked arm in arm down the hall toward the kitchen.

"I'll pour the coffee if you'll get the paper." Mrs. Jenkins pulled two cups from the cabinet.

Audie hesitated. "No good news in that paper. Why don't we just talk?"

"Child, I know what's in the paper and I want to read it. If the rest of the world is going to read about my family, so am I." Mrs.

Jenkins cocked her head to the door.

Audie obliged and stepped outside into the stillness of the morning.

Mrs. Jenkins was already sitting at the table, two cups of coffee poured and set on the table when she returned. She delayed handing over the paper until her mother glared at her.

Mrs. Jenkins took the paper, unfolded it and smoothed it out on the table. She took a sip of coffee, set her jaw and let her eyes cascade through the headlines.

*   *   *   *

Hunter frowned. "What the hell do you think you're doing cat? You know better than to get on the table." He stood, lifted the large mass of fur off the table and set him on the ground. This elicited a long, low mew. "What?" He shrugged at the cat as if he expected an answer.

When he opened the paper, multiple headlines hit him like rolling punches to the gut.

Jenkins Family Still Looking For Answers.

ACLU Calling For Independent Investigation.

Police Shooting Victim's Funeral Today.

This was the first time he'd seen a newspaper since the shooting. He'd been so distracted with his emotions and so focused on the Logan case, he hadn't thought about the potential media backlash.

His throat constricted as he forced himself to scan through the black words on the white paper. He locked in on the story about Brandon Jenkins' funeral. A person was being buried because he'd pulled the trigger on a gun. A young man with a seemingly bright future.

How did this happen?

Heat flushed into his face, but he couldn't stop reading. The graveside service was scheduled for 9 AM. Almost on autopilot, his hand reached for his phone and he keyed in a text to Sanders letting him know he'd be late.

He paused only briefly as he dropped the note on the table, packed up his laptop, grabbed his gun and his badge and headed toward the garage. Once again, he had to step around Panther on his way out.

That cat seems hell bent to get in my way this morning.

It was a little after seven when he pulled onto Western Center. He had some time to kill but he knew that he'd have to get there early. It wasn't like he was going to be able to actually attend the service. He needed to be able to position himself where he could observe without being seen.

*   *   *   *

A knock on the door broke the silence that had settled into the small living room. Audie and Mrs. Jenkins had finished their coffee and were now dressed in black and waiting.

Audie stood and answered the door. "Hey Uncle Max." She stepped back and let Professor Maxwell Arnett step through the door.

He hugged Audie and let her linger on his shoulder as a short burst of sobs racked her thin frame. His hands patted her on the back as he looked to his sister. "Valerie, the limousine is waiting outside to take us to the funeral home whenever you're ready."

She didn't move, her eyes fixed on the bookshelf across the room where Brandon's smile taunted her from inside a picture frame. She'd been staring at the photo for several minutes. This was the fifth morning she'd woken up without her son and part of her still expected to see that smile again.

Arnett and Audie waited without speaking. After a few more moments of silence, Valerie Jenkins stood, smoothed her dress and straightened her shoulders. She turned and walked toward the door. "It's time to bury my son."

*   *   *   *

For most of his life, he'd questioned the usefulness of cemeteries. He really didn't understand the concept of paying homage to plots of earth that contained lifeless bodies. Even with Gina and Frank both buried here, he rarely visited. This morning he pulled into the front entrance of Mount Olivet Cemetery, his coffee warm in the cup holder.

This morning, his view of the place seemed different. Cemeteries were the ultimate and final American melting pot. With rare exception, modern public cemeteries catered to all ethnic groups and religions. No matter what your view of race, gender, faith or sexual orientation, the chances were good that everyone would spend eternity buried close to people of all variations.

Cops and criminals and victims all shared a few acres of finely manicured grass. If there was an afterlife, God clearly had a sense of humor.

Following the signs for the Jenkins funeral, he ended up near the north west corner. Although it was near the train tracks and 28th Street, it was in a grove of beautiful old oak trees, tranquil and serene with the late morning light.

He drove past the portable awning set up for the service and found a secluded spot where he wouldn't be noticed. Circling back so that he faced the awning, he pulled to the curb, cut the engine and waited in the silence that only a graveyard can induce.

*   *   *   *

The limousine pulled up and stopped outside Calvario Funeral Chapel at the corner of Northside Drive and N. Main Street. Under the carport stood a gleaming hearse and another limousine matching the one carrying the Jenkins. Mrs. Jenkins' entire body stiffened at the sight of the two waiting vehicles.

"I want to get out."

"Valerie, there's no need." Maxwell furrowed his brow. "The service is going to be at the graveside. We're just stopping here so that we can..." He cleared his throat. "Escort Brandon home."

"I want to stand out there when they carry him out." Her jaw was set and her eyes were unblinking.

Maxwell nodded his head, acquiescing without much of an argument. He opened the door, stepped outside and assisted his sister and niece. The three of them stepped to the back of the hearse, its door already open.

A moment later, a shining silver casket rolled through the open double doors. Flanked on each side by three of Brandon's friends, none of which looked up to meet her gaze. At the sight, her grip tightened on Maxwell's arm and a knot swelled in her stomach.

Stepping forward, she forced them to stop just shy of the vehicle. She placed one hand on the casket. In spite of the warmth of the morning, the metal was cold and a chill raced through her veins.

An unrecognizable sound came from her throat and Maxwell caught her before she realized her knees had buckled.

"Mama, are you okay?" Audie helped her uncle support her. "Let's get back in the car."

She could feel her head absently nod as they almost carried her to the limousine. Through the window, she watched the six young men perform the first step of their duty.

*   *   *   *

This was a bad idea. Why did I come here?

The past thirty minutes had crept by as his mind replayed that night over and over. Without the engine running, he had no air conditioning and sweat soaked his shirt. He had watched the mourners begin to arrive and crowd around the area. There were dozens. So many that the crowd seemed to swallow the small covered area reserved for the family. The crowd was diverse. Old, young, black, white. Many took meandering walks as they paused at various headstones, often hugging one another for support.

Just before nine, a white hearse and two matching limos slowing inched their way through the grounds. When they stopped at the site, he realized his heart was pounding and he was breathing as if he'd just run a mile. He closed his eyes and focused on relaxing to get himself under control.

When he reopened them, he saw a woman being escorted from the limo. He assumed Mrs. Jenkins. A thin, teenage girl Hunter recognized from pictures to be her daughter Audie, supported her on one side and a tall middle aged man bearing a family resemblance, was on the other. Although she was projecting a strong, stoic air, even from a distance, he could see the pain wash across her whole being.

As the pallbearers extracted the casket from the hearse, Hunter's attention was drawn to a throng of media that had arrived and were setting up shots for the evening news. He hadn't thought about that possibility and began to fidget in his seat.

This was a really bad idea.

*   *   *   *

"My friends." The preacher's voice boomed. "We are here today to say goodbye to our brother Brandon Jamahl Jenkins as he finishes his journey to his final home. We all…"

The crowd drew closer, hanging on the words of comfort. The preacher's purple silk robes swayed in the light morning breeze and fluttered as he waved his arms and held tight to his Bible.

"…An innocent man cut down in the street. A young man taken well before his time. He was…"

The words ran together and the edges of the scene blurred as the final reality set in for Valerie Jenkins. That wasn't just a silver casket. That was the casket that contained her only son.

"…And we will not forget. No, we will not forget."

*   *   *   *

Hunter couldn't hear what the preacher was saying, but the effect on the congregation was palpable. Emotion surged through the crowd as people leaned on each other for support.

He could barely breathe. His anxiety swelled as his attention alternated between the emotional crowd and the media vultures. When his phone rang, he jerked back so hard his head audibly slapped the headrest. He saw Sanders' number on the screen.

"Hunter." His voice sounded foreign even to him.

"Cowboy? Are you all right?"

He took a deep breath to slow his heart rate. "Yeah, I'm fine. What is it?"

"I know you said you'd be in a little late, but I've got something you need to see right away."

Hunter closed his eyes and silently thanked Sanders for giving him an excuse to leave. He cleared his throat and hit the ignition.

"I'm on my way."

Chapter 26

The image of Brandon Jenkins' mother tormented Hunter the entire drive down I-35 and into the city. He was responsible for the pain etched on her face. After pulling into the rear parking lot for the Central Division Station, Hunter sat for a moment and fought back the emotions welling up in him.

His phone rang. When he saw that it was Reyes, he let it go to voicemail. He wiped his brow with a leftover fast food napkin he found in his console and blamed the sweat on the heat outside. A few deep, calming breaths later, he headed into the building.

When Sanders saw Hunter walk through the door of the conference room, he shook his head slowly without breaking eye contact. "Cowboy, you don't look so good. Man, if you need the day off..."

"I don't need anything." His voice was almost a bark.

Sanders held up his hands in surrender. "No problem. Don't get me wrong. I'm glad you're here."

Hunter dropped his laptop bag on a table and swiped his hand through his hair. "You said something about ballistics?"

His phone rang again. Reyes. He let it go to voicemail again. He knew he should pick up, but his priority was in front of him. "Sorry, you were saying."

"Yeah..." Billy picked up a manila folder and handed it to Hunter. "According to this, the gun that shot Logan, the gun that Brandon Jenkins had in his hand, was used in an armed robbery a little over two years ago."

"Okay. It was used in a previous, unsolved crime. What's so

earth shattering about that?"

Sanders scrunched his face and shook his head. "That's just it. The crime wasn't unsolved. We got the guy. He's down in Huntsville. And here's the headline. We also got the gun."

Hunter looked up from the report and looked at Sanders as if he'd just stated the obvious. "Well of course we have the gun. We got it Friday night at the scene."

"That's not what I meant. According to our records, we've had it all along. Based on the evidence inventory for the robbery case, that gun is sitting in the FWPD evidence lock up. Has been for over two years."

Hunter arched his eyebrows. A slow grin spread across his face but it was interrupted by his phone ringing again. Hunter sighed when he saw it was Reyes. He looked at Sanders. "Jimmy's about to wet his pants. I need to get this." He punched the accept button. "This had better be good."

"If by good, you mean bad, then, yeah, it's good." Reyes was clearly worked up about something.

Hunter wasn't. "Okay Jimmy, I know English is hard for you, but what the hell are you talking about?"

"The ballistics on the Tyler case came back."

"And?"

"We got a match."

"That's good. Let me know when we can go arrest someone."

"That's the problem. The guy who last owned this gun has been sitting in Huntsville for two years."

Hunter stopped, his face went flat and he eyed Sanders while he spoke. "Let me guess the punchline. It was a robbery case and the gun is supposed to be in the FWPD evidence lock up."

The phone was silent for a long moment before Reyes spoke. "How the hell did you know that?"

"It seems to be going around. Email me the ballistics report. I want to compare it to Logan case. Make it quick. I want to see it before Billy and I go over to the lock up."

He clicked off. "Well now. This just got interesting."

"Don't tell me.." Sanders' eyes were wide. "The same gun was used for both Tyler and Logan."

"We'll find out when we get that email, but the odds sure look good."

"That means we've got two murders tied to a gun that theoretically, is sitting in the FWPD evidence lock up."

"Exactly." Hunter nodded. "Looks like someone's got some explaining to do." He glanced at this watch. "As soon as we get that email from Reyes, you have time to drive over to the warehouse?"

"Thought you'd never ask."

* * * *

While the exterior of the warehouse looked very ordinary, drab gray concrete walls and no signs, the level of security around it was anything but. Ten foot high cyclone fence with razor wire on top. Cameras on each of the four corners of the fences as well as of the building. Two heavily armed but nondescript guards dressed in all black with K9 partners roamed the open space between the fence and the building.

There were no outward signs that this building had any association with the Fort Worth Police Department. Even the guard manning the booth at the gate wore all black with no FWPD patches or insignia.

The building had no parking spots near it so Hunter had parked in a public lot around the corner. He and Sanders walked the few hundred feet through the heat to the booth, produced their badges and signed into the log sheet. Because of the nature of the facility, they were required to leave their weapons with the guard. He radioed to his counterpart inside to let them know the two detectives were on their way.

Hunter felt the eyes of the patrol guards on him as he and Sanders walked the few steps from the guard shack to the front door.

When they entered they were met by another guard behind thick glass. "I need to see your identification, then log in using that keyboard. Please provide the case number for the evidence you'll be viewing." He directed them to a kiosk.

Both men complied, showed their badges and logged in with their names and the case number for the armed robbery. The guard then pointed to uncomfortable looking plastic chairs. "An escort will be up in a minute."

Hunter remained at the window. "Officer, can you please provide me with a list of all officers who have accessed this case number since it's been here?"

The guard nodded, let his fingers tap a number of keys and looked at the display in front of him. "No one, detective."

Hunter scrunched his forehead. "In the entire two years? You're sure?"

"Positive. You're the first."

"Thank you." Hunter nodded and stepped over to the chairs.

Once seated, Sanders leaned toward Hunter. "This place is like Fort Knox."

Hunter smiled. "I guess this is your first time over here. They take evidence security seriously here."

Before they could continue, the door leading into the facility opened and a guard motioned for them to enter. He was dressed the same as the rest of the guards and seemed about as friendly. "Follow me. I'll take you to your case evidence."

The warehouse was larger than it looked from outside with at least twenty rows of pallet racks, each three sections high. The rows went back at least a hundred feet and were packed from floor to ceiling with boxes marked with case numbers. With its stale, dusty cardboard smell, it always made Hunter think of it as an unfriendly Costco.

Midway back on the seventh row, the guard pointed to a box on the floor. "Case number 975681. Looks like it's just this one box." He stepped back but didn't leave.

When Hunter noticed him still standing there, he looked over to him. "We've got it from here."

"If it's all the same to you Detective, I'll wait here."

"Suit yourself."

While the warehouse was neat and the floor was clean, the box had a thin layer of dust on it. Hunter wiped his hand across the top to see the inventory label on the front. He let his finger fall down the short list of items until it stopped on the line with the Smith and Wesson 9mm. "It says it's here. Let's see what's behind lid number one."

He popped the lid open. Did a quick scan. There were only a handful of evidence bags. No gun. Hunter stood up and looked to the guard. "Officer, we have a problem. The gun is missing from this box."

"Excuse me?" The guard squinted his eyes at Hunter. "That's not possible."

Hunter stepped back and gestured toward the box. "See for yourself."

After emptying the box and verifying the contents against the label three separate times, he checked each box in the stocking location to confirm there was only one box for that case. The guard stood and spoke into his shoulder mic. "Curtis, send Sergeant Thompson down to my location immediately. We've got a missing firearm."

Like a television rerun, the Sergeant repeated the verification the guard had done. The results were the same including the wide eyes and loss of color on his face. "Detective, we will launch an immediate investigation to locate the missing gun. I can assur−"

"We know where the gun is Sergeant. That's not the problem."

The Sergeant's mouth dropped open. "What?"

Hunter continued. "The problem is that it was used in a murder five days ago. What I need to know is how the hell it got out of this building?"

Sergeant Thompson's face flushed and he wiped his brow. "According to our records, no one has accessed this case since the day it got here. When evidence arrives, it's inventoried and signed off by two guards. I checked this case before I walked down here. We followed procedure and I can assure you that gun was in that box when it arrived. I know because I was one of the two guards who inventoried and signed off."

Hunter tilted his head. "That's unfortunate Sergeant." He chewed on the inside of his cheek while he let the stifling silence linger for a moment. "Just for grins, can you check something for me?"

"Certainly, detective," he answered with surprising eagerness.

"Can you see if Detective Bonner Hopkins has accessed any cases in this area in the past two years?"

Thompson nodded and relayed the request into his shoulder mic. He adjusted his earpiece as he waited. He closed his eyes and his shoulders slumped when he got the answer. "Six months ago, he accessed a case on this row about two pallets down."

Hunter looked at the Sergeant and then to his escort. "Do your escorts always stay with detectives when they're looking through evidence?"

The Sergeant fidgeted for a moment. "Our standard procedure is for the escort to stay with them. However, there are occasions, depending on traffic, where the escort might step away for a moment."

"Is there any way to know if that happened when Hopkins was here?"

Instead of answering immediately, the Sergeant spoke into his shoulder mic. "Curtis, can you check the logbook volume for the day Detective Hopkins was here?"

A moment passed before a voice crackled on the speaker. "Pretty heavy day that day sir, especially around the time he was here."

"Thanks." Sergeant Thompson looked at Hunter. "It's possible he could have been left alone, but there's no way to know."

Hunter shook his head at Sanders. "Looks like we get to go visit the boss."

Chapter 27

Getting out of the evidence warehouse was harder than getting in. Being the ones who had discovered that the gun was in fact missing from inventory, Hunter and Sanders spent the balance of the morning filling out reams of paperwork and being interviewed by progressively higher levels of rank. By the time they left, the Sergeant and his team were engulfed in a full official investigation. Hunter and Sanders were just ready for lunch.

Hunter retrieved his Glock from the guard in the booth and rolled his neck and shoulders to loosen up. His patience for process, procedure and bureaucracy was gone. With the confirmation of the gun's origin and the realization that Hopkins at least theoretically had access to it, Hunter's sense of urgency was growing. The thought that an undercover cop may have killed two people amped up his twitchiness.

They grabbed a quick fast food lunch on the way back to the station. This was more out of courtesy to Billy. While Hunter had initially been hungry, his sense of urgency overpowered his appetite and he barely touched his food. He spent most of the time tapping his foot and starring off into space. His mind processed the fact that Hopkins had been to the evidence lock up, that he'd accessed a box just a few feet from where the gun was stored and that there was a strong possibility that he'd been left alone long enough to get the gun. He also knew that, as tight as the security was at the facility, it was not standard procedure to search detectives on their way out.

When they finally made it back to the station, the engine was still knocking as Hunter jumped out of the SUV. His long strides required Billy to jog in order to keep up as they crossed the parking lot. He maintained his pace as they bolted through the back door, blew past the Sergeant on duty and climbed their way to the second floor.

"He's on a call." Paige McClaren's voice pierced Hunter's focus just before he barged into Lieutenant Jeff Sprabary's office.

He stared at the closed door and clinched his jaw before turning to Paige. "I'll wait."

"Might be a while."

"I'll wait."

As Paige shrugged in her best 'I don't give a shit' attitude, Sanders smiled, clearly amused at the interplay. Hunter never noticed either reaction as he began to pace in front of Sprabary's door mulling over the implications of the new information. His initial impression of Hopkins may have been wrong. It was possible that he'd let the fact that Hopkins was a cop cloud his judgment.

I should have seen this as a possibility. Undercover cop turned corrupt. He completely duped me.

"Hunter. Stop wearing out the carpet." Sprabary stood in the open doorway. "This had better be important." Without inviting them in, he stepped back and sat at his desk.

Sanders followed Hunter into Sprabary's office and closed the door behind them. Sprabary drummed his fingers on the desk and glared at them. Hunter started to speak but then caught himself. "Billy should catch you up since he's the lead on the Logan case."

Billy shot him a thanks-for-throwing-me-to-the-wolves look but straightened in his chair and faced Sprabary. "Lieutenant, we've made some progress on the case but there are two new developments we wanted to bring to your attention. One has created an internal issue."

Sprabary motioned his hand for Sanders to continue.

"We've received ballistics matches on the gun that killed Logan and the one that killed Tyler."

Sprabary furrowed his brow. "Who?"

"The Monticello Park case." Hunter interjected.

Sanders took a deep breath and continued. "First, it turns out that the same gun was used in both cases."

Their boss's eyes widened as he leaned forward. "Well now, that's interesting."

"The second issue, and most concerning, is that the gun was used in an armed robbery from two years ago. It's a closed case and the weapon was recovered and stored in evidence inventory at the time." He stopped to let that sink in.

The silence in the room seemed to grow in pace with the increased color of Sprabary's face. He leaned forward and squinted his eyes. "Let's be perfectly clear. You're saying that this murder was committed with a weapon that was supposed to be in the control of the FWPD?"

Sanders nodded in a way that made him look like an six year old getting scolded by the principal. He fought to keep from smiling. Any humor flew away when Sprabary directed his glare at Hunter.

"Are we sure?"

"Positive." It was Hunter's turn to nod like a bobble head. "We validated the ballistics, the make and model as well as the serial number. Before we brought it to you, we even went to evidence storage and confirmed the gun isn't there."

Hunter and Sanders both stared as Sprabary processed the information. Eventually his expression turned to the lowest common denominator — *the shit storm just turned worse.* He adjusted in his chair blew out a long breath. "This is not good gentlemen."

The two detectives exchanged glances before Hunter continued. "Well, sir, unfortunately, there's more. It seems that Detective Hopkins, Lieutenant Carlson's undercover guy, AKA Vance Harvey, appears to have had access to the weapon about six months ago. When you combine that with the fact that Logan provided the drugs that killed Hopkins' girlfriend, it looks like we may have kicked him prematurely."

Sprabary shook his head before Hunter finished his sentence.

"This just gets better and better." He looked from Hunter to Sanders and back. "So the guy we had in here for questioning earlier today. The guy who, if he hadn't been a cop, we'd have held on suspicion of murder. It now turns out that he had access to the murder weapon. Does that sum it up?"

Now both detectives' heads nodded once.

"I'd suggest you find him immediately and get his ass back in here." He reached for the phone. "In case we're wrong, we need to keep his cover solid. Make sure everyone involved knows that he's a cop, but make the detainment look like any other drug dealer. I'll call Carlson and tell him his boy's in deep shit and if he can contact him, he needs to turn himself in now." He stopped as his hand was about to punch in the extension. "What the hell are you two waiting for, an engraved invitation? Get the hell out of my office and find that son of a bitch."

Chapter 28

Sanders was on the phone to dispatch before Hunter had a chance to bark an order. He requested a BOLO under both names, Vance Harvey and Bonner Hopkins.

When Sanders hung up, Hunter started to interject, but Billy held up his hand as he hit speed dial. "Zeke? Hey this is Billy Sanders. Can I get you and your team to back us up on a raid?"

By the time Billy had given the SWAT Leader all the pertinent information, he and Hunter had made it back to the conference room. Billy hung up, stopped in the doorway and looked at Hunter. "You wanted to tell me something?"

Hunter smirked. "Yeah, I was going to suggest that you call dispatch to get a BOLO out on Hopkins and that you call SWAT to arrange for backup."

"I guess we're good then."

"I guess we are." Hunter held up his keys. "I still get to drive."

Sanders smiled and gestured toward the door. "Age before beauty."

Hunter moved through the door shaking his head and muttering something about getting too big for his britches. Sanders smiled and followed.

Hunter and Sanders met Zeke Dickson and the SWAT team around the corner from the target location in order to plan the raid. In this case the target was Hopkins' apartment and the planning location was the parking lot of Oakhurst Park, a block west of N. Sylvania.

SWAT Leader Zeke Dickson, looking every bit like a tax accountant, nodded to the two detectives when they pulled up. Even though they'd parked the SWAT truck under a shade tree and had kept it running with the AC blasting, with all of his gear on, a sheen of sweat had formed on every inch of Zeke's exposed skin.

"Cowboy, Billy, it's been a while." Dickson reached out and shook their hands when they stepped over. "What do we have going today?"

Sanders stepped over, spread a street map out on the hood and walked Zeke through his thoughts. When he finished, he looked at Dickson. "Let's not forget that this guy is a cop. That means he's going to be armed and he knows how to use a weapon." He paused. "It also means that we don't fire unless we absolutely have to."

Zeke nodded. "Understood." He looked around the group making eye contact with each of his team members. "Let's roll gentlemen."

Within minutes, a SWAT team member with a battering ram was positioned to the right of the front door. Two additional SWAT members with body shields and automatic weapons were flanked on each side. Sanders and Hunter had their vests on and weapons drawn.

Sanders nodded and without warning, the battering ram crashed into the door and blew it open with the efficiency of a bomb. The two SWAT members with shields breached the door first, followed immediately by Hunter and Sanders.

A half dozen voices yelled over each other. "Fort Worth Police. Search Warrant." The frenetic entry into the tiny apartment ended almost as abruptly as it began when Hunter and Sanders took a few steps into the apartment, rounded the corner into the living room and froze in their tracks.

They could hear shouts of 'clear' as the SWAT members progressed through the bedroom, bathroom and kitchen, but neither of them moved or said a word as they stared at Detective Bonner Hopkins sitting in his recliner. His gun was on the ground to the right of the chair. There was a neat black hole in his right temple, and the left side of his head was gone.

Chapter 29

Time seemed to grind to a stop for Hunter. People were talking, moving, but all he could do was stare at Hopkins' eyes, open but hollow. The smell of cordite and burnt flesh filled his lungs and turned his stomach. He glanced to Hopkins' left shoulder and saw liquid still oozing from the head wound.

We missed him by minutes.

"Cowboy?" Billy's voice sounded like it was in a tunnel. "Hey Cowboy."

Hunter felt Billy's hand on his shoulder and the world came back into focus. "What?"

"I've called it in. The ME and CSI are on their way. I've got a couple of patrol units taping off the area. We need to step out and debrief with Zeke's team before they pack up and roll." He tilted his head toward the front door.

"Yeah, let's go." Hunter's voice turned raspy and his stare lingered another moment before he turned to follow Billy out the front door.

The mid-afternoon heat shocked Hunter back into focus when they stepped out the front door. The crime scene tape was up and a crowd of neighbors had already begun to gather and gawk. Even with the bright sun beating down, the red and blue from the patrol car racks washed over everything. Hunter gazed up and down N. Sylvania and could see more coming. In another twenty minutes, this would be a full blown circus.

"Sorry it turned out this way Cowboy." Zeke frowned. "I hate to see a cop go south."

Hunter's head snapped up and he snarled. "Hopkins was a detective with the FWPD and until we prove otherwise, he was a cop doing his job." He poked his finger at both Zeke and Sanders. "We need to keep this out of the press and I don't want to hear another word about him being dirty until we know for sure." He paused and glared. "Understand me?"

Both men nodded.

After a moment and a deep breath. "Why don't we sit in my truck and debrief? That way we won't melt." Hunter reached into his pocket for his keys as he moved toward the curb.

Dickson and Sanders followed and the three spent the next twenty minutes reviewing what they had done step by step. Billy made notes and filled out an incident report.

His prediction of a full blown circus had blossomed into reality by the time they stepped out of the SUV. Hunter thanked Zeke and his team for their efforts and then he absorbed the scene for a moment. He had seen Doc and his assistant enter the apartment a few minutes earlier. The CSI team was setting up a shade tent in the front yard.

Stacy caught his eye, her expression one of concern. He flashed her the okay sign. She didn't seem convinced, but went back to directing her team.

Hunter blinked when a bead of perspiration rolled off his forehead and hit his eyelash. Standing in the sun for just the few minutes required to survey the action and he was sweating like he'd just finished a marathon. He loosened his vest and walked back into the apartment.

"Tell me something beyond the obvious, Doc."

"Ah, Detective Hunter, how nice of you to call me out on such a lovely spring day."

"Butter me up later. What have you got?"

"Well, if you insist on something beyond the obvious, it's going to be a short conversation." He pointed to Hopkins' body. "Single gunshot wound to the right temple. Appears self-inflicted.

Time of death must have been minutes before you arrived, certainly not more than an hour."

"Is there anything that says this wasn't suicide?"

Doc shook his head. "I'm afraid not. No sign of a struggle. No defensive wounds."

Hunter folded his arms across his chest and looked down at the floor. "As soon as Stacy's team has everything they need, you can transport him."

Doc started to step away, but Hunter stopped him. "Keep in mind, he's…he was a cop."

"He will be handled with the utmost respect, Cowboy."

"Thanks."

Hunter stood in the middle of the chaos. He noted the position of the gun, Hopkins' hands, where he was sitting, the clothes. The details poured into his brain and while they all pointed to the same conclusion, he hated the thought. He'd met this guy. He'd interrogated him. He'd spent over an hour looking him in the eye and talking. The scene seemed to add up, but his gut wasn't on board.

"Hey, Cowboy." Stacy's voice pierced through the noise in the room. He looked toward the doorway to the single bedroom and saw her smiling and holding up an evidence bag with something in it.

"What did you find?" He squinted.

"The eyes are the first to go." She smiled and walked toward him. "It's a cell phone. I'm guessing it's a burner." She held out the bag, jiggled it and tossed it to Hunter. "That's not the big news. Read the outbound text on Friday night."

Hunter smoothed the plastic so he could read through it. His breath caught in his throat as he read.

Got the source for the bad X. Meet me at the place 9:20 tonight.

"Did we check the number?"

"Brandon Jenkins'."

He reread the text two more times. "Interesting." The word

was said more as a verbal thought than a response to Stacy.

"That's not all. We also found a box of ammo that matches what was used to kill Logan and Tyler."

Hunter heard her and nodded, but his mind was spinning a thousand miles an hour. *Why wouldn't he have tossed the phone or at least deleted the message? Why would he keep the ammo?* He shook his head to clear his mind but the thoughts kept popping. Everything was falling into place. *He had access to the gun, matching ammo and a burner phone with a text to Brandon. He apparently killed himself.*

Doc's ME team had bagged the body, had it on the gurney and were maneuvering it gingerly through the tight hallway. Hunter watched them as his mind processed. "Hey, Doc. Can you hold for a second?"

Doc stopped and turned toward Hunter looking at him over the top of his glasses. "Yes?"

"Did we do a GSR test on his hands?"

"We bagged the hands and planned to do it as part of the autopsy."

"Can we do a preliminary now?"

Doc held his jacket lapels and stared at him. "If you think it's important Cowboy, certainly." He looked over at Stacy. "I assume your team has a GSR kit?"

"Sure. Let me grab it."

A moment later Stacy returned. They unzipped the body bag and Cowboy watched intently as Stacy swabbed Hopkins' right hand. She took the swab, processed it and got the expected results. "Gunshot residue is positive."

Stacy started to zip the bag up but Hunter stopped her. "Can you check the other hand?"

She tilted her head and furrowed her brow. "Cowboy. The bullet went in his right temple. The gun was laying by his right hand. He would have had to have been a contortionist to have shot himself with his left hand."

"Humor me." Hunter continued to stare at the body.

"Okay." She shrugged and went back through the same process. The results were once again as expected. "No GSR on the left hand."

Hunter nodded. "Thanks." As they zipped up the bag one more time, he moved past them and toward the front door. "I need some air."

They had been there all afternoon. It was now shortly after six and the blistering heat had started to wane. He was still jolted slightly with the blast when he stepped outside.

In spite of the heat, he began to pace in the front yard, replaying the scene in his head. He couldn't put his finger on it but something was out of place. As he moved , he felt sweat rolling down his forearm and pooling under his watch. He reached over with his right hand and wiped it away. When he did, his mind clicked.

He spun on his heels to see the ME loading the body in their van.

"Hold up guys." He was almost sprinting across the lawn.

Doc's shoulders dropped and he held his palms out. "What is it now, Cowboy?"

"I need to look at him one more time."

Doc sighed. "Let's at least get him loaded so we don't have an audience."

Hunter nodded. He stood and fidgeted as he watched them load the gurney. As soon as it was in, he crawled in after it and unzipped the bag. He reached in and grabbed Hopkins' right arm. "That's it." His eyes were wide when he turned to Doc who was looking at him like he'd lost his mind. "Doc, what kind of people wear their watch on their right hand?"

Doc's mouth opened to speak but closed as he looked down to see a watch on Hopkins' right arm. "How interesting." He rubbed his chin. "Why would a left handed person shoot himself using his right hand?"

Hunter nodded. "He wouldn't."

Chapter 30

Hunter watched the ME's van disappear south on N. Sylvania, his mind swirling around the implications of Hopkins being left handed. As Doc had so aptly put it, 'why would a left handed person shoot himself with his right hand'.

It made no sense. Under any circumstance, killing yourself isn't easy. Nobody would purposely make it even more difficult. His head spun around this thought as the sweat accumulated on his forehead. Even though the sun was beginning to sink over the trees to the west, it was August which meant the ambient temperature wouldn't start to drop for the night for several more hours.

Between the heat, investigating the death of a fellow officer and the lack of sleep over the last week, fatigue plagued his entire body. As much as he wanted to continue searching for every scrap of evidence on the scene, every part of him screamed for a break.

Maybe I can convince Billy and Stacy that the rest of the scene can wait until tomorrow.

When he stepped back into the small apartment he realized there wouldn't be too much convincing needed. Stacy appeared to be already packing up her equipment and dispatching her team. When she looked up and made eye contact with him in the hallway, her hair had fallen over her face and her makeup was splotchy. She looked as drained as he felt.

She blew a few strands of hair out of her face and walked over to him with her hands on her hips. He smiled at her, reached over and tucked one last errant strand behind her ear. "Don't suppose I could talk you into a quiet evening at my place?"

"Thought you'd never ask. Let me finish packing up and I'll meet you there a little before eight."

"Sounds great." He let his hand linger on her cheek for a moment before pulling away and pointing toward the bedroom. "I'm going to talk with Billy for a moment and then get out of here. See you soon."

He found Sanders taking one last look around the bedroom. "Find anything else interesting?"

Billy shook his head. "What else do we need to find? We've got a gun registered to him with one bullet fired sitting beside his body. The wound appears self-inflicted. We've got a burner phone with a text message to Brandon Jenkins suggesting to meet him someplace about the time Jenkins was found at the Logan scene." He shrugged his shoulders and glanced around the room. "Add to that, the matching ammunition and it seems pretty straight forward." He shook his head. "What a shame."

"You know..." Hunter stopped. His shoulders ached with exhaustion and he thought about a quiet evening with Stacy. "Well, you just never know." He shrugged. "I've got another session with the shrink in the morning so I'll catch you after that."

After his thirty minute drive home and a quick shower, he was catching a second, or maybe third wind. Stacy showed up at the door with a takeout bag from Pei Wei. He supplied the wine and the two of them relaxed and obeyed their self-imposed rule of no shop talk at home.

"I think he's missed us just hanging out as much as I have." Panther rubbed his head against Stacy's arm, demanding affection and purring.

"He's just jealous that I'm taking you away from him." Hunter playfully pushed Panther away and picked up the TV remote. They'd had the Rangers game on in the background but hadn't paid much attention to it. It was the ninth inning and the home team's bull pen was coming up lame again. Hunter was ready to give up on them. It was ten o'clock and Hunter wanted to catch the news.

His timing was just right. As he flipped to Channel 5, the camera was panning in on the anchor desk.

"Good evening and welcome to NBC 5 Local News, I'm Amy Johnson." Her smile was as dazzling as ever and her golden hair reflected the perfect amount of studio lighting.

"And I'm Steve Crawford. Tonight we start our program with an on location report from Misty Covington. Misty." He made sure to get one last rugged look into the camera before it cut away.

"Steve, I'm here at Mount Olivet Cemetery standing in front of the freshly covered grave of Brandon Jenkins..."

Hunter stared at the TV, the breath evaporated from his lungs. His vision tunneled to the point that all he could see was the picture on the screen. The reporter's voice distorted in his ear canal where he couldn't understand what she was saying.

Stacy's tight grip on his arm startled him as if he'd forgotten she was there. He sucked in air like a diver breaking the surface of the water and the voice of the reporter came back.

"Hundreds of family and friends stood in the early morning heat today to mourn the loss of this twenty year old college student. He was fatally wounded by Fort Worth Police late last Friday. The question on everyone's mind here today was, has Fort Worth joined Ferguson, Baltimore and South Carolina? This is Misty Covington for NBC 5 News. Back to you Steve."

Stacy reached for the remote but Hunter pulled it away. "Cowboy, just turn it off. Stop torturing yourself."

Hunter didn't speak. He just gestured for her to be quiet as the shot switched back to the anchor desk.

"Thanks Misty. To help us answer that very question, we welcome two guests to our studio this evening. Star Telegram columnists John Ray Phillips and J. R. Lambert."

Hunter's stomach twisted in knots as the camera panned back to show the two columnists, Phillips sitting to the left of the anchors and Lambert to the right.

Crawford turned toward Phillips. "John Ray, how does this

situation compare with the number of other recent police shootings?"

"Unfortunately for Fort Worth, we have joined a group of cities where it's no longer safe to be a black male. How many times do we have to see this kind of shooting—"

"You can't compare this situation to those." Lambert cut in waiving her hands. "The Fort Worth Police have clear video evidence that Brandon Jenkins pointed a gun at the officer."

Phillips snorted. "I haven't seen that video yet. They haven't released it to the public."

"What? Now you're accusing the FWPD of lying? Are you kidding me?" Lambert eyes went wide.

"All I'm saying is I'm perfectly capable of determining what is or isn't clear video evidence. So show me. Besides, this isn't about one incident. Did you know that black males are twenty-one times more likely to be shot by the police than their white counterparts?"

"Could it be because blacks are arrested for over 40% of the violent crime even though they're only 13% of the population?"

The debate continued but Hunter had tuned out. He sat, nonresponsive, the images from the TV reflecting in his glassy stare. Stacy grabbed the remote and turned off the TV. She slid over beside him reached over and gently pulled his head to her shoulder. "I won't let you continue to beat yourself up over something you were forced to do."

He buried his face into her neck and wrapped his arms around her. His voice scratched at his throat. "He was just a kid."

Chapter 31

Dr. Murray gave Hunter a concerned look and sighed. "Not to start things off on the wrong foot this morning, but you look like shit detective."

Hunter had dragged himself through his Thursday morning routine fueled by extra caffeine and the memory of a night spent in Stacy's arms. It had been a wonderful, momentary distraction. He only wished his mind had been as engaged as his body.

Now he found himself sitting in a comfortable chair across from the casually dressed psychiatrist, or as they both preferred, shrink.

A forced grin spread across Hunter's face. "It's been a tough week." His voice sounded as drained as his soul.

"Problems sleeping?"

Hunter nodded.

"I can prescribe you something if you'd like."

Hunter shook his head. "I'll pass for now."

Dr. Murray nodded, jotted a notation. "Other than what happened last Friday, is there something else keeping you awake?"

The room went quiet as Hunter looked down and anxiously played with his fingers. He cleared his throat twice as the doctor waited. "It's just that... Things seem to..." He took a deep breath. "This case has led to another death and..." Hunter's voice strained. "This time it was a cop."

"Oh." Dr. Murray put his pen down on his notepad and adjusted in his seat. "I hadn't heard of an officer fatality. I'm so sorry."

"You wouldn't have heard. He was undercover and the scene appeared to be a suicide."

"You don't sound convinced."

"I'm not. We're still processing evidence. We'll know more today."

"Do you feel responsible?"

Hunter leaned back in his chair and looked over at the bookcase as he processed his thoughts. "I'm not sure. I just know that it's all a chain of events that were set in motion when I pulled the trigger."

"Do you think you did something reckless or inappropriate?"

Hunter shook his head.

"So despite your 'Cowboy' nickname, you feel like you followed procedure and acted appropriately based on the situation?"

This time a real grin spread across Hunter's face. "I think you're misinterpreting my nickname. I didn't get it because I'm some renegade. I'm so 'by the book' that I've sometimes been accused of squeaking." Hunter relaxed for the first time that morning. "No, I followed procedure."

Dr. Murray arched his eyebrows. "So, we've found a topic that makes you smile. Let's stick with it for a moment. If you didn't get your nickname because of your rogue behavior..." He gestured toward Hunter's clothing. "And you certainly didn't get it because of the way you dress. Just exactly how did you get your nickname?"

Hunter leaned back in his chair and waived him off with his hand. "It was just a stupid incident from when I was a rookie on patrol. Not worth the time to tell it."

"But good enough to earn you a nickname that stuck around for a decade." He put down his notepad. "Besides, the department is picking up the tab for my time."

"All right." Hunter shrugged and relaxed into the couch. "I'd been on the force for a year and it was one of the first times I'd ridden solo. Late that afternoon, I got a call for a car wreck up on I35 near Loop 820. It turned out to be an 18 wheeler hauling cattle rear ending another tractor trailer rig.

"A complete mess. The driver of the cattle hauler was trapped in his cab, the paramedics hadn't arrived, traffic was backing up..." Hunter's eyes drifted as he shook his head and remembered. "I was so focused on getting the driver out and getting the scene under control, I didn't notice that the latch on the trailer had broken." He grinned at the thought. "By the time the paramedics arrived, there were a dozen head of cattle scattered all out in the grassy median."

"Only in Texas." Dr. Murray smiled.

"Oh yeah." Hunter nodded. "It was a mess. And hot. That trailer smelled like it hadn't been cleaned out in a month. Cars were honking. The traffic backup went miles on I-35 and was starting to back up even on 820." He was getting animated now, talking with his hands. "I knew if I didn't get those cattle rounded up fast, there'd eventually be a bovine fatality."

Hunter sighed. "I had no idea what to do. I thought I could just herd them back up into the trailer." His head drooped. "That was not a good idea. I'd forgotten that it had rained heavily the night before. So when I went running out in the grass, the next thing I knew I was ankle deep in mud, slipping and sliding like I was at a water park."

He rubbed his face. "There I was, chasing cows in every direction, skidding and falling, yelling and clapping my hands. But the damn cattle only managed to scatter farther apart, and I got covered from head to toe in mud. Made a complete ass of myself, and it was all caught on live TV from the overhead helicopters.

A broad smile had come across the doctor's face.

Hunter sat back in his chair and shrugged. "Not exactly one of my finer moments."

"So how did it turn out?"

"Well, I also didn't know that one of the paramedics had noticed the cows when they pulled up and had already called dispatch to get some mounted officers to come out and round them up. About the time I was completely covered in mud and manure, I looked up and saw their trailer rig pull up. Once they managed to get their laughter under control, it took them about twenty minutes to get all the cattle loaded back on the trailer and waiting to be transported."

"So, were they the ones who gave you the nickname?"

He shook his head. "After every cop in the city had seen me on every news station in the area, the next morning, the entire precinct just spontaneously started calling me Cowboy. Fifteen years later, here I am." He shrugged and grinned.

"I bet most of the cops on the force today don't even know the story." Dr. Murray sat back with a big smile on his face and stopped talking.

Hunter cut his eyes at him. "What?"

"It's nice to see you smile. I think we're done for today."

Chapter 32

"Uncle Jake!"

Jessica's voice cut through the normal chaos of the squad room and stopped Hunter in his tracks. It was almost eleven in the morning. He'd just returned from his session with Dr. Murray and was about to walk into the conference room to meet with Stacy and Billy.

"Uncle Jake. Wait up."

He turned to see the beautiful young woman his niece had turned into, navigating through the obstacle course of desks and people, flashing a smile that lit up the room. Her shoulder-length, brunette hair trailed behind her as she launched herself into Hunter's arms.

"What on earth?" Hunter hugged her back. His smile reflected hers and for the first time in a week, he wasn't thinking about Brandon Jenkins, murder cases and suicides. He was just happy to see his niece. "What are you doing here?"

She pulled away slightly but kept her hand on his arm. "Long story. Actually here on business but I thought I might catch you."

The commotion of their connection had stopped much of the chaos in the room. Detectives strained to see who could get that kind of reaction out of Hunter. Hunter turned to see both Stacy and Billy standing in the doorway of the conference room, wide eyed and slack jawed.

Hunter's face flushed. "Oh guys, you haven't met." He gestured between them. "Stacy, Billy, this is my niece Jessica Hunter. Jessica, this is CSI Stacy Morgan and Detective Billy Sanders."

She confidently stepped forward to shake their hands. They both still looked stunned. . "Nice to meet you both. I've heard a lot about each of you. By the way, everyone calls me Jess."

Stacy stammered slightly as she shook her hand. "Nice to meet you… Jess." She shot daggers at Hunter.

"Same here." Billy had recovered and was now smiling at Stacy's reaction. He reached out and shook her hand as well. "Nice to finally meet someone from Cowboy's family."

Everyone looked at Hunter. He just shrugged. "So, to what do we owe the pleasure of your company?"

"I'm here to see, uh…" She dug a notepad out of her bag. "Lieutenant Carlson. I was given his name by the Media Relations Officer as someone who might speak at an anti-drug symposium."

"Hm…" Hunter cringed. "If anyone can get him to, it's you. But your timing isn't good. He just lost one of his undercover detectives."

Her face dropped. "I'm sorry to hear that. Was he undercover working narcotics?"

Hunter put his finger to his lips. "Can't officially say. We're investigating his murder."

Billy cocked his head at the word murder but with a quick sign, Hunter let him know he'd fill him in later.

Jessica shook her head. "What a shame. How many good cops have died trying to stop drug trafficking? It's a hell of a cost."

Hunter nodded. "It is."

The conversation stalled for a moment before Jessica spoke up again. "I don't suppose you could give me directions on where I could find this Lieutenant Carlson?"

"I'll do better than that. I'll escort you there myself."

She turned to Stacy and Billy extending her hand. "It was wonderful meeting both of you. I hope to see you again soon."

Hunter pointed Jessica down the hall and spoke over his shoulder to Stacy and Billy. "I'll be right back." Billy was still grinning while Stacy stood with her arms folded across her chest and one eyebrow arched.

As they walked down the hall, Jessica's smile drifted away and her eyes tightened. "How are you doing Uncle Jake?"

"Oh, I'm fine."

She stopped and held up her hand to stop him. "Seriously. Grandpa Charlie told me what happened. He and Grandma are worried sick about you. Are you sure you're okay?"

Hunter put his hands on her shoulders, leaned down and kissed her on the forehead. "I'm fine. I promise to call Dad and Mom tonight."

A triumphant smile blazed back across her face. "Good. Now where's this lieutenant?"

"Follow me."

Carlson looked up from his desk when Hunter knocked. His face was pale and the bags under his eyes more prominent than when Hunter met him a few days earlier. "How can I help you, detective?"

Before Hunter could respond, Jessica stepped into the office and extended her hand. "I'm Jessica Hunter. I represent CADC, Communities Against Drugs Coalition. I was directed to you by the Media Relations Officer. She indicated you might be able to help me." She gestured back toward Hunter. "It just so happens that Detective Hunter is my uncle, so he guided me to your office."

She smiled at Hunter, stepped over and gave him a hug. "Thanks for the escort, Uncle Jake. Don't forget that phone call."

"I won't forget." He looked at Carlson. "Don't let her get you in too much trouble. She's a force to be reckoned with."

He smiled, gave a mock salute to both of them and made his way back to the conference room. As he walked in the door, he started to speak but Stacy's voice cut the air.

"You have a niece? We've been together how long and you never thought to mention you have a niece?" Her fists were balled on her hips and her foot tapped the tile floor.

Billy headed for the door. "I'll see you two after lunch." He cocked an eyebrow at Hunter on his way out. "Good luck."

Hunter fidgeted. "Speaking of lunch. Can we discuss this over a sandwich?"

Chapter 33

"I'm sorry. It just never came up."

"How long have we been together?" Stacy stopped him from answering when she jutted out her held up palm. "How can it not come up that you have a niece?"

Hunter swallowed, and snuck in a deep breath. "It's not something I like to talk about."

They had decided on Potbelly Sandwich Shop in Sundance Square after Stacy had just huffed when Hunter had asked her lunch choice. If it wasn't August, they would have likely taken a nice walk through downtown to get there. Instead, they opted for a very frosty drive.

Stacy almost dropped her sandwich into its basket. "What's so horrible about having a niece? Especially one who seems as lovely as Jessica?"

He nodded. "Jessica's wonderful. She's amazing really. Especially considering…" He cleared his throat. "Talking about her is easy." His eyes blinked rapidly and he wiped his mouth with a napkin. "Talking about my brother is more difficult."

"Brother?" The wheels were clearly spinning, the realization washed across her face. "You have a brother?"

"Had."

"Oh… God…" Stacy reached over and took his hand. "I'm so sorry, Cowboy. I didn't know… It didn't dawn on me." She looked up at him, her eyes glassy. "Look, if you don't want to talk about it, I understand. Whenever you're ready."

Hunter shook his head. "No. This is as good a time as any

and you're right." He squeezed her hand. "We're together. You should know my history."

"My brother… Jordan was eight years older than me." He'd completely given up on his sandwich and had his elbows on the table with his hands clasped in front of his chin. "He was Mr. Everything. High school football star, Student Council President, Honor Roll. You name it. He owned it. He was everything I ever wanted to be. To say I idolized him would be an understatement."

"Sounds like he was pretty amazing."

"He was." Hunter rearranged his sandwich remnants. "By the time I was sixteen and in high school, Jordan was twenty four and was well into his life. He'd gotten married when he was twenty and was already a father. Jessica was three." He smiled. "In spite of getting married early, he'd managed to graduate from the U.S. Naval Academy in Annapolis and had been commissioned as a First Lieutenant in the Marine Corps. Seeing him in his dress blues…" He stared off for a moment and bit on the inside of his lip. "It was like seeing Superman."

Stacy didn't say anything. She just let her hand rest on his forearm.

"In the Fall of 1990, Operation Desert Storm, Gulf War I, was about to begin. He kissed his wife and daughter goodbye and went to serve his country."

Hunter's face went dark. "His platoon was deployed to the Gulf in January of 1991. When the Coalition's Air Campaign started to tail off at the end of January, Iraq went on the offensive and attacked the city of Kafji with two Divisions. The Marines and the Army Rangers were the first Coalition troops engaged.

"I've never been in battle, but from everything I've been able to discern, it was four days of pure hell. The Coalition forces won the day but in the process had forty three killed and another fifty two wounded. Jordan was one of the wounded. He was shot up pretty good, took two rounds in his torso and a third round shattered his right femur."

Stacy's eyes were wide with anticipation. "But he lived, right?"

Hunter nodded. "Oh yeah, he lived, but he was a mess." He pursed his lips. "Multiple surgeries, well over a year of rehab, chronic pain, depression." Hunter shook his head as his voice strained. "He was ultimately given a medical discharge and he, his Purple Heart and his Bronze Star went from war hero to unemployed and semi-disabled civilian overnight.

"When he came to my high school graduation, he was still walking with a cane. He'd lost so much weight he was just a shell of himself. His skin was pale and his eyes were hollow. Even as a self-absorbed teenager, I could see that he was emotionally messed up. Post Traumatic Stress Disorder wasn't a commonly used term at that point so there was no formal diagnosis, but I knew he was suffering.

"His next nine years were just a downward spiral. Through all of his surgeries and rehabs, he'd become addicted to pain killers. When the doctors stopped prescribing them, he bought them on the street or used whatever he could find to try to self-medicate. He lost everything, his wife, his daughter, his will to live.

"When the towers fell in 2001, it was the final straw. A week later they found him in a cheap hotel. He'd put a bullet in his head and left a rambling note about how he'd failed everyone."

Hunter's vision was blurred with tears. When he stopped talking, he was staring down at his hands while they absently picked apart a napkin. He was spent.

Stacy reached over and took his hands in hers. "I'm so sorry Cowboy. I never knew."

"She's remarkable, you know." Hunter sat up straighter.

"Jessica?" Stacy squinted at him.

Hunter smiled softly. "She barely knew her Dad before the war. She spent most of her formative years mostly without her father and when she did see him, he wasn't much more than a street junkie." He tapped his finger on the table to emphasize his point. "Despite that, look at her now. She's twenty-seven. She graduated early from UT with a bachelors in Psychology and graduated last year from UT's Law School."

He leaned forward, pride welling up. "She's now an intern at a major law firm and has convinced them to sponsor Communities Against Drugs Coalition and let her spend a portion of her time supporting that organization."

"In honor of her Dad." Stacy smiled.

Hunter's voice was raspy. "In honor of her Dad."

Chapter 34

Sanders looked up to see Hunter and Stacy walk into the conference room, Hunter's hand was placed lightly on the small of Stacy's back, guiding her into the room. Both seemed content. "Glad to see lunch was good."

"It was enlightening." Stacy drifted past him, found a chair and sat.

"Speaking of enlightening..." Sanders looked at Hunter. "What was that stuff about Hopkins being murdered?"

That comment broke Stacy out of her lunch mood. She also turned to Hunter. "Yeah, what did you mean with that?"

Hunter nodded and smiled. "Yesterday I kept looking at the scene and thinking something was off. But I couldn't put my finger on it until Doc and his boys were loading up. I finally figured it out." He held up his right arm and pointed to his wrist. "Hopkins was wearing his watch on his right hand."

Stacy cocked her head. "Oh my."

Billy looked from Stacy to Hunter, scrunched his forehead. "So?"

"You don't wear a watch, do you?" Stacy looked at his wrist.

"Why would I wear a watch? I've got a phone."

Hunter shook his head. "Youngsters." He held up his left wrist and showed Billy his watch. "Almost everyone who wears a watch wears it on the non-dominant hand. Hopkins wore his watch on his right wrist so chances are he's left handed and lefties don't shoot themselves with their right hand."

"You're serious." Billy frowned.

"Absolutely. Check his personnel file and I'll buy the beer if he's not left handed."

Sanders turned in his chair, clicked a number of keys on his laptop and leaned forward to read the screen when it popped up. "I'll be damned." He shook his head, spun around and smiled at Hunter. "Looks like I'll have to buy my own beer. You're right." He paused. "But is that really enough to declare it a murder?"

"Not sure, but I asked Doc to rush the tox screen. Why don't we give him a buzz?"

They gathered around the speaker phone and Billy punched in Doc's office number. "Dr. Grimes, how may I help you?"

"Doc, this is Detective Sanders. I've got Cowboy and Stacy with me in the conference room. I understand that you were going to put a rush on the initial tox screen for the Hopkins case. Any luck?"

"One moment." The sound of paper rustling and then keys clacking. "Yes. Let's see… Oh my." Doc paused causing the team to exchange glances. "According to my report, he had extremely high levels of diazepam in his system. In fact, so high that had he not been killed by a bullet to the brain, he might have died from an overdose."

Sanders bounced his glance from Stacy to Hunter and back to the speaker phone. "How does that impact your findings? Could he have just used that as chemical courage to pull the trigger?"

"I don't think so. With this much already in his system, I can't imagine him being able to sit up straight, much less operate a weapon effectively."

Stacy jumped in. "We found no evidence of drugs, drug paraphernalia or empty bottles in the apartment or the trash."

"Doc, we were able to confirm that Hopkins was left handed." Hunter frowned and shook his head at Billy. "Sure makes this suicide look suspicious."

"More than suspicious Cowboy." Doc paused. "Looks to me like you have a murdered detective."

After a long pause where everyone seemed to absorb the news, Hunter leaned forward onto the table. "Shit. Doc, let us know what else you find with the full autopsy. We need to go have a conversation with a couple of lieutenants to let them know our bad news just got worse."

Hunter punched the speaker phone off and began to pace. His jaw muscles tightened with every step. "This is not good. Not only does this trash any thoughts that Hopkins killed Logan and Tyler, now we've got another murder to solve."

"And this one's a FWPD detective." Stacy's voice cracked.

"Someone not only killed a cop, but they tried to frame him for two murders." Sanders rubbed his shaved head. "And they almost got away with it."

"They didn't get away with the frame up and I'll be damned if they're going to get away with the murder." Hunter's eyes were like lasers. "Stacy, we need to get all the evidence collected at the scene back up here so that we can go through it again. This time knowing it was a murder, not a suicide."

He looked at Sanders. "Billy, I want the three of us back at the scene first thing in the morning to scour it one more time." He closed his eyes and rubbed his forehead. "This is going to be a nightmare to handle in the press."

Billy exhaled and shook his head. "Guess we get to go see Sprabary to let him know this thing has turned to shit."

Hunter smirked. "More like diarrhea."

Chapter 35

The smell of death had settled into the space. Dried blood, fingerprint powder and spent gunpowder had combined with two days of heat and no air circulation to make the trio recoil as they entered Bonner Hopkins' apartment.

Hunter and Billy had helped lug Stacy's evidence kits and the two boxes of evidence collected from the scene on Wednesday. They planned to go through all the evidence previously collected item by item and reinterpret it now that this was a murder scene. In addition, they planned to scour the scene for anything they might not have considered evidence when they thought it was a suicide.

After cutting through the yellow police tape, Hunter held open the hastily repaired door for Billy and Stacy. "Set everything on the kitchen table. We'll use it to sort through the boxes."

After settling into their chairs, both Hunter and Sanders reached for an evidence box. "Stop." Stacy swatted at their hands. "We're going to do this the right way." She took out her evidence list. "Let's talk about one item at a time and check them off the list."

Hunter smirk. "Okay boss, where do you want to start?"

She cocked an eyebrow. "Let's start with the easy things to rule out like fingerprints and DNA." She looked at her list. "There were ten unique prints collected and three different DNA samples. Those are already being processed and we expect results back today."

Sanders nodded. "Great, maybe we'll get a hit."

"Won't matter." Stacy frowned. "We collected them as part of our standard procedure but even if we get a hit, all it will mean is that sometime in history, that person was in this apartment. None of the prints or DNA were on the weapon or the body."

"That's why we can rule them out. Gotcha."

The process dragged on for the next two hours. They looked at the gun, the ammo and the burner phone. All were likely planted but none held any clue to where they came from or who left them there. It now seemed more interesting that the phone and ammo were completely clean, no fingerprints or DNA. There were fiber samples that might mean something once they have a suspect but on their own weren't leads.

Stacy blew an errant strand of hair out of her face. "All we've got left are the crime scene photos. I downloaded everything to my tablet. Why don't you guys slide around and look over my shoulder?"

Both men stood, stretched out the kinks from sitting for so long and joined Stacy on the other side of the table. She punched on her tablet, pulled up the folder for the Hopkins crime scene and tapped on the first thumbnail. "Here we go."

She scrolled slowly through dozens of photos, lingering on each for several moments as all three stared at the screen. Every few shots, someone would ask about the picture. Why did they shoot it? What angle was it from? They discussed the story each photo told in context of the murder.

An hour into the process, they'd found nothing of interest. Finally, Hunter stopped her on a photo of a faint shoe print. "Why was this shot taken?"

Stacy reviewed her notes. "It was an outlier. It was clearly fresh. Whoever made it stepped in something wet and the moisture picked up the dust off the floor. Most people, even men…" She eyed the two of them. "Would clean it up after a day or two. Or it would just wear off."

She shrugged. "We also knew it wasn't made by our team. It's not the right tread for the SWAT team. They all wear the same make of boot. And it's a size 11 which doesn't match either of you." She looked at Hunter. "You're a size nine and a half." Then to Billy.

"And you're a size thirteen."

Sanders smirked. "I guess size really does matter."

"Hey." Hunter looked at him indignantly. "Is that some kind of crack about my little feet?"

"If the shoe fits…" Sanders laughed.

Stacy mockingly stroked Hunter's shoulder. "I like your feet just the way they are."

After a moment of continued laughter, Hunter calmed them. "Okay, but what does this tell us?"

Stacy got serious again. "It's a fairly unique shoe pattern and a specific size and we know that whoever left it had to have been in the house within a day of the murder. It's kind of like Cinderella. Find the person who's wearing those shoes and you can at least place them at the scene."

Hunter nodded. "Well, that's more than we had before."

They finished up the rest of the photos with no new revelations and took a break for lunch. After lunch, they were back at the apartment, this time intent to search inch by inch to find anything they'd missed before.

Stacy touched Hunter's shoulder. "Before we get started, can you help me carry the two boxes of existing evidence down to my van?" He grabbed one box and she took the other as Billy sat down. They started down the sidewalk but she slowed and looked at him. "It's been a long week, huh?"

"One of the longest in my life." He shook his head in disgust. "A week ago today, I shot an innocent kid. Two days ago, I watched his mother bury him."

Stacy stopped in her tracks. "Oh, Cowboy, you shouldn't have done that."

"Yeah…" He continued walking. "I know."

After securing the evidence in the locked van, they made their way back to the apartment. At the front door, Hunter stopped. "I know we shattered the door on entry Wednesday but did anyone ever check for forced entry?"

"No. Once we saw the scene, it didn't seem relevant."

He opened the door and looked at the striker plate and both the door knob and the dead bolt. "Look at these scratches." He point to the two locks.

"They look pretty fresh, like someone used a lock pick recently."

"Get some pictures of those. They may be relevant."

After taking shots of the scratches on the door, the three of them scoured every square foot of the apartment using flashlights, ultraviolet lights and magnifying glasses.

By late afternoon, they were all exhausted and frustrated with having found absolutely nothing new to add to the evidence boxes. Billy took out a handkerchief and wiped his head. "Guys, there's nothing in this apartment we hadn't already found."

Stacy nodded dejectedly, but Hunter perked up. "Billy, you're right. There isn't anything in this apartment. But what about outside? Did either of you notice any security cameras?"

"I didn't." Billy shook his head.

"Neither did I." Stacy glanced between Billy and Hunter.

"All right then. Let's go look." Hunter turned for the door.

It took only a few minutes for Billy to spot a camera hanging from under the eaves of a neighboring building. The angle wasn't great, but it would likely have caught a glimpse of someone approaching Hopkins' door.

Billy told Hunter and then headed over to the building to find the manager. When he got back, Stacy and Hunter had finished packing up her evidence kits. He held up the DVD. "Got a copy of all footage for the last week."

"Bingo." Stacy snatched the disc, dropped it in an evidence bag and logged it onto her clipboard.

"It's late." Hunter rolled his shoulders. "Stacy and I'll spend some quality time with that security footage over the weekend to see what we can find."

Billy nodded. "Hopkins' phone records should be in my

inbox. I'll do the same with those to see if there's anything out of the ordinary."

"Sprabary wants us to brief him and Carlson on Monday morning. I'll make a call on my drive to get that scheduled. We'll reconvene earlier that morning to compare notes." He looked at both of them. "This may have been a long and not overly productive day, but we're going to keep at it. Whoever did this has left a trail of bodies and one of those was a cop. That's unacceptable."

Chapter 36

In addition to compulsively watching the dashcam footage, he immersed himself in the security tapes over the weekend and continued to review the photos from the Hopkins scene. Anything to keep his mind occupied and churning on the case. Idle time led to contemplation and that invariably took him to a dark place.

His immersion, while frustrating to Stacy, was mildly productive and his focus over the weekend had his mind racing as he drove down I-35. Their preview meeting was scheduled for 8 a.m. He left in time to beat rush hour and would be early, but at least they'd have something to talk about.

After hitting a Starbucks drive through to get coffee for the team, he pulled into the station well before eight. He made his way up to the conference room and stuck three grainy black and white pictures to the whiteboard before Stacy and Billy arrived.

"Looks like someone's been productive." Hunter stood by the whiteboard looking at the pictures. "Are these from the security camera?"

"Yep. Not great, but at least something." Hunter joined him at the whiteboard.

"Oh, thank God you got coffee." Stacy rushed in, her hair looking windblown. "I was running late and haven't had any." She stopped and realized Hunter was smiling at her. She quickly finger combed her hair and straightened her blouse. "What is it? What's wrong?"

Hunter's smile grew larger. "Nothing. You look... Great." He reached over and poured her a cup of coffee.

Sanders held out his open palms. "So, where's mine?"

Hunter just handed him the Starbucks cardboard jug. "Here you go. Help yourself."

Sanders shook his head and poured a cup. He pointed back to the photos on the whiteboard. "What have you got?"

"Those are the three best shots." He stepped over and tapped the photos. "Not great. We really can't see his face, but this is definitely our guy. The timestamp is shortly before our estimated time of death and he's wearing gloves and a hoodie in the middle of the day in August."

"That's just a bit suspicious." Stacy smirked and then looked closer at the pictures. "Hey, in this one you can see his shoes pretty clearly."

"How does that help?" Billy joined them at the whiteboard.

"You remember the shoeprint, right?" Stacy stepped over to her bag and pulled out a folder as Billy nodded. "This may surprise you, but the FBI actually has a database on shoe treads. I called in a favor over the weekend and got our shoeprint run." She pulled out a picture of the sole of a running shoe. "We got a hit."

"No shit."

"Yep. It matched a high end specialty triathlon brand called Altra. This particular tread matches their Zero Drop Instinct style. See how the tread on the shoe mimics the pattern of a bare foot with the toes."

Sanders nodded. "Looks like a match to me."

She pulled out a side view picture of the shoe. "Now compare this to the shoe Mr. Hoodie is wearing."

Both Hunter and Billy smiled.

Stacy continued. "These aren't shoes you'll find at your typical Foot Locker. You either have to go to a store that specializes in triathlon equipment or buy them online. Trust me, you're not going to find these in the closet of your average jogger."

"On top of that..." Hunter raised his eyebrows. "They have a fairly distinctive look. If he's wearing these, we'll be able to spot them from a block away."

"Outstanding." Sanders nodded. "What else did you notice in these shots?"

Hunter stepped up. "Unfortunately, you really can't see much of the guy himself. Could be white. Or Hispanic." He pointed to one of the pictures. "In this one, he has his arm raised and his sleeve is riding up. See the gold chain bracelet. Don't think you're going to see too many guys wearing one of those."

"So we've got a couple of very distinctive fashion statements." Sanders tapped his pen to his chin. "Once we find our guy, this will help nail him." He sighed. "At this point, it doesn't really point us to someone."

"No it doesn't." Hunter frowned. "What did you find in his phone records?"

Sanders scrunched his forehead. "Kind of interesting. I ran the last three months for his home phone, his cell phone and the burner we found in his apartment." He shrugged. "The home phone was like every other home phone I know. Outbound calls were to a Chinese takeout place around the corner. There were a number of inbound calls, none lasting more than a minute and all from either toll free or out of state numbers. We can have someone run them all down, but I'm sure they're all telemarketers."

"Agreed. How about the cell phones?"

"The burner was only activated last week. It had very little use, a handful of texts and calls. All were to other burner phones except the one text to Brandon Jenkins." He shook his head. "Unless we find those other burners, we don't know anything new."

Sanders picked up a folder and pulled out a number of pages. "This is the last three months for his cell phone." He dropped the pages down on the table. "About what you'd expect from an undercover guy infiltrating a drug operation. There were a few calls to local businesses, but most calls were to and from burner phones."

"Any of them the same burner phones as the other cell?"

"No crossover at all."

"Do we know where the phones were purchased?"

"Haven't had a chance to run the records, but based on serial numbers and brands, my guess is that they were all over the place."

Hunter frowned.

"But..." Sanders held up one finger to make a point. "There was one anomaly. There were about a half dozen calls to a cell number registered to Carlos Calderon."

Hunter cocked an eyebrow. "Do we know who that is?"

"I didn't have time to run a full background but I did a quick search." He pulled out another folder and dropped it on the table. "I can't find any obvious ties to the organization Hopkins was working, but this guy was definitely in the drug trade. He has eight different arrests, all for drug related offenses, none that got him anything more than probation."

Stacy cleared her throat to get their attention and looked at her watch. "I need to get back to the lab and you two have a date with the brass."

"At least we've got something to talk about." Sanders packed up his files and stepped toward the door.

Hunter followed but stopped at the whiteboard. "Carlos Calderon..." He mouthed the name as he wrote it on the whiteboard. "Who the hell are you?"

Chapter 37

No matter how many meetings Hunter had with Lieutenant Sprabary, there was always a sense of stepping in front of a firing squad. This morning was no exception. When he and Sanders rounded the corner, they could see Lieutenant Carlson sitting in the office. It appeared as if the two of them were old buddies sharing war stories.

Hunter noted they had already brought in an extra chair. It was going to be cozy. As a formality, he stopped at Paige McLaren's desk. "We're here for a meeting with the two lieutenants."

"They're waiting for you." She paused just long enough for him to turn. "I saw them sharpening their fangs earlier." He cut his eyes back at her as she cackled, not unlike the wicked witch of the west.

He reached his hand up to knock on the door, but Sprabary motioned him in before he could. "Detectives, have a seat." He gestured to Carlson. "I believe you both have met Lieutenant Carlson. He heads up our Narcotics Division."

"Yes sir." They responded almost in unison and both nodded toward Carlson as they sat down.

Sprabary turned to Hunter. "What kind of update do you have on the Hopkins situation?"

Hunter cleared his throat, leaned forward and spoke in his most professional tone. "On Wednesday of last week when we discovered the body of Detective Hopkins, we believed two things…" He ticked off his fingers as he continued. "First, that he was responsible for the murder of Michael Logan and James Tyler, and second, that Detective Hopkins' death was self-inflicted. As we discussed late last week, there were some evidence anomalies that put those two beliefs into question. Based on additional evidence we found at the scene and the findings from the ME, we no longer believe that Detective Hopkins committed either murders nor do we believe that his death was a suicide."

Carlson almost spilled his coffee rocking forward in his chair. "Excuse me?" His jaw clenched and his voice rose. "I reviewed the initial reports on Thursday morning and everything indicated suicide."

He paused, held up his hand to keep anyone from speaking. "I'm sorry. I don't mean to sound upset. This is actually great news. It's just that I've been stonewalling his family, not really knowing what to tell them." He rubbed his forehead. "After all, up until this minute everything I'd seen indicated that he was dirty. Now..." He let the sentence trail off as he shook his head.

"Yes sir." Hunter nodded. "My apologies for the delay. It wasn't until late Friday and over the weekend that we were able to confirm our beliefs." He turned to Sanders. "I'll let Detective Sanders run through the specifics."

Carlson, his eyelids at half-mast and shoulders slumped, looked stricken but gestured for Sanders to keep rolling.

Sanders nodded. "Sir, it really comes down to four components." He counted them off on his fingers. "The Medical Examiners report. Evidence that the locks on his door had been picked. A shoe print that indicated an unknown person was in the room shortly before his death. Lastly, footage from a security camera showing a subject entering and leaving his apartment at times that coincide with the time of death."

"So your team went back out to the scene after the initial processing on Wednesday?" Carlson furrowed his brow.

"Yes sir. On Friday."

Carlson nodded. "So, walk me through the details."

Sanders pulled out his folder and over the next thirty minutes walked both Sprabary and Carlson through the Medical Examiners report showing high levels of diazepam, the photos of the footprints and the photos of the scratches on the doorknob and deadbolt.

When Sanders mentioned the security camera on a neighboring building, Sprabary seemed to be suppressing a smile of a proud parent. Billy laid out the three pictures showing the best shots of the suspect and started to walk through them. "We've been able to confirm the specific brand and style of shoe and if you look at photo three, you'll see a distinctive gold bracelet."

Before he could continue, Carlson grabbed one of the pictures and began examining it closely. "Wait a minute, detective. What brand of shoe did you say?"

"Uh, I didn't, but..." Sanders flipped through his papers. "The brand was Altra and the style was called Instinct."

Carlson smiled and leaned back in his chair, still looking hard at the picture. "Holy shit." He looked up. "Gentlemen, I think I might know your suspect."

Three heads popped up in unison and they all turned to look at Carlson. He turned the photo around as if to display it. "Gentlemen, this is Carlos Calderon."

"You're kidding." The shock of hearing that name overrode Hunter's normal decorum in the company of ranking officers. "I mean... I'm sorry. It's just that we ran across that name in our investigation this morning."

"How's that?"

Hunter gestured and Sanders jumped back into the conversation. "Well sir, we analyzed Hopkins' phone records and we found a number of calls made to and from a cell phone registered to Carlos Calderon, including one made about thirty minutes before the suspect enters Hopkins' apartment." He pulled out another folder. "A quick background revealed very little other than a few drug related arrests."

"Can you give us any insight into Mr. Calderon?" Hunter looked at Carlson.

Carlson nodded slowly as if he were collecting his thoughts. "I can..." He paused. "It's just that his name popping up seems strange in this context because he wasn't the target of Hopkins' investigation. That target was Dalton Foster and his organization. Carlos Calderon is actually the head of another TCO." He pursed his lips.

"A TCO?" Hunter interjected.

"Transnational Criminal Organization. Another narcotics wholesaler. I'm not sure you'd classify them as competitors or rivals, but they are definitely not cooperating interests."

"Why would Hopkins be in contact with a rival dealer?"

"Damn good question. I have no idea. Maybe he'd played his part so well that Calderon was reaching out to him in some sort of takeover move." He shrugged. "Whatever was going on, he hadn't reported it internally."

Hunter nodded, absorbing the new information. "How do you know this is Calderon? His face isn't visible."

"It's the shoes." He smiled. "We keep a detailed database on all the players we're tracking. Everything from what they like to smoke, drink or eat to what they wear. He's known for wearing this brand of running shoe. As you said, it's kind of a unique brand."

Hunter scrunched his face. "A drug dealer who is a triathlete?"

"Oh hell no." Carlson laughed. "He probably couldn't run a block without passing out. Apparently, he just likes the shoes."

Sanders grinned and nodded. "You mentioned that these guys are competing distributors. What are we looking at, cocaine? Heroin?"

"Well, they're certainly into that..." Carlson leaned forward. "But these days, it's more about CPD's and Designer Drugs than the old standbys. Yearly deaths involving CPD's outnumber cocaine and heroin deaths combined and there are more Ecstasy users now than there are cocaine users."

Hunter held up a hand to stop him. "CPD's?"

"Sorry." Carlson grinned. "I'm used to talking with narcs. Controlled Prescription Drugs. That includes Valium, Quaaludes, Oxycontin and anything else that can be legally prescribed by a doctor."

"Gotcha."

"No problem. It's an ever evolving landscape. Whether we're talking about the classic products or the new stuff, it's still an epidemic. The number of drug overdose deaths per year in the U.S. has surpassed motor vehicle deaths as the leading cause of injury deaths."

"Thought we were in a war on drugs." Hunter smirked.

"Yeah, well, we may win a few battles here and there but that thirty year war is long from over." Carlson nodded toward Hunter and Sanders. "And I can assure you that whatever we're seeing in the narcotics world is affecting how busy you are in homicide land. Almost 60% of individuals arrested for all crimes test positive for drugs and over 50% of prison inmates are clinically addicted."

Hunter smiled. "Now I see why Jessica wanted you to be her guest speaker for her event."

Carlson smiled and waved him off. "As for Calderon and Foster, they're two of the biggest dealers in the region. Historically, they've respected each other's operations and have rarely tangled." He shrugged. "But who knows…"

By the time they closed out the conversation, Hunter was anxious to get moving on the new information. "Lieutenant, thanks for all your help."

"No problem. Reach out to Detective Chambers from my team. He'll put together information packets on both operations for you."

All four men stood and shook hands. Hunter and Sanders turned for the door but Carlson stopped them. "One last thing guys, what made you question the initial suicide determination?"

"Hopkins was left handed."

"Huh?" Carlson squinted at Hunter.

"He was left handed but he shot himself in the right temple."
Carlson nodded. "Go figure. Good work."

Chapter 38

Hunter moved fast down the hallway as he and Sanders left Sprabary's office. "What was his guy's name for the information packets?"

"Chambers."

"Let's call him from the conference room." His hands were waving as he walked. "I want a BOLO on Carlos Calderon issued immediately. Let's get his picture out on the network."

Sanders was nodding, walking and trying to take notes all at the same time. They got to the conference room, dropped their notebooks and files and Billy grabbed the phone, punched on the speaker and then the number for the Narcotics team room.

The phone was answered by one of the detectives and Billy requested Chambers. There was a moment of shuffling before a gruff voice answered. "Chambers here."

Hunter was up pacing and let Billy do the talking. He introduced the two of them, mentioned that they'd just finished meeting with Carlson and made the request for the information packets.

"Hmm. Okay, I can get that for you, but it'll take a little time to put it together." There was a pause. "Is tomorrow okay?"

"This is related to the Hopkins case." Hunter barked from across the room. "We think we have a lead and need this information to follow up."

"Hopkins case?" Hunter could almost see Chambers snapping to attention on the other end of the line. "I'll get that over to you in a couple of hours. Better yet, if we can do it right after lunch,

I'll hand deliver it and brief you myself."

Billy turned to Hunter who nodded. "Sounds like a plan. Thanks." He hung up, impatiently tapped his fingers on the table. "I'll have a full history pulled on Calderon and request a trace on his cell number to see if we can use his GPS tracking." He paused. "What else?"

Hunter continued to pace, his arms folded across his chest. "Do we have a last known address?"

"We do, but I wouldn't put much stock in it."

Hunter looked at his watch. "Worth a drive while all the rest of this is simmering."

Thirty minutes later, they pulled up to the curb and looked out the window to see nothing but weeds and trash. Hunter put the truck in park and let it idle. "You sure about that address?"

Sanders check his notes, looked up and perused the neighborhood. "This is 2015 NE 36th Street." He frowned.

"He doesn't live here unless he lives in a tent." Hunter snickered.

"What a waste of time."

Hunter pointed at the outside temperature gauge in his car which read 102. "At least it's a nice cool day today."

Sanders shook his head.

"Let's go grab some lunch." Hunter put the SUV in gear. "The Taco Shak's just around the corner."

They got back to the conference room a few minutes before one and found Detective Chambers and another detective standing by the whiteboard talking. They each had large folders in their hands.

"Gentlemen." Hunter nodded when they turned to his voice. "I'm Jake Hunter." He pointed to Billy. "This is Billy Sanders."

They shook hands as Matt Chambers introduced himself and his partner Travis Nix. At least based on body type, they looked a bit like Abbott and Costello. Matt Chambers was heavy set with big jowls, mostly gray hair and pale eyes. Nix was tall and thin and sported a seventies style bushy moustache.

Chambers held up two thick folders. "We thought it might go faster if we both briefed you." He purposefully caught Hunter's eye. "Bonner Hopkins was a friend of ours. He wasn't dirty. And we want his killer found."

Hunter nodded. "Sounds like we all want the same thing."

All four detectives moved to chairs around a central table. The two Narcotics detectives launched into a lengthy session bringing Hunter and Sanders up to speed on everything they knew about the two drug organizations. They put special emphasis on specifics about Carlos Calderon and the number of locations he and his associates were known to frequent.

After over two hours, Hunter leaned back and stretched. He looked at his very full pages of notes. "By my count, we've talked about three houses, two business fronts, four warehouses and five apartments. He could be at any of them."

"Or none of them." Nix shrugged. "This guy is constantly on the move."

Hunter was up and pacing, rubbing his neck. "So how do we find him?"

"You don't, but..." Chambers leaned back in his chair. "There is another alternative."

Hunter stopped, tilted his head and waited.

"We could just methodically roll up his boys one location at a time until someone either gives him up or we get lucky." He shrugged. "If nothing else, we'll put a hell of a dent in his operation."

Sanders rocked forward in his chair. "Do we have anything to justify warrants for these places."

A sly grin spread across Chambers's face. "Oh, trust me. Give me a few hours and I'll have signatures on warrants for every place on that list."

Hunter looked at his watch. It was well past three. "Do we try to ramp up to start hitting these places tonight or do we time it for the crack of dawn?"

"If you want to actually catch people instead of empty

buildings, we need to do it tonight. These guys are nocturnal. I'd time it for after dark."

"Got it. If you'll take care of the paper, Billy and I'll coordinate with SWAT. We'll plan on hitting the first site at nine." He looked to each of the men. "Let's go find a cop killer."

Chapter 39

The plan was simple. They would hit the warehouses first with the expectation that the bulk of the organizations criminal activity would be centered around the larger facilities. While the Narcotics Division had basic intel on these locations, due to limited manpower, they had not actively reconnoitered them. It was going to be a crap shoot as to whether anyone would be at the locations.

By a few minutes after nine, the sun's last remnants were just visible on the western horizon and the team was in place at the corner of NE 34th Street and N Pecan. They were in three vehicles, the SWAT truck led, followed by Hunter's SUV and then Chambers' FWPD unmarked sedan.

Their first target was a small tan metal building in the 3500 block of N. Grove Road. It backed up to the railroad tracks and was the only building on the west side of the street, flanked on both sides by gravel covered fields containing a strange mixture of parked trucks, junk and equipment.

In one swift synchronized maneuver, the three vehicles turned right on N. Grove, sped a half block and converged on the small parking lot in front of the building. The officers were out before the cars stopped rocking. Two SWAT officers flanked the glass door for just a split second before a third officer used the battering ram to destroy the door's aluminum frame and send shattered glass fragments blowing into the building.

The four detectives followed the six man SWAT team through the gaping hole, through a short hall and into an open storage area. Ten officers yelled their identification simultaneously and crashed down the dark hallway. The chaos froze the three suspects in their tracks. By the time they thought to react, they were staring down the barrels of a half dozen Colt M4 Carbines held by the SWAT team and four detective's Glock 9mm's.

Within seconds the men were on the ground and cuffed. Then the rest of the facility was cleared and the SWAT team took up security positions. The Narcotics detectives searched the building while Hunter and Sanders lined up the suspects for interrogation.

While Hunter and Sanders ran into an immediate brick wall with all three men requesting lawyers before even admitting their names, Chambers and Nix gave loud, excited whoops.

Chambers stepped out from behind a set of storage racks. "You gotta come check this out." He motioned to Hunter who shook his head in disgust and walked around the corner. Chambers pointed to a stack of cut open boxes. He couldn't contain his exuberance. "Every one of these is full of CPD's. Calderon may not be here, but when he hears about this take down, he is gonna be pissed."

"How fast can we get this wrapped up and move to the next location?" Hunter's lack of enthusiasm cooled the tone.

Chambers pursed his lips. "I wasn't really expecting to find this kind of stash. We'll need to get an evidence team out here to properly disposition this stuff."

"Shit." Hunter yanked his phone out of his pocket and punched in a number. "Harry, this is Hunter. I need two patrol cars and a CSI team dispatched to my location immediately. I've got three suspects and a warehouse full of narcotics that need to be transported. I'm going to leave a detective and two SWAT guys here to keep the site secured while the rest of the team moves on to another location."

He finished with the details and hung up. "Zeke, let's leave two of your guys here while the rest of us move on to the next address."

Zeke frowned, surveyed the situation. "It's not optimal, but as long as we survey the next site thoroughly before we move, I'm good.

Hunter nodded. "Will do." He turned to Chambers. "Who stays, you or Nix?"

Chambers shook his head and turned to Nix. "Get these guys and this stuff booked." He wagged his finger at him. "Don't you take all the credit. I'll kick your ass."

"Billy, Zeke, let's load up." Hunter gestured for them to wrap up and headed for the door.

Hunter wanted to kick himself for not anticipating the potential need for prisoner and evidence transport. He remedied that on the way to the next location by requesting patrol units in advance. It turned out not to be necessary for the next two locations. They were empty of both people and contraband.

Midnight came and went by the time they were ready to hit the fourth location. Nix and the two SWAT officers had caught up with them and the team staged themselves around the corner from their next target on N. Commerce Street.

They were one block east of N. Main Street in the heart of a heavy industrial area known for junk yards and scrap metal recycling, the humid August night gave off a day-after-the-apocalypse vibe. Hunter half expected to look around and see Mel Gibson in his Mad Max costume.

Hunter had driven by their target earlier to do an initial survey of the layout. It was a strange looking combination of office and warehouse with a two story frontend that almost looked residential. The mustard yellow and muted red wooden structure had a concrete parking area surrounded by a chain link fence that was in serious disrepair but was still standing enough to be a significant barrier to entry.

A number of vehicles sat in the parking area, and the windows clearly emitted internal light. Unlike the last two places, there was going to be a welcoming committee. Due to the layout, the perps would have plenty of time to react.

In anticipation of this being more difficult, Zeke called in two additional SWAT resources, both snipers. Perched on opposite roofs, covering all their asses. Each were lined up on large windows in the front structure.

Once those resources were in place, Zeke nodded to Hunter and Hunter gave the go signal. As before, three vehicles raced in unison. This time, they went west on NE 34th Street for a short block and north on N. Commerce. At forty mph, the SWAT truck steered hard left and crashed through the locked chain link gate. It flew off in dozens of pieces.

The other two vehicles followed and in seconds, all the officers were out and moving. They followed the same plan as with the other locations, each officer taking a predetermined path to spread manpower in as many directions as quickly as possible.

Hunter and Sanders followed into the doorway and saw a stairway leading to the second floor. As they heard officers shouting their identification, they took the stairs without hesitation. Gunfire erupted from the ground floor. They rounded a corner at the top of the stairs and moved through a doorway into a large open room cluttered with furniture, boxes and storage cabinets.

Each swept the room, looking for threats. Hunter moved right, Sanders left. Hunter heard Sanders bark. "Freeze! Police!" He turned to his left, his Glock 17 leading the way. He sensed movement before he actually saw it. A man emerged from behind a desk staring at Hunter, the gun in his hand moved up into firing position.

The world slowed to a crawl. Hunter's brain told his finger to move from the trigger guard to the trigger and pull, but his finger didn't respond. The suspect's weapon was pointed directly at him but Hunter's finger still didn't respond. His eyes widened and he looked down the barrel of the gun. He blinked and the man's head mushroomed into a bright pink and red plume of mist.

Time warped back to full speed as the perp's body fell. Sanders cuffed a suspect on his left and Hunter noticed shards of window pane spread all over the floor, some still tinkling across the concrete.

Hunter still held his gun outstretched. His entire body was drenched in sweat, his heart was pumping so hard that he couldn't tell if the gun battle on the first floor had ended.

"Cowboy...Cowboy!" Hunter turned toward Sanders' voice. He flashed the okay sign as he spoke into his radio. "Second floor clear, one in custody, one down." He looked at Hunter. "You okay?" He smiled. "Damn good thing you and Zeke deployed those snipers."

"Yeah..." He mustered a weak smile and tried to conceal how hard he was breathing. "Damn good thing."

The next thirty minutes was a blur of activity as the team rounded up the remaining suspects. Hunter powered his way through the cleanup, letting Zeke and Billy take the lead. The final toll was sobering—two suspects killed, one seriously wounded and five more in custody. One SWAT officer, with a wound in his shoulder, argued with the paramedics about transferring him to the hospital.

Chambers and Nix were almost dancing they were so giddy as they rummaged through the storage area opening boxes and laughing like it was Christmas morning. The narcotics haul was going to be epic.

In spite of all the good news, Hunter's stomach twisted. None of the suspects, dead or alive, were Calderon. With the level of carnage at this site and the late hour, there would be no more raids before sunrise. Out in the parking lot, he forced several long breaths of warm, early morning air, the smell of rusted metal and oil filling his nostrils.

His brain processed the madness swirling in his mind. He'd frozen. At the moment of truth, he hadn't reacted. The only reason he'd walked out of that building alive was the skill of a long range sniper. The reality pressed in on him like a vice.

Chapter 40

The clock in Hunter's SUV blared 4:16 am when he pulled into his driveway and he was back at the station well before eight. The brief time at home didn't matter. There was no sleep for him anyway. In just over nine days, he'd shot and killed an innocent college kid, watched his family bury him, and discovered a murdered fellow police detective. To top off his list of life changers, he'd frozen at the critical moment of a raid. As he nursed his third cup of coffee in the conference room, he thought he might never sleep again.

When Sanders walked in, Hunter knew he wasn't the only one looking somewhat frayed. "You look almost as bad as I do."

"God, I hope not." Sanders smirked as he walked over to the TV, turned it on and flipped it to the news. "Check out our fellow rock stars from Narcotics."

The picture came on with a split screen. On the left side the classic press conference staged in the lobby of the Tarrant County Courthouse. There was a row of local dignitaries standing behind a make-shift podium with a bundled group of microphones. On the right side was a live feed showing sporadic police activity at the fourth location. As Lieutenant Carlson spoke, the dignitaries, including the Mayor and the Police Chief smiled and fidgeted in the background.

"Tonight's coordinated raids on four locations were the result of an ongoing investigation by FWPD Narcotics Division." Carlson spoke, flanked by Chambers and Nix his moustache twitching. He began to explain the logistics of the raids and the statistics around the arrests and confiscated drugs.

Sanders shook his head. "Ongoing investigation my ass."

"Couldn't exactly tell the truth." Hunter shrugged. "We've already lost the element of surprise with Calderon. Fortunately, Hopkins' real identity hasn't leaked to the press yet. As soon as it does, everyone who's ever met Vance Harvey is going to scatter like cockroaches when the light comes on."

"Yeah." Sanders folded his arms across his chest. "What do you think? Only a couple of days before it gets out?"

Hunter humphed. "Could be an hour, could be a week." He nodded toward the TV. "We need to drive this thing to the ground before then."

When Hunter's phone rang, he looked at it, smiled and punched the accept button. "Detective Jake Hunter, how may I help you?"

"Why do you still answer your phone as if Caller ID had never been invented."

"How are you this morning, Jessica?"

"Not as good as your buddies over in Narcotics. Are you watching the news?"

Hunter looked across the room to the scenes of the news conference being flashed on the screen. The camera panned across a long row of tables full of guns and drugs. It was like one of those DEA press conferences at the culmination of a six month long investigation. "Yeah, I've caught a bit of it. Looks like quite a haul."

"How come my favorite uncle isn't ever on TV like that?"

"Because your only uncle is in homicide, and even when I do my job great, people are still dead and that usually doesn't leave anyone in the press conference mood." He switched gears on her. "Carlson looked good on camera, and based on a conversation I had with him the other day, I think you picked the right guy to be your presenter."

"Speaking of which, that's why I called. We've lined up a number of guests including Carlson and Dr. Liam Anderson, the head of John Peter Smith's Emergency Services." Hunter grunted in response and she continued. "We're trying to cover the topic from three perspectives. The law enforcement angle covered by Carlson, the health impact view covered by Anderson, and the social impact context. That brings me to this call. There's another guy I'd like to ask but I wanted to check with you first."

"What on earth would I have to do with it?"

She hesitated. "It's Maxwell Arnett."

Hunter didn't respond for a moment. "Who?"

"He's a professor from UTA who's an expert on Mass Incarceration and the social impact of the War on Drugs on the black community." She paused. "He's also Brandon Jenkins' uncle."

Hunter's mind flashed back to the funeral, the tall thin man Brandon's mother was walking with. His heart rate instantly surged and he was short of breath.

"Uncle Jake?"

Until Jessica spoke, Hunter didn't realize he hadn't responded. "Uh, yeah." He cleared his throat and took a deep breath to calm his pulse. "Jessica, you get whoever makes sense for your evening. It'll be fine."

"You're sure?"

"Yep. Hey, I need to run. Great talking with you. Good luck with your seminar." After quick goodbyes, he punched off, leaned forward on the table in front of him and closed his eyes.

The press conference on the TV continued in the background as the Mayor congratulated the FWPD on a job well done. Sanders was still glued to the set. Finally he turned to Hunter. "So what now? Continuing to execute raids on Calderon locations isn't going to get us anywhere."

"Nope." Hunter shook his head. "He's so far underground by now, we may never find him." He looked at his watch. "Why don't you head back to the final location? Stacy and her team should be wrapping up pretty soon. See if there's anything tying all this to Calderon, or anything pointing to his next hideout."

Sanders nodded.

"Meanwhile, I've got an appointment. We'll meet up after that and figure out a plan."

"You got it." Sanders packed up his gear and left.

Finding Calderon had just gotten exponentially harder. While their plan looked successful on the morning news programs, as far as he was concerned, it had backfired terribly.

Chapter 41

"Last time I saw you, I thought you couldn't look much worse. Clearly I was wrong." Dr. Chapman Murray leaned back in his chair and perused Hunter with a worried look.

"So, I'm guessing that positive reinforcement theory wasn't part of your training." Hunter had settled into the couch and tried to smirk but it came off more as a sneer.

Murray smiled. "At least you haven't lost your sense of humor." He paused. "Well, sort of."

"Based on the past two weeks I've had, that's as good as it gets."

"Why don't you walk me through it?"

Hunter nodded but didn't immediately start talking. He churned the week's events in his head. As he did, he felt his face flush and a sheen of sweat began to form on his forehead. He ran his hand through his hair and shifted in his chair.

"Take your time." Murray voice was purposely calm and low.

He nodded again, this time more vigorously, as if willing himself to start talking. "Well, let's start with last Wednesday..." His hands fidgeted around as if he didn't know what to do with them. "In our last session, we got so wrapped up in the story about my nickname that I didn't mention that..." The words caught in his throat and he had to force them out. "I went to Brandon Jenkins' funeral."

Dr. Murray's entire body shifted in his seat. "Brandon Jenkins? The young man who was killed?"

"The one I shot. Yes."

"Detective..." He started, but paused a moment. "Why on earth would you do that?"

"I... Uh..." The flush on his face now felt like a sunburn and the light sheen of sweat had grown to a tidal wave. He unbuttoned his sleeves and rolled them up to his mid-forearms. "I guess I just needed to see what I'd done."

"Did it help?"

"No." Hunter stared down at the scraped hard wood floor, getting lost in the dark swirls of the grain. He finally shook his head and continued. "All it did was give my mind more fuel to burn."

The frown on Dr. Murray's face was that of a disappointed school teacher, a little discouraged but mostly empathetic. "I'm sure. Where did you stand? Did any of his family members notice you?"

Hunter shook his head. "I watched it from my car."

After a few more questions but no real suggestions, Dr. Murray changed tacks. "What other events from the last two weeks are troubling you?"

"Yeah. I mentioned a fellow detective's death last time I was here. As it turns out, my suspicion at the time that it wasn't a suicide was confirmed. He was murdered."

The doctor jotted some notes, but didn't speak.

"The worst part is, the department isn't acknowledging his murder. Since he was deep under cover, they're waiting to see if we can find his killer first."

Dr. Murray nodded. "And he had a family..."

"He wasn't married, but his parents are being delayed the opportunity to have their son buried with a full Police funeral." His voice went quiet. "He deserves that."

"Yes. I can see why this is weighing on you, but..." He drew his eyebrows together. "Both of those events happened before our last session. You seem much more upset this week than you did on Thursday. Has something else happened?"

"Last night..." Hunter sighed. "What I say here is

confidential, right? It doesn't go in a report to my lieutenant, right?"

"Correct."

"Will it affect my ability to continue working?"

Dr. Murray paused, appeared to contemplate his answer. "These sessions are not intended to determine your fitness for duty. No one has questioned that. They're intended to help you deal with the shooting." He hesitated. "If, however, I conclude that you may be a danger to yourself or to others, I am required to report." He looked up and caught Hunter's eyes. "I would never do that unless the situation was extreme and clear. Based on our few sessions and your record as an officer, I don't expect that to be the case."

Hunter absorbed his answer and sat for a moment. In the silence he weighed the consequences of talking about the night before. He couldn't imagine his world without being a cop, but continuing to be a cop without fixing this problem wasn't likely.

"Last night..." He stopped, started again. "Did you see the news this morning about the multiple narcotics raids?"

"Yes."

"They weren't really narcotics raids. I mean, yes, there were narcotics seized in the raids and the target was a major wholesaler. But that wasn't the reason for the raids."

"You were involved?"

One side of Hunter's mouth twitched up. "We were trying to find the guy we think might be responsible for the undercover cop's murder."

"Did you find him?"

"No. That's one of the reasons we had the Narcotics guys take the credit for everything. We didn't want our suspect to know that we'd connected him to the murder. We wanted him to think it was all about the drugs."

"Okay. But according to the news reports, even without finding him, the raids netted several suspects, an enormous amount of contraband and there was only one officer hurt and that sounded fairly minor." Dr. Murray squinted at Hunter. "That doesn't sound so bad."

"I froze." The words jumped out of Hunter.

"Sorry?"

"I froze, Doc. I had a suspect in my sights. He pointed his gun directly at me and I froze. I didn't squeeze the trigger. If it hadn't been for a SWAT sniper, I'd be dead right now."

"Oh."

The whoosh from the air conditioning vent sounded like a freight train.

Dr. Murray set his notepad down, leaned back in his chair and intertwined his hands together across his abdomen. "Detective, what you do is incredibly dangerous. Things happen in a split second. Being a little hesitant, especially in light of recent events, is perfectly understandable."

"It's perfectly unacceptable is what you mean." Hunter's voice roared in the tiny office. "I should have fired. I could have died. Worse yet, someone else on my team could have."

"But you didn't. And nobody else did either. The team worked as it was designed and all the good guys walked away." Dr. Murray leaned forward. "Detective, this thing is going to take some time. You feel like you made a mistake with Brandon Jenkins. Your natural tendency is to be more cautious."

Hunter chewed on the inside of his mouth and absently shook his head.

"I have a number of suggestions for you." He stopped, tilted his head. "Have you fired your gun since the incident?"

"No."

"Go to the range. You need to get used to your gun again and understand it's there to protect you."

Hunter rolled his eyes.

"Don't give me that look. Consider it doctor's orders. Also, I'm prescribing you something to help you sleep. Walking around like a zombie will not help your brain process. Besides, you need sleep not only for critical situations, you need it to solve the case."

"Okay."

"Lastly, even though today is our final mandatory session, I'm going to strongly recommend that we keep visiting on at least a weekly basis. Going forward, I'd like to work with you on deep relaxation and visualization. I think it will be helpful."

Hunter nodded, looked at his watch and stood to leave.

Dr. Murray waited for his reply.

"I'll do whatever you tell me to. Whatever it takes to keep being a cop. "

Chapter 42

"Well, if it isn't our resident rock stars." Hunter smiled at Chambers and Nix when he walked into the conference room. After leaving Dr. Murray's, he had taken a little time to have a quiet lunch by himself and to collect his thoughts. He hadn't come away with any epiphanies, but he was at least ready for the afternoon. "I thought you two would have already signed a book deal and sold the movie rights."

"I'm waiting on a call from my agent." Chambers deadpanned and pulled out a felt tip marker. "If you'd like an autograph, I'm happy to oblige, assuming it's not on a body part."

"I got your autograph..." Hunter made a mildly obscene gesture and pulled up a chair. He glanced at the paperwork across the table. "What do we have going?"

"Assuming Calderon has gone underground, hitting the rest of his locations isn't going to get us much." Sanders pushed a folder across the table to Hunter. "We've been combing through all of his known associates. We thought we'd narrow down the list to those who might know where he's at."

"And?"

"We started with over forty possibilities." Chambers jumped in. "When you subtract out last night's total—"

"You mean the eight we arrested, the two fatalities and the one we put in the hospital from that Narcotics raid?" Nix snickered and gave Chambers a high five.

Hunter shook his head, but couldn't quite suppress his grin.

"Boo-ya." Chambers nodded. "We whittled it down to

twelve. Now we're working on last known addresses, places of employment and known hang outs."

"Do we have any that are actionable?"

"These top four are ready to be chased down." Sanders pointed to the names on the list. "It takes a little time to build a file." He pointed to Chambers and Nix. "It's mostly these guys using their tribal knowledge and calling their informants."

Hunter nodded. "Divide and conquer?"

All three detectives looked at Hunter like he was crazy. Sanders arched his eyebrows. "Uh, you did hear that part about tribal knowledge and drug informants, right?"

"Yeah, I caught that." Hunter smiled. "Meaning we let Chambers and Nix continue to apply their 'tribal knowledge' while you and I go chase down these scumbags?"

"Oh sure. Leave us here to do the shit work while you have all the fun." Chambers shot him a sarcastic smile. "You're just jealous."

"Just optimizing resources." Hunter smiled.

Nix shook his head. "Sucks when he's right."

After twenty minutes of coordinating, Hunter and Sanders were in his SUV with information packets on two of Calderon's known associates. The plan was that by the time they tracked those two down, Chambers and Nix would have two more ready. They'd find them, detain them and see if they can't get them to give up Calderon. Worst case, they'd continue to put pressure on his ability to do business.

Finding known felons who aren't legally employed rarely involves knocking on their front doors. Most of them don't have permanent front doors upon which to knock. More often, it involves knowing where they hang out and with whom.

"So, who's our first contestant to play 'Where's Carlos'?" Hunter pulled out of the parking lot and began navigating the one way streets in downtown. Since most of Calderon's known associates lived in or near the Diamond Hill Jarvis area, he planned to hit Main

Street and go north over the river and through North Side.

Sanders put on his best Don Pardo voice. "Johnny Garcia, come on down." He turned and addressed Hunter as if he was Bob Barker. "Bob, Johnny has no permanent address nor legal employment so we'll have to look elsewhere for him today. All indications are that if you find Johnny's girlfriend, you'll likely find him."

"Well, Don, where can we find Johnny's girlfriend?"

"Bob, I thought you'd never ask. Based on our best information, she is a tattoo artist at Spinning Needles Tattoo's and Body Piercing on N. Main just south of 28th Street."

Hunter shook his head and grinned. "Her parents must be so proud." He steered the SUV passed the courthouse and crossed the Trinity River. Twenty minutes further up N. Main Street, they were passing through the tourist and party area known as the Stockyards. Once they crossed Exchange Street, Los Vaqueros Restaurant was on their left.

"Spinning Needles should be about a half block further up." Sanders nodded in the general direction and Hunter slowed the truck.

"Do we know what Johnny drives?"

"You mean rides." Sanders pointed to a small standalone tan building with a shingle awning over a narrow front porch. It housed two store fronts, a thrift shop and the tattoo parlor. "It's a custom Harley that looks just like that one."

"We must be living right." He drove past, took a right into the 7-Eleven parking lot and looped around so they could approach from the north. "I'll park on the side of the building. You go around to the back. There's only two doors in that place and my bet is that when I walk in the front door and flash my badge, he's going to rabbit out the back."

"And I get to be his welcoming committee." Sanders smiled. "Sounds like a plan."

Two minutes later, Hunter strolled through the front, held his badge up and bellowed. "I'm Detective Jake Hunter with the Fort Worth Police. I'm looking for Johnny Garcia."

Almost before he finished the sentence, he heard a crash of commotion and a blur of movement. He saw the back of a large, dark haired man in a black leather vest moving fast. The man pushed the back door open, took one long stride and ran into Billy's outstretched forearm. The big man landed with a thud that shook the back porch. Billy just looked down at him and smiled. "I'm Detective Billy Sanders. You must be Johnny."

As Sanders cuffed Garcia, Hunter called for a patrol backup and convinced Johnny's irate girlfriend that she needed to calm down or she'd get to join him. She finally got the message a few minutes later when the patrol car pulled up.

They dragged Johnny outside and leaned him against the car. Their search of his pockets netted a small baggie of white powder and a nasty looking knife. Hunter dropped the items on the hood of the car and turned him around. "Johnny, today's your lucky day. Instead of charging you with narcotics and weapons possession, I'm going to give you an opportunity to walk back in there and continue playing kissy face with your sweetie."

Garcia glared at him.

"All you have to do is tell me where we can find Carlos Calderon."

Garcia spoke slowly and over enunciated. "Fuck you. I want my lawyer."

"Have it your way." Hunter sighed and turned to the patrolmen. "Book him on everything you can come up with."

As fast as they'd arrived, they were back in the SUV turning left out of the parking lot. Sanders was on the phone with Chambers feverishly jotting down notes.

Hunter squinted against the afternoon sun and flowed north with the traffic on N. Main. Sanders signed off and looked over at him. "Our Narcs have us a couple more opportunities."

"Nice of them to let us have some of the fun."

Sanders smiled and rubbed his forearm. "Good news is our next stop is right up the road, a little place called Durango Bar." He nodded forward. "Might get a chance at more than one. It seems this fine establishment is a hangout for several of Calderon's crew."

"Then we'll need some backup before we go in." Hunter dialed dispatch and requested two patrol units. They arrived a few moments after Hunter and Sanders pulled past the chain-linked fence surrounding the weathered asphalt parking lot.

The Durango Bar was located about seven blocks north of the tattoo shop near NW 35th Street in an industrial area southeast of Meacham Field. It wasn't much to look at, especially in the harsh sunlight of the afternoon. The squat brick building was painted an ugly purple with white trim.. The black metal front door was built for security, not curb appeal.

Several older model cars sat scattered throughout the parking lot, blending into the bleak surroundings.

The building had no windows or security cameras so he wasn't worried about spending a few minutes in the parking lot briefing the patrol units. He positioned two officers at the front of the building and two in the rear. He and Sanders would go in through the front door, announce themselves, watch the cockroaches scatter and see if any of their targets landed in the net.

The plan worked as expected. Before their eyes could even adjust to the dark rooms, the sounds of feet moving fast came from several directions. "Fort Worth Police. Don't move!"

Several of the clientele with slower reflexes gave up on the idea of breaking for the door and assumed the position. Two were already down the back hall. Bright daylight flashed when the back door opened. Shouts from the patrol officers demanding they stop and get on the ground rang down the hall.

"Like carving a boneless chicken." Hunter shot a glance to Sanders. "Why don't you get our compadres from out front and process the slow group? I'll head out back and take care of our sprinters."

"Works for me." Sanders stepped to the door and motioned the two officers to come in.

Behind the bar in the parking lot, the story was different. There were two men cuffed and on their knees sweating on the steaming asphalt. Hunter studied their driver's licenses and sneered at them. He looked up and saw Sanders. "No luck, huh?"

Sanders shook his head. He had finished talking to the half-dozen afternoon drinkers in the bar. They were nothing more than a collection of unemployed misfits and hardcore alcoholics. None were on the list of potential Calderon associates and all claimed never to have heard of him. "Just a depressing trek through society's leftovers. How about you?"

"I'm not nearly as philosophical, but I did find two of Calderon's boys." He shrugged. "Of course, they used uncalled for profanity and lawyered up immediately." He turned and handed the licenses to one of the officers. "Book 'em," He directed Sanders' attention to the collection of contraband laying on the hood of the patrol car. "Fortunately for us, they're just as stupid as the last guy and we've got enough to take them off the streets for a while."

The rest of the afternoon was rinse and repeat. They searched for eight of the twelve known associates on their list. They found six. In each case, the target immediately asked for a lawyer. None answered a single question. All had enough contraband on them to warrant a trip downtown.

Shortly after five, worn out from a hot afternoon of frustration, Hunter and Sanders popped back into the conference room. Chambers and Nix, while slightly less sweaty, looked just a beat.

Chambers rubbed his temples. "We continue to throw people in jail but haven't made any progress on our real objective."

"Mama said there'd be days like this." Hunter shrugged. "We'll hit it again tomorrow. We'll either find this bastard or we'll have run him out of business." He looked at his watch. "I'm going to go spend some time with someone much prettier than any of you."

Chapter 43

"You want to go blow stuff up?"

"Mm, Cowboy, I love it when you talk dirty to me." Stacy giggled on the other end of the line. "I'll need to stop by my place and pick up my toys."

"Works for me." He looked at his watch. "I'll wrap stuff up here and swing by in thirty."

Shortly after six, Hunter escorted Stacy down the sidewalk in front of her house. He had two handgun cases while she carried a third and two sets of earmuffs. Hunter couldn't conceal his smirk. "You need three guns when you go to the range?"

"Variety is the spice of life." She winked.

He shook his head and opened the passenger door for her. On the drive up I-35, he relayed the frustrating results from the afternoon. As they exited on Golden Triangle Boulevard and circled back under the freeway, she reached over and held his hand. "We'll get him. We always do. Sometimes it just takes longer."

When they pulled in the parking lot of the Shoot Smart Gun Range, she squeezed tight and smiled. "Let's go pop some caps and pretend the targets are perps."

He gave her a wry look. "You might enjoy this a bit too much."

She smiled and hopped out of the SUV. They carried Stacy's cases into the shop and after some quick shopping for supplies, checked in with the Range Marshall and set up in a bay.

Stacy quickly opened all three cases, pulled out the three pistols and checked and loaded each one. The whole time Hunter patiently watched her. Once she had everything laid out to her liking, she looked at Hunter. "You going to get ready?"

He patted his Glock 17 in his shoulder holster. "I am ready."

Stacy rolled her eyes. "All right, hotshot." She gestured toward the target. "Give it a go."

As the explosion of rounds echoed off the walls around them, Hunter reached under his jacket, unsnapped his holster and pulled out his weapon. He ejected the magazine, checked the load, slammed it back home and racked the slide. Stepping up to the firing line, he raised his gun. The black silhouette target fifteen yards away narrowed in his sights. He paused as his pulse suddenly jackhammered.

Stepping back, he let his arm drop and shook it out to relax. He cleared his throat, rolled his shoulders and took a deep breath. Once again, he stepped forward, raised his weapon, squinted to focus on the target and waited, readjusting his grip several times.

"Cowboy? Is something wrong?"

"I'm fine." He continued to take aim.

"It's only a paper target. Just pull the trigger."

He nodded, took another deep breath and pulled the trigger once. The explosion seemed louder than normal and he lowered his weapon. When he looked down range at the target, the hole had barely clipped the torso.

Until Stacy touched his shoulder, he didn't realize he was staring. He blinked several times and coughed out a laugh. "That wasn't very good, was it?" He cleared his throat when he heard how raspy it sounded.

Stacy wrapped her arms around his waist from behind and squeezed. She whispered in his ear. "Go again. Empty it."

He nodded, quickly raised the weapon and popped off thirteen straight shots. By the time he finished, he felt out of breath and his hand was shaking. He set his gun down and gripped the table so Stacy wouldn't notice.

"That's better." She pointed to the target with holes grouped sporadically throughout the torso. "Not bad." She grinned. "Not your best, but not bad."

Hunter ran his hand through his hair and frowned playfully. "Why don't you pick one out of your arsenal and give it a go?"

Trying to lighten the mood, she smiled. "Just because they won't let me carry at work doesn't mean I can't when I'm on my own time."

"Now that's all we need. A bunch of CSI's packing heat."

Stacy pushed him away. "Step back and let me show you how it's done." She looked at her four guns. "Let me see... I could go with my little Smith and Wesson Bodyguard. Nothing quite like a .38 Special revolver." She smiled, then ran her hand across a .40 caliber Smith and Wesson Pro Series. "Or I could go with my cannon."

Hunter faked a shiver and she laughed.

"Nah. I'll warm up my Ruger LC9." She picked up the compact, slim line 9mm semiautomatic. In a quick motion, she stepped up to the firing line, racked the slide and popped off seven quick rounds. The target suffered a tight grouping of holes right in the center of the chest. She smiled.

"Good Lord." Hunter laughed, reloaded his weapon and took his turn. This time, he was more relaxed and his grouping was a little better, but not nearly as good as Stacy's.

They continued to take turns, Stacy alternating between her options but consistently outshooting Hunter. She teasingly poked him in the ribs. "What does it mean when the cop's girlfriend has better aim than the cop?"

"My aim is just fine when it counts." The playful smile fell off his face as the last words came out. They both went silent as the implication hung in the air.

Stacy didn't say anything, she just stepped over and hugged him. "It's okay, baby."

Hunter nodded and held her tight.

She kissed him on the neck and whispered. "Why don't we pack up these toys? I've got another idea."

Chapter 44

"Don't give me that look. You're just jealous." Hunter reached over and rubbed Panther's head. The enormous black cat purred hard enough to vibrate the kitchen table. A genuine smile spread across Hunter's face, one of the first in a week and a half.

Stacy walked up and hugged him from behind. She was fresh from the shower and dressed for work. He inhaled deeply as her scent blended with the aroma from his coffee. The mixture reinvigorated him better than any caffeine drink.

"What's on your plate for today?" Stacy poured herself a cup.

"Meeting with the narcotics guys at nine, and then spend the rest of the day arresting what's left of Calderon's boys." He turned to see her leaning against the counter blowing on her cup. His smile grew. "And you?"

"Same old stuff, different day." She put down her cup, stepped over and tugged on his lapels. "Just processing anything and everything to put bad guys in prison."

By the time he strolled into the conference room, he was almost relaxed, a feeling he'd almost forgotten. Chambers, Nix and Sanders were already heads down comparing notes and lists. He nodded to them as he put down his laptop. "Gentlemen."

"You won't find any of those here." Chambers snickered.

"No doubt about that." Hunter sat down, began to unpack. "You got us some targets ready?"

Sanders stood up. "Got six lined up. No need to get comfortable. I'm ready to roll whenever you are."

"Well okay." Hunter stood back up and repacked. "Let's

move."

As he and Sanders stepped toward the door, a beefy desk sergeant appeared in front of them. "Hey Cowboy, glad I caught you. There's a couple of characters out in the lobby asking for you." He looked at his note. "Some guy named Calderon and his attorney."

"Excuse me?" Hunter's eye widened.

"You're kidding me."

"Holy shit."

"No way."

Sanders, Nix and Chambers's responses tumbled over each other.

After their initial reactions, all four of them gaped at each other. Finally, Hunter laughed and shook his head. "Well, Sergeant. Please escort our guests to an interview room and tell them I'll be with them momentarily."

"Will do. They'll be in number three."

When the sergeant left, Hunter turned to the group. "This is sure as hell a first for me." He shrugged. "I guess we'll go have a chat with Carlos Calderon."

Five minutes later, the infamous Carlos Calderon sat realaxed and jovial next to his attorney in the interrogation room. Clearly unconcerned with the gravity of the possible charges. Hunter and Sanders watched him through the observation window. His attorney, while not exactly playful, certainly didn't look tense. Their mood was in stark contrast to the harshness of the interrogation room. Sanders folded his arms. "Damn. Look at his attorney's suit. Handmade. Must have cost more than your entire wardrobe, Cowboy."

Hunter's face remain passive.

"That's a thousand dollar pair of shoes," Sanders added.

"That he bought with blood money." Hunter set his jaw. "Let's get this party started." Hunter burst through the door, cuffs in his hand. "Mr. Calderon, stand up, turn around and put your hands behind your back."

Calderon leaned back, surprised, but before he could move,

his lawyer stood up, calmly held his hand out in front of him. "Don't move Mr. Calderon." He looked at Hunter. "Who are you and what are the charges?"

"I'm Detective Jake Hunter and I'm arresting this man for the murder of Bonner Hopkins." He turned back to Calderon. "Now stand up."

"Don't move, Mr. Calderon." His voice louder but still calm, he glared at Hunter. "I'm Antonio Flores. This man is my client and we are here voluntarily —"

"And we greatly appreciate you helping us locate him, Mr. Flores. We've been searching for Carlos for two days." He pointed to Calderon. "He's been quite elusive."

"Detective Hunter." Flores purposely lowered his voice. "We're here to answer any questions you have. Afterwards, if you still believe you have reason to arrest my client, I will not interfere."

Having set the tone, Hunter stared at Flores for a long moment and then gestured for him to sit. "Very well, let's start off with some simple ones." He looked at Calderon. "What size shoes do you wear?"

Calderon paused until Flores nodded. "Size eleven."

"Please show me your shoes."

He pulled his feet out from under the table so that Hunter could see them. As in the security camera pictures, he was wearing the Altra triathlon shoes. Hunter picked up a large plastic baggie he'd brought in with him. "Please take them off and put them in this bag."

Flores sat up straight. "Excuse me."

Hunter yank a folded paper from his jacket pocket. "I've got a warrant for them. I've been carrying it around with me for two days as we tried to find your client." He pointed to Calderon's wrist. "And while you're at it, I've got a warrant for the gold bracelet on your left wrist."

Flores grabbed the paper, examined it, sighed and nodded to his client to comply. Calderon started to object but Flores cut him off with a glare. After registering his dismay with a look to Hunter, he took off the shoes and bracelet and placed them in the appropriate baggies.

"Now..." Hunter slapped down two photographs, one of Logan, Tyler and one of Hopkins. "Do you know either of these three men?"

Calderon looked at the pictures and shrugged. "They look familiar, but I don't know them." He grinned. "No offense, but I don't exactly hang with that many Anglos."

Hunter showed no reaction to his comment. "Can you tell me where you were between 3pm and 10pm on Friday, August 7th?"

"I need to check my calendar." He picked up his phone, tapped a few times and smiled as if at a happy memory. "That was the night my cousin Miguel got married." He tilted his head and looked at Hunter. "If I need an alibi, I've got a couple hundred people who saw me there. It was an all day event. Hell, since I was his best man, I'm probably in hundreds of snapshots." He tapped a few more times. "Here are some selfies."

He handed the phone to Hunter who took it and scrolled through several pictures. All were date and time stamped from that Friday and all had Calderon's smiling face in them.

After looking at several, Hunter took advantage of having permission to look at the phone and casually searched for other data of interest. "What about Wednesday, August 12th?"

Without hesitation, as if he was expecting that question. "I was in Mexico visiting family."

Flores reached in to his briefcase and tossed a passport on the table. "You can note the exit and entrance stamps. He left on Monday and came back on Friday." He reached in again. "Here's his boarding passes from both flights. I'm sure if you ask, DFW Airport will provide security footage from those gates and you can confirm his departure and arrival."

Hunter felt his stomach drop but he wasn't ready to give up. As he looked at the passport and the boarding passes, his mind raced through the evidence.

The shoes and bracelet are a match to the photo, but you can't see a face in it. What else? Oh yeah, the phone.

"Mr. Calderon, what's your cell number?"

He rattled off a number, but it didn't match the number Hopkins had called shortly before his death.

As a last resort, Hunter took his cell phone out of his pocket and punched in the number Hopkins had called. In his ear, the phone rang but there was no corresponding ring from the phone in Hunter's hand. He slid it across the table to Calderon. At least he was smart enough not to have brought that phone with him.

Hunter was at a loss. With apparent airtight alibi's for both murders, matching the shoes and bracelet to a faceless man in a photograph wasn't enough to hold him.

As if reading Hunter's mind, Flores made a show of closing his briefcase. "If there's nothing else, Detective, Mr. Calderon and I will be leaving now. Here's my card should you need to have any further conversations with my client." A smug smile ran across his face as he got up. "We always want to cooperate with law enforcement."

Flores and Calderon left Hunter standing alone in the interview room and staring at the open door. The feeling in his stomach had now transformed into a volcano. He didn't believe a word that had been said, but without something solid, he was stuck.

He ran his hand through his hair and stepped toward the door.

And this morning started out so promising.

Chapter 45

Sanders tried to catch Hunter as he bolted from the interrogation room. He was still tailing him when he walked into the conference room, grabbed a stapler from off the table and threw it across the room. It disintegrated upon impact with the far wall.

"I'm guessing the conversation didn't go as expected." Chambers eyed Hunter appearing concerned for the safety of other office supplies.

"Son of a bitch." Hunter's brisk walk now turned into a brisk pace. "Bullshit."

Chambers glanced at Sanders. "What happened?"

Sanders exhaled and shook his head. "Calderon has airtight alibis for all three murders."

"Bullshit." Hunter turned and poked at the air. "Airtight my ass. I don't buy it for a minute." He resumed his pacing but kept talking. "I want to see the security footage of him getting on and off both of those flights. I also want to run facial recognition on the passengers for every DFW to Mexico City flight in between."

When Sanders looked confused, Hunter continued. "He could have flown back here under a false identity, shot Hopkins, and returned to Mexico."

"Gotcha." Sanders nodded.

"I also want our pictures of him analyzed at a deeper level. I know we can't see his face, but let's confirm everything else we can. Height, weight, build, whatever."

"We don't have the tools to do that, but I've got a buddy with the Bureau who might be able to help me." Sanders jotted down several notes.

"Could he have hired someone to do it?" Chambers chimed in.

Hunter snapped his fingers, but then paused and shook his head. "Why hire someone to dress like him for the hit?"

"Good point on Hopkins, but he could have had any of his guys take out Logan and Tyler."

Hunter nodded and the four detectives continued to brainstorm while he paced and fumed until late morning. When it was time to break for lunch, Chambers and Nix decided to head back to Narcotics so they could check in with Carlson.

The heat wave that had sent temperatures above a hundred for most of the month of August had finally broken. That meant a lunchtime temperature in the mid-nineties, bearable enough for Sanders and Hunter to walk over to the Sundance Square area and grab a burger at Five Guys.

Hunter spent most of the meal nibbling on fries while he disassembled and rebuilt his burger several times as if there was something wrong with it. When not playing with his food, he stared out the window. The only conversation Sanders could evoke from him were monosyllabic words and grunts.

By the time they got back to the conference room, any burst of energy had completely dissipated. They were at a dead end and it ate away at Hunter's gut. He would have them chase every possibility with Calderon, but disproving eyewitnesses, photos, passport stamps and boarding passes was a near impossibility.

Most of the afternoon was spent in silence as they each filled out paperwork, researched the occasional brain fart and reread their files hoping to see something new. But it was all more old news, and empty trails.

Late in the afternoon, Hunter, with his jacket off and his sleeves rolled up began pacing again. "Are we looking at this right?"

"What do you mean?"

"I'm just trying to think of the why behind it all."

"Who knows?" Sanders tapped his pen on the table. "Since when do drug wholesalers need a logical reason to do anything?"

"Always." Hunter stopped and looked at Sanders. "Look, these guys may be lunatics and soulless scum, but at the end of the day, they are businessmen."

"Okay, so what does any of this have to do with their business?"

"Maybe that's the question we need to answer." Hunter raised his finger in the air. "You know the old saying, follow the money?"

Sanders nodded but didn't speak.

"Well, let's tweak it a little and look at each event from the view of who benefitted. Go back to the first domino. When the three kids got the bad batch of Ecstasy."

"You think that's what triggered everything?"

Hunter nodded. "I do, because that was the only apparent connection between Jenkins and Logan." He tapped a picture of Logan on the whiteboard. "That's what put them in the same room together."

"So, who would possibly benefit from three young people ending up dead or on life support?" Sanders stood up and walked to the whiteboard, looked at the various pictures taped there and the names written. "Logan certainly didn't benefit. Neither did Tyler."

"No. He merely got blamed for it."

"Likewise, Dalton Foster looked bad because it was his product and reputation that were tainted."

"Precisely." Hunter nodded. "Which means, by default, Calderon benefitted. Whether on purpose or by accident, if your competitor falters, your business gets a bump."

Sanders put a check by Calderon's name. "I can't think of anyone else who'd benefit from kids dying."

Hunter paused and chewed on the inside of his cheek. "What about an anti-drug organization?"

"Wow, were you born that cynical or did you witness Santa

Claus murder the Easter Bunny when you were a kid? Damn dude. Seriously?"

"What happens every time something like this makes the headlines? There's a temporary decline in drug use and the fund raising for anti-drug organizations sky rockets."

"Yeah, but... You're not saying that an anti-drug organization deliberately tainted a drug supply to kill kids just so others would be persuaded not to use." Sanders looked like he might puke. "I just can't wrap my head around that."

"Reality is, neither can I but it's not unprecedented. The U.S. government poisoned alcohol during prohibition to scare people into not drinking. Killed close to ten thousand people." Hunter shrugged.

"Holy crap." Sanders cringed.

"I just wanted to open our thought process to all possibilities."

"Well, you certainly did that. Shit." Sanders shook his head.

Hunter nodded. "Let's move on to the murders of Tyler and Logan. Who benefitted?"

"Several people." Sanders started writing on the whiteboard. "First, each victim's family. They got to see the perceived culprit die. Second, Calderon again because it's more turmoil in his competitor's organization. Third, Hopkins in his role as Vance Harvey, because he'd be positioned to move up a notch. Finally, how about Dalton Foster? He gets to look like he's cleaning house and doing something about the tainted drugs issue."

"Damn, it's a wonder Logan and Tyler lasted as long as they did." Hunter raised an eyebrow. "Realistically though, considering Hopkins was next on the hit list, he doesn't make sense. And Calderon is a long shot because it was unnecessary. Logan and Tyler being alive were more damaging to Foster."

"Good points. So who benefitted from Hopkins' death?"

Hunter thought for a moment. "The only person that makes sense is Foster, and even that assumes he either found out Hopkins was a cop or he's beyond paranoid and wanted to get rid of anyone on Logan's team."

"You're right." Sanders nodded. "Calderon wouldn't bother with someone that low on the totem pole. He probably didn't even know who he was. As for the families, only one of them really knew him."

"Okay, not that I believe Calderon, but..." Hunter rubbed his chin. "Let's pretend for a moment that his alibis are as solid as they sound. That means someone wanted us to chase him. Who would benefit from us suspecting Calderon?"

"Well, in the last two days, we've almost destroyed Calderon's ability to do business and confiscated enough of his inventory to put him out of business for at least a few weeks."

"Exactly, the only person who benefits is Foster."

Sanders stared at the board for a moment. "With the exception of the original drug related deaths, Foster benefitted from everything else that's happened."

"Exactly. Dalton Foster." He tapped on the board. "Let's make his life uncomfortable."

Chapter 46

Where do we go from here?

Hunter shuffled down his dark hallway at 3 a.m. on Thursday morning trying not to step on Panther. Sleep had not come. It wasn't thoughts of Brandon Jenkins but the realization that the trail was going cold.

He made some coffee and thought about the 9 a.m. status meeting with Sprabary and Carlson. They were almost at the two week mark and this would once again be a mixed bag of little victories that had gotten them no closer to solving either Logan or Hopkins' murders.

Sprabary bypassed small talk when Hunter and Sanders sat down. He gestured toward Lieutenant Carlson. "I know you guys have given my colleague here a reason to be brush up on his TV skills, but I haven't heard that you've booked anyone on murder charges. Are we close?"

Hunter cleared his throat. "No sir. Our most promising suspect, Carlos Calderon, voluntarily came in yesterday…"

"And he's not behind bars today?" Sprabary leaned forward.

"No sir. Based on our interview with him, he was able to provide extremely strong alibis for all three murders."

"I thought we had pictures of him at the scene."

"We have pictures of someone who appears to be him. That doesn't seem to be the case now."

Hunter went on to detail how Calderon was out of town during the Hopkins' murder and had a couple of hundred people who can vouch for his whereabouts during Logan's and Tyler's.

"I assure you, we are checking every angle to verify that his alibis are legit." Hunter's jaw was set so tight, he almost ground his teeth as he made the statement.

"Anything you need, let me know." Carlson nodded. "I not only have access to the FWPD resources, but DEA has already called to volunteer assets if it means putting Calderon behind bars.

"We'll be sure to do that."

"One thing's for sure." Carlson smiled almost uncontrollably. "We put one hell of a dent in his business plan. We confiscated a regular smorgasbord of narcotics valued on the streets at well over $5 million. Between the inventory and the number of soldiers that are currently guests of Tarrant County, he won't be able to service many of his clients for weeks."

"That brings me to another possibility." Hunter could tell that he had gotten their attention. "What if Calderon really isn't our guy?"

Sprabary fidgeted in his chair. "I thought we were pretty sure about him."

"We are, but most of that was based on the shoe prints, phone records and security camera footage. Since none of that includes DNA, fingerprints or a facial view, it all could have easily been staged."

A frown swept across Sraybary's face. "You mean framed him? Sounds like something out of a movie. Who would go to so much trouble?"

"Only one man with the motivation and means, Dalton Foster." Hunter opened his palms out. "Calderon's biggest competitor."

Carlson shook his head. "Those guys have peacefully coexisted for years. Seems a bit farfetched."

Hunter spent the next several minutes walking them through the logic about who benefitted at each point in the cycle.

"Well, Detective," Carlson rubbed his chin. "I like your thought process, but we're pretty confident that Hopkins' cover was intact. We haven't heard any chatter on the street about someone taking out an undercover. In fact, the little we are hearing is that Foster is pissed about losing three guys."

He leaned forward and continued. "We're still keeping very close tabs on Foster's organization. Based on what we're seeing, it doesn't look like he's moving to take over additional territory." He shook his head. "Quite the opposite, more like battening down the hatches and laying low. He appears concerned that he could suffer the same fate as Calderon."

After fifteen minutes of discussion around Foster and his organization, Sprabary pointed to Hunter. "Keep investigating Foster, but don't make any specific moves without clearing it through Lieutenant Carlson and me."

The room went quiet but the look on Sprabary's face told Hunter they weren't done. After a moment, Sprabary tapped his finger on the desk and leaned forward. "There is one more topic we need to discuss. It's been over a week now since Hopkins' murder. Keeping it out of the press this long has been a miracle, but we really can't delay any longer. The Chief and Hopkins' family are insisting that we go public with the information and that we schedule a full honors funeral."

Sprabary's normally serious demeanor now looked beyond severe. He let the Lieutenant continue without interruption.

"Under normal circumstances, I would be the first to honor a fallen brother. My concern is that the minute we do, the little we have to go on will evaporate like flash paper."

Carlson held out his hands. "If you think Foster is laying low now, wait until he learns that his organization was infiltrated. He will burrow deeper than a groundhog."

Hunter and Sanders both just nodded. There wasn't much for either of them to say. This was a decision way above their pay grade. Their only option was to react to whatever fallout might occur.

"At the end of the day, sir..." Hunter paused. "Hopkins died in the line of duty doing one of the most dangerous jobs out there. As far as I'm concerned, he was a hero and deserves to be honored as such. If that makes our job a little harder, so be it." He shrugged. "Whether they know or not, as it stands, we've got absolutely nothing that implicates Foster other than a theory."

Sprabary narrowed his eyes. "Sounds like you two have some work to do."

Chapter 47

Hunter shot out of Sprabary's office like a bottle rocket. Instead of being dejected because of the lack of progress, he was jacked up with possibilities. Maybe it was being reminded that they were hunting a cop killer. Maybe it was because he knew that as soon as it hit the media, the pressure to solve the case would explode .

"We're going to take Carlson up on his offer for help." He pointed to the phone as he and Sanders bolted into the conference room. "Call Chambers and Nix, see if they're still available. I'm going to enlist Jimmy's help. We're going to hit this hard."

It was early afternoon by the time the two Narcotics detectives and Jimmy Reyes were able to join Hunter and Sanders in the conference room, but Hunter had been alternately pacing and writing on the whiteboard since their morning meeting.

"Okay, gentlemen..." Hunter stood at the front of the room twisting a dry erase marker in his hand. "I don't have to remind any of you that we're hunting someone who murdered one of our own. As it stands..." He pointed to the whiteboard. "We've got three possibilities. First, Carlos Calderon's alibis are bullshit. Second, Dalton Foster is cleaning house and trying to blame it on Calderon. Or third, someone else has gone out of their way to frame Calderon. We've got to investigate all three tracks." He gestured toward to the guys sitting in the room. "That's why you guys are here. Extra manpower."

Reyes got Hunter's attention. "So I'm the new guy here, but aren't we working three different murders?"

"Yes we are."

"Are we assuming they were all killed by the same person?"

Hunter pursed his lips. "We have been, unless someone has alternate logic."

"I don't see how it's not one person." Sanders stood. "They were all part of Foster's crew. Logan and Tyler were responsible for the tainted narcotics. Hopkins was investigating that incident and ended up dead while we were investigating him for the Logan and Tyler murders." He shook his head. "These are all tied together."

"I agree. This is all one guy." Hunter surveyed the room and saw all heads nodding. "Chambers, Nix, I want to use you guys on stuff related to Calderon and Foster since you already have built in knowledge of their operation."

He pointed to Chambers. "You've got all the information on Calderon's alibis. I want you to find anyone who was at that wedding to confirm he was there. Get pictures. We've already got folks checking security tapes for both airports. Chase them down."

"You got it."

"You get Foster." He nodded to Nix. "Find him. Bring him in and see where he was during our murders. Dig into his phone records and financial records and see if you can track his movements over the past two weeks."

Nix nodded. "Will do."

He turned to Jimmy and Billy. "That leaves us to chase down the framing theory."

"How do we do that?" Jimmy was all business.

"Well, I figure if it was a setup, it was based around our four core pieces of evidence." He ticked off his fingers as he spoke. "The shoes, the bracelet, the surveillance camera photos and the cell phone registered to Calderon."

Sanders smiled. "If we can find someone who bought those items, we'll find the person who framed Calderon which logically will be our murderer."

Reyes started laughing. "Okay, I can see the cell phone as a possibility, but tracking who bought a bracelet or a pair of shoes.

How do you plan to do that? It's not like either has a serial number."

"Watch and learn my friend. What do we know about the shoes?" Hunter pointed to Sanders.

"We know the size, brand and style."

"Correct. And that brand happens to be only available over the internet. All we need is for the company to provide us with a list of all the size 11, Altra Instincts shipped to Tarrant County addresses in the last three months." Hunter held out his hands as if to say 'see there'. "Once we have that list, we can compare it to our suspect pool and see if there's a match."

Reyes still wasn't sold. "That list could have thousands of names on it."

"Doubt it. Niche brand and highly specialized shoes. Once we narrow the size and style, I'd be surprised if the list was more than fifty names."

"All right. I'll give you that, but what about the bracelet?"

"Same basic process, but with real stores. We figure out the manufacturer. Contact them to see who distributes locally and go knock on the doors to see who's bought this style bracelet in the last three months." Hunter smiled.

"Look at you go." Sanders grinned. "But how do we find who bought the phone? All we have is a number. We don't even know the carrier much less what store."

"T-Mobile."

Reyes and Sanders exchange doubting looks before both looked at Hunter and crossed their arms.

"Carrierlookup.com. You can find anything on the internet. Do I have to teach you guys everything?"

That brought a round of laughter from the room. "Jimmy, you take the shoes. Billy, you've got the bracelet. I'll track the phone. Don't be surprised if the companies require subpoenas. Most organizations guarantee some level of data privacy for their customers. Just get the paper and get them moving."

"One last thing." Hunter held a finger. "Billy, did you hear back from your Bureau guy about the photo analysis?"

"I did. According to their experts, the guy in our photo was around six foot tall and probably close to two hundred pounds." He shrugged. "Calderon is at least two, maybe three inches taller than that and is probably in the one-nineties."

Hunter smiled and pointed at Sanders. "So, someone was specifically trying to look like him." He cocked his head. "Maybe our frame up theory isn't so crazy after all." He looked at his watch. It was almost four. "Keep me posted on your progress. We'll touch base in the morning. I'm going to go chase down another thought."

He picked up his phone and headed for the door as he punched in a number. "Hey Jess. It's your Uncle Jake. Got a minute?"

Chapter 48

"So, I get to see my favorite uncle twice in a span of a week." Jessica greeted Hunter at the door of the Starbucks with a hug. "Have I been living right, or what?"

"Your only uncle feels the same way." He gestured toward the line. For five o'clock in the afternoon on a hot August day, the line was ridiculously long. "Let's get something and then we'll fight for a couple of seats."

They got lucky and found two cushioned chairs in the corner. As they settled in, Jessica squinted one eye at Hunter suspiciously. "What's up?"

"How's the planning for your meeting going?"

"Challenging, but good. Our three key speakers are confirmed. Plus, it looks like a number of industry folks will be there to participate in a question and answer session."

"Industry folks?"

"Yeah, law enforcement, border patrol, journalists who cover the topic and my counterparts from other anti-drug organizations."

Hunter nodded. "I'm guessing anyone related to the anti-drug movement is pretty busy these days."

She scrunched her forehead. "Why do you say that?"

"With all the publicity over the past few weeks." He sipped his coffee. "I mean, there were the three cases of tainted Ecstasy, the murder of some drug dealers and the raids on Calderon's warehouses. My guess is that your phones have been ringing off the walls."

"You sure you're a cop? You sound more like a marketing

executive." She smiled but then it faded. "You're right, though. No one really pays attention to this until something bad happens, and it's plastered all over the news."

"Probably helps with fundraising, though?"

She nodded. "Unfortunately, yeah it does."

"When news hits like those young people dying, how big of a bump do you get?"

She paused, set down her coffee. "Why are you asking, Uncle Jake?"

"Just trying to understand the bigger picture surrounding my cases. After all, everything I'm working on right now seems to have been triggered by the tainted Ecstasy."

She arched an eyebrow at him. "You're a really lousy liar. I don't know how you ever get anyone to confess. "Now tell me the truth, why so interested?"

He sighed. "I'm working three connected murders, all associated with a major drug wholesaler, and all linked at some level to the tainted Ecstasy. We've got a couple of suspects that we are turning upside down, but at least so far, we've got nothing solid. When we were brainstorming about who might benefit from everything that's gone on lately, the suggestion was made that someone within the anti-drug world might."

She glared at him for a long moment. "What kind of cynical asshole would suggest something like that?"

"Uh…" He cleared his throat.

"You?" She set her coffee down hard enough that drops shot out of the hole in the lid. "You're kidding me. My uncle thinks that me or one of my colleagues would kill people in order to make fundraising easier?"

"Well, when you put it that way…"

"How else would you put it?"

"I'm looking at all leads, no matter how small. That's my job." He was back peddling fast now. "And when you think of it, it's not unprecedented. We have people all the time who stage crimes to look like the victim so that they can blame it on someone else. Death threats have been made against political candidates by their own staff so that they can blame the other candidate to get a bump in polls."

By the look on her face, he wasn't winning the argument. In fact, as he looked at her, he realized he was just digging a deeper hole. "Look, I'm sorry. I shouldn't have even brought it up."

She wiped the table clean with her napkin, took a drink and sat quietly for a moment. "Just for the record, I think you've been working homicide too long. Suspecting the very people who work so hard to help the police." She shook her head. "The fact that our fundraising has skyrocketed the last two weeks is the positive out of all of this chaos and tragedy. In fact, I'm not sure how we would have funded the symposium without the increase."

A slight smile started to creep across his face.

"Don't even think about smiling. Just because the numbers are what they are doesn't mean someone would do something that awful just to pad our pockets."

Hunter nodded quickly. "I just wanted to see if there was a cause and effect."

"There is."

"Is it localized?"

"What do you mean?"

"Do local organizations get a bigger impact when something bad happens close to home?"

"Yes. The national organizations live off bigger donors and off annuity philanthropists. Our donations fluctuate with events and level of effort. I spend more time asking for money than I do educating against drugs."

"How many local organizations are there?"

"Several, but only two or three that would be impacted by what happened?"

"Would you be offended if I asked for a list of organization names and the people who run them?"

"Yes." She sipped her coffee and looked away. "But I'll send them to you anyway." She frowned. "Please don't let them know I gave their info to you. Or that we're related."

She stood and grabbed her purse. "Don't forget that Grandpa and Grandma asked us out for dinner on Sunday. Make sure you bring Stacy. She seemed really nice."

"Glad you reminded me."

She spun and left without saying goodbye.

Chapter 49

Fridays for detectives aren't like Friday's for the regular working world, especially if they're in the middle of a case that's not going anywhere. Hunter wasn't working for the weekend. He was up early, antsy and hopeful that today would be the day when they finally caught a break.

As he drove down I-35 at 8 a.m., he was already on the phone to T-Mobile and was working his way from one customer service rep to another, slowly climbing up the food chain. It was going to take a while and was undoubtedly going to try his patience.

"No, no, don't put me on... Hold." For the fourth time now, he was listening to horrid hold music. *What kind of self-respecting musician records this shit?*

"Hello, this is Mr. Johnson. I'm the Customer Service Manager. How can I help you?"

"As I've told the last four people, I'm Detective Jake Hunter with the Fort Worth Police Department. I need to know where a specific phone was sold and to whom."

"Sir, I'm afraid I can't provide that information to you without clearance from our Legal Department and I'm quite certain they will tell you they need a subpoena."

"Fine. Can you give me the name and number of someone I can contact in Legal? I'll have a subpoena for them when I call."

Hunter was walking through the conference room door as Mr. Johnson was providing the information. He grabbed a marker and wrote the name and number on the whiteboard.

*   *   *   *

"You should already have the paperwork in your inbox. I hit the send button ten minutes ago." Sanders looked up and watched as Hunter walked into the conference room with the phone to his ear and stepped straight to the whiteboard. He nodded a few times as he listened. "Okay, thanks."

The two detectives clicked off their calls almost in unison. Billy set his phone down and gestured to the whiteboard. "Who's that?"

"That is who wants a subpoena before T-Mobile will give me any information."

"Get in line. I just put in my request. She said I'd have mine within the hour."

"Duly noted. Sounds like you're making progress."

Sanders laughed. "At least I know who to send the subpoena to. Getting the information will be more involved. They're a small company and their systems aren't exactly user friendly. Going to take a few days to get it together."

"At least you've got it in the works. If you want, you can roll with me as I go to the T-Mobile store and we can brainstorm along the way."

"Works for me."

*   *   *   *

Jimmy Reyes scratched his head as he stared at the gold bracelet in the plastic baggie. It was two tone with circular links. He wasn't much of a jewelry guy, but he actually kind of liked it. There was an engraved logo on the backside of the clasp that was difficult to read.

He dug through his desk, pushing aside the years of accumulated crap, until he found a magnifying glass. As he was squinting through the glass at the bracelet, Blaine Parker strolled by and laughed. "Going old school, Sherlock Holmes?"

"That's right." Jimmy didn't miss a beat. "But you sure as hell aren't my Dr. Watson."

"You know, we have these magical things called microscopes now. Or digital cameras with zoom lenses." Blaine continued to laugh as he walked away.

Jimmy refocused on the logo. Two intertwined letters, G and M. He knew this was Carlos Calderon's bracelet so clearly, these weren't his initials.

With that in mind, he pulled up his search engine and started clicking away. He tried a number of variations of combinations including men's jewelry, gold and bracelets. After several tries, he stumbled on a website for a company named Golden Mine. Once there, it didn't take long to find what he was looking for, a White Pave Curb Cuban Link Bracelet in two tone 14k gold.

"Old school works," Jimmy smiled. "Just like the government to suggest a $1500 resource when a $1 tool works just fine."

*　　*　　*　　*

"I guess there are some advantages to dealing with large corporations. He said he'd have the store information in five minutes." Hunter held on the phone.

"Sweet." Sanders started to say something else but Hunter held up a finger for him to hold.

A moment later Hunter hung up the phone and looked at Sanders. "Well that's convenient. The store location is close, on West 7th, right there where it connects with Camp Bowie, University and North Side Drive."

"Every once in a while, the stars align." Sanders smiled.

"Let's hope they keep aligning." Hunter grabbed his notepad and nodded toward the door. "Let's roll."

*　　*　　*　　*

"Reyes, R-E-Y-E-S. Yes, I'm a Fort Worth Police Detective."
He closed his eyes and rested his head on his hands.

"Sir, we don't sell directly to the public."

"I don't want to place an order. I'm trying to track down who
might have ordered one of your items."

"Sir, as I said, we don't sell directly to the public, so I
wouldn't have that information. Thank you for calling."

"Wait. Hold on."

There was a heavy sigh on the other end of the line. "Was
there something else I can help you with?"

"Yes. If you don't sell over the phone or online, can you
provide a list of Fort Worth area stores where someone could buy
your products?"

The long pause was almost painful. "Please hold."

It was now Jimmy's turn to listen as someone desecrated a
classic song. After two minutes of synthesized violins playing the
Rolling Stones, the woman clicked back on. "There are three jewelers
in your area that carry our products."

"Great." Reyes grabbed a pen feverishly wrote for the next
minute before sarcastically thanking her for her time and service.

*   *   *   *

Since the T-Mobile location on West 7th was right around the
corner from a Chipotle, Hunter and Sanders grabbed an early lunch
before dropping in on the store. After watching Sanders eat a burrito
the size of a football, Hunter shook his head. "How the hell do you
eat like that and still look like you do?"

"It's called a gym. You should try it sometime."

"The concept of sweating on purpose makes no sense to me."

Sanders smiled. "You're lucky you have the genetics to get
away with that. If I didn't exercise, I'd look like the night desk
sergeant."

Hunter scrunched up his face. "Ouch."

They pulled into a tiny strip mall. T-Mobile front and center. Hunter stepped in through the door and let the cold blast of air conditioning wash over him. Even though the recent oppressive heatwave had passed, it was still August in Texas. A perky sales clerk greeted them almost before the door shut. She seemed slightly shocked when they displayed their badges and asked to see the manager.

A moment later, a woman in her early thirties stepped over. She was wearing khaki pants, a hot pink T-Mobile golf shirt and a name tag: Susan Nicholson, Manager. "Good afternoon gentlemen. How can I help you?"

*   *   *   *

Reyes mentally scratched two of the four names off the list. He'd save them for last because they were so far south. Based on where Calderon operated, it wouldn't make any sense for or anyone associated with him to shop there. That left two locations, one of which was a short drive over near the courthouse.

Haltom's Jewelers downtown location was located on Main Street right in the heart of the Sundance Square area. The Haltom name was well known for high end retail jewelry in the Fort Worth area. They had multiple locations around town but this one was the flagship.

When Jimmy stepped through the door, the sales clerk's facial expression went from faux exuberance to barely concealed annoyance. Clearly, he didn't meet her expected criteria as potential buyer.

Her tone didn't do anything to hide her preconception. "Can I help you?"

"You sure can." Jimmy amped up his excitement to purposely annoy her. He displayed his badge, identified himself and pulled the bagged bracelet out of his pocket. "And you are?"

"Ashley." She said it as if she was smelling something awful.

Reyes smiled. "Ashley, I need to know if this bracelet was bought in this store. It's from a distributor named Gold Mining."

She didn't reach for the bag, she merely looked down her nose at it as Reyes held it out. "I have no way of knowing if that particular item was purchased here. But I did sell one just like that about a week and a half ago."

"No kidding. You remember it that clearly?"

Her frame stiffened. "Well, it was just… memorable."

"How so?"

Ashley hesitated. "Well…" Her eyelashes fluttered. "The man's appearance didn't seem to match his name."

Jimmy raised a brow.

"What I mean is that he had a Hispanic name but he didn't look…Hispanic."

A big smile spread across Jimmy's face. "Oh, you mean he was a white guy?"

"Uh, well, yes."

"Can you describe him beyond that?"

She shrugged. "Not really. He was kind of normal." Her face scrunched. "Dark hair, jeans and a polo shirt. You know, normal."

Reyes jotted down the information. "What was Mr. Normal's name?"

"Let me check." She stepped over to a computer. After a few clicks, she looked up. "Carlos Calderon."

He stood up straight. "Did you get that from his credit card?"

"No. Paid in cash. That was the name he wrote on the receipt. For a cash sale, we don't require anything beyond providing a name."

Reyes frowned, looked around the store as he thought. His eyes noticed a security camera in the corner behind the counter pointed directly at him. That brought a smile to his face. "Then I'll need a copy of the camera footage for the day he was in."

"Unfortunately, I don't have that. The camera is on a seventy two hour cycle. Anything past three days gets deleted automatically."

*   *   *   *

"Susan, I was directed to this store after I provided a subpoena to your Legal Department." Hunter handed her a copy of the document. "We need to get all the information we can on who purchased a phone in this store."

"Sure. Anyway I can help."

He handed her a piece of paper with the number on it. "When was this number set up, and by whom?"

"Certainly." She stepped around behind the counter and tapped a few times on a keyboard. "It was set up a week and a half ago by a Carlos Calderon."

"Did Mr. Calderon pay with a credit card?"

She ran her finger across the display to guide her eyes. "No. This is a prepaid phone and he paid in cash."

Hunter frowned. "Is there anything else you can tell me about the person? An address? A picture? Anything?"

"We always ask for ID, so he had to show something. But on cash purchases, we don't keep a record of it." As she spoke, her eyes scanned the computer record. "Hang on. Mark was the sales rep on this transaction. He's in the back. Maybe he can remember something about the guy."

A moment later, she was back with a floppy haired, college aged boy in tow. "Hey. What's up?"

Hunter went back through the whole story while Mark hung on every word.

"Oh yeah. I remember that guy. First, because of the name. I'm taking Creative Writing at school and the name, Carlos Calderon, is what they call an alliteration." His excitement was obvious. "It kind of just rolls off your tongue."

When he stopped and didn't go on to his second point,

Hunter looked at him. "And?"

"Oh yeah. Also because…" He stopped. "Please excuse my stereotyping, but he didn't really look like a Carlos Calderon."

"What do you mean?"

"Well, uh…" He pointed to Hunter. "He looked more like you."

Hunter frowned. "In what way? Height? Weight? Color"

"He was a white guy, dark hair, casual. Kind of forgettable.

"How was he dressed?"

"Kind of like a… No offense, but like an old dude on a Saturday."

"What the hell does that mean?"

"You know, faded Levi's, grimy sweat shirt, ball cap." Mark shrugged.

Sanders couldn't contain his snicker. Hunter just rolled his eyes and closed his notebook.

Chapter 50

Saturday morning found him back in full work mode and in the conference room. As he had done every day since the shooting, he spent a few minutes staring at the small laptop screen, watching the images from the webcam. It had become almost an obsession.

Friday night's quiet evening with Stacy, Panther and a few cold beers hadn't helped clear his head. It was clear that would only happen when he solved this case.

He hadn't asked the team to come in, but he did ask them to have their phones in case he called. Some were running things down from home. With his take out Starbucks on the conference room table, he stood for a moment absorbing all the information on the whiteboard.

The original two cases, the murders of James Tyler and Michael Logan, had now slipped past the two week mark. They had done a tremendous amount of work, so many leads, and even permanently taken several scumbags off the streets. But none of them were Tyler's, Logan's or Hopkins' murderer.

Hunter pounded his fist on the table, his frustration mounting.

Most murders get solved in the first 48 hours. We're way past that and we're still spinning in circles.

His laptop dinged with a new email. He clicked it open and saw a curt note from Jessica providing him with the names of the top five local anti-drug organizations and their leaders. Nine all together. With her own at the bottom.

Good girl.

Before he started working down that list, he needed to get caught up on the activities of the team. He punched in Chambers' number and it rang.

"Chambers here."

"Matt, Jake Hunter, sorry to interrupt your Saturday.

"No worries. What's up?"

"Just wanted to get a quick update on your progress with Calderon's alibis."

"Wish I had better news. A half dozen people who were at the wedding confirm he was there. Apparently, he was the life of the party. Every one of them sent me phone pics with Calderon in them."

"Sounds like his alibis for Logan and Tyler are solid."

"As a rock."

Hunter shifted the phone to his other ear. "Did you get a chance to check on his trips?"

"Yep. Running facial recognition on all the days in between his departure and return is going to take some time, but it's in progress. As for the flights he gave you, video surveillance confirmed."

"Okay. Looks like a dead end. Let's connect again on Monday. Enjoy the rest of your weekend." He signed off, crossed Calderon off the list on the whiteboard.

His mind started processing the board again. Even the silence of the conference room, which normally helped him focus, wasn't revealing new possibilities.

After a few more frustrating minutes, he went back to his phone and called Travis Nix in Narcotics.

"I was able to locate Foster yesterday morning and he was surprisingly cooperative, didn't even insist on a lawyer. According to him, he, his girlfriend and a number of friends spent that Friday out on his boat on Eagle Mountain Lake. The alibi checks out with the friends. They all said they were at the lake until past ten that evening."

Hunter leaned back in a chair, and set his leg up on the table.

If he was going to continue to get bad news, at least he'd be comfortable. "Where was he when Hopkins was killed?"

"That's the interesting part. Just like Calderon, he was out of town. He was on a flight to LAX the day before Hopkins' murder and he returned the day after."

"How convenient."

"That's what I thought. Almost like he knew to be gone that day. At the very least, it was too much of a coincidence."

"Exactly, my experience is that it takes a lot of planning to create a good coincidence. Call me with any other updates." Hunter hung up the phone and once again found himself in a silent hole.

It took him a while to get self-motivated enough to reopen Jessica's email and start working through his own cynical theory. Like everyone else, he had no desire to go down this path. But as he watched the other alternatives evaporate, he had no other choice. If, for no other reason, it gave him something to do.

Eventually, he reread the email, and started investigating them. In spite of her insistence, he didn't bother with Jessica's. Over the next few hours, he methodically pulled off histories for each.

The more he read, the harder it was to continue. With rare exception, each person had a similar story. Somewhere along the way, their normal lives were tragically interrupted when someone close to them was devastated by illegal drugs. The lucky ones still had some version of their loved ones alive. The others only had memories. And vicious scars.

His mind drifted back to the interviews he and Sanders had done with the families of Martina Ruiz, Tyson Hancock and Juarita Chaler. Each one was damaged at an unimaginable depth. *Normal* would never exist for them again.

Watching his own family had proven that. Ten years had passed since they had buried his brother. A full military funeral was hard to forget. Especially true when the idolized, older brother he grew up with was the one beneath the flag.

Even so, those visuals weren't what Hunter remembered

most when he thought about his brother, Jordan. It was seeing his father crumble right before his eyes. The toughest man he'd ever known openly crying, his muscular shoulders shaking like the weight of the world crushed them.

It was the first time in his life he'd ever seen his father cry. The first time he realized his father wasn't indestructible. Even now, when he saw Charlie, if you looked deep into his face, there was a sadness that had never left.

Hunter refocused on the list. Anything to keep his mind from diving into that dark place. Two individuals happened to be co-leaders of the same organization with fairly new entrance into the industry. But unlike their counterparts, their lives before benevolent advocacy were marked by significant troubles with law enforcement.

He jotted down the names and listed out some of their histories.

Breaking and entering, possession with intent to sell, grand theft auto. Hmm… Hello there red flags.

Chapter 51

"So, just so I'll know, there's not going to be a surprise nephew there tonight, right?"

"Give me a break." Hunter rolled his eyes as he steered his truck west on I-30 toward Weatherford.

Cool August weather in Texas is a relative concept, but Sunday evening was beautiful with perfectly clear blue skies, a light breeze and a thermometer drifting down below ninety. As much as possible, Hunter had put his frustrations on hold after his long Saturday and was feeling pretty good, in spite of Stacy not letting him off the hook for the Jessica surprise. In Hunter's defense, he had reminded her that they'd only been dating for nine months and between shootings, kidnappings and hospital stays, they really hadn't interacted much with the respective families.

Tonight was going to be different, they were going to have dinner with Hunter's parents, Charlie and Olivia. Jessica would be there as well so it would be an opportunity for Stacy to get to know her.

Stacy snickered, reached over and grabbed his hand. "I'm really looking forward to dinner. I've only met your folks a couple of times and it's always been brief. Maybe tonight, I'll get to hear all the little Cowboy stories."

He shook his head. "You know I wasn't called Cowboy when I was a kid. In fact, my parents may look at you strange if you call me that. To them, I'm just Jake." He grinned. "Which is an improvement over some of the terms of endearment my Dad used for me when I was a teenager."

"Ah, a troublemaker in your youth?"

"I had my moments."

She smiled as they exited the freeway. "My, I am learning so much about you this week."

"That's probably not a good thing."

Their conversation had them both smiling when they pulled up to the curb in front of his parent's home. Hunter pointed to a shiny black BMW in driveway. "That's what having a law degree from the University of Texas buys you."

"Not bad, but I'm more of an Explorer kind of girl." Stacy gave him a quick kiss and opened the door.

The aroma of spices hit them like a wave when they walked through the front. Stacy breathed in deeply as she greeted Hunter's mother with a hug. "Oh my God, Olivia, that smells wonderful."

Olivia's dark eyes smiled as she waved off the compliment. "It's a recipe my grandmother from Monterrey taught me. I hope you like tilapia."

"What a lovely home." Stacy seemed to absorb the dark woods, stonework and western themed art as they walked through the family room.

"Thank you. Charlie may have designed the house, but the interior is my turf." Olivia directed them to the kitchen.

Hunter smiled as he observed their interaction.

Jessica was putting the final touches on a tray of stuffed jalapenos while Charlie was nursing a cold beer. He stopped in mid-sentence when he saw Hunter and Stacy. "Stacy, you look beautiful." He gave a light hug before he shook Hunter's hand. "Jake, you know where the beers are. I was just telling Jess a story."

Stacy and Jessica said their hellos as Jake stepped to the fridge and Charlie jumped back into a story about his early days with the Texas Rangers. The conversation never slowed through the entire delicious meal. All of her meals were delicious.

"Apparently, one more thing that Cowboy failed to tell me was that you're an amazing cook Olivia." Stacy cut her eyes and smiled at Hunter as she spoke to his mother.

Hunter just shrugged and grinned. This was the most relaxed he'd been in two weeks.

Jessica speared a piece of her apple pie with her fork and gave Hunter a wry look. Then finally turned to Charlie. "So, Grandpa, did Uncle Jake tell you that he's investigating me?"

"What?" Charlie eyed his son.

Hunter sighed. "Oh come on now, I—"

"All right boys." Olivia cut him off. "You know the rules. No cop talk at the table."

Jessica giggled as Charlie pushed back his chair. He looked at Hunter. "That's all right, Jake. I've got some Don Julio waiting for us upstairs. You call tell me about throwing your niece in jail up there."

Hunter looked at Stacy. She shooed him away. "You go. Jessica and I will help your mom clear the dishes, and then I'll get her to tell me some Little Jake stories."

Olivia smiled. "Oh dear, we'll be here all week."

His parents had custom built this home for their retirement. Forty acres of Texas prairie sat just outside of the bay windows in the dining room. The pride of Weatherford. Charlie had a third floor observation room built with windows looking out in all directions. On a clear night like tonight, the East sky was filled with the lights of downtown Fort Worth just peaking over the horizon.

After Charlie had poured each of them a tumbler of Don Julio 1942 Tequila, he toasted his son. His smile faded and his eyes set on Hunter. "I heard what happened son. How are you doing?"

Hunter sipped his drink, stared out the window and absorbed the stars bursting from the black sky. "I'm getting through."

"I know it's tough." Charlie spoke softly. "My first fatality..." He shook his head. "Almost quit the force."

"You did?" Hunter turned to him. "I didn't know. Was he innocent?"

Charlie laughed. "Oh, hell no. He was the meanest snake this side of the Guadalupe Mountains. Killed three people. Those were just the ones we knew about." He looked away. "Even so, taking someone's life is a hard thing."

"Yes, it is."

"You know, if you stay in this game long enough, there are going to be others. It's the nature of your job. You get to deal with the dark side of humanity day in and day out. Sometimes fatal consequences are unavoidable." Charlie put his hand on Hunter's shoulder. "It doesn't get easier, but you learn how to cope with it better."

"God, I hope so."

There was a momentary pause before Charlie continued. "So, the news reports say there was dashcam footage."

Hunter nodded his head.

"How often have you watched it?"

"Every day."

"Has it helped?"

"Not one damn bit."

"Didn't think so." Charlie shook his head. "Are you at least making progress on the case?"

"Unfortunately, not enough."

Hunter spent the next thirty minutes laying out everything they knew about all three murders. He explained about the first two murders being done by the same gun and talked about the weak list of suspects.

"Ballistics for both of the first two murders came back to a gun that was supposed to be in the FWPD evidence lockup?"

Hunter nodded.

"And you're sure that the Hopkins murder was either done by the same killer or was ordered by the same person?"

"Pretty sure. All three victims are connected and whoever killed Hopkins went out of their way to make it look like he killed Tyler and Logan." Hunter thought for a moment. "And took extra measures to make it look like Carlos Calderon killed Hopkins."

Charlie nodded. Hunter had already told him about the shoes, bracelet, cell phone and security photo. "So, your killer somehow got his hands on a gun, that theoretically only a cop could access. They knew enough about crime scenes to stage a pretty convincing suicide and planned it thoroughly enough that if that fell apart, they already had a frame job in place to point to Calderon."

"Yeah, if I wasn't trying to arrest the guy, I might actually be pretty impressed with him. I mean, who thinks like that?"

Charlie didn't say anything. He just stared at Hunter as if the answer to his question was obvious.

"What?" Hunter shrugged.

"Your killer had access to the gun, could stage a suicide and could build a convincing frame."

Hunter started, then stopped. "Oh...shit. You don't..." He looked down at his glass, then took a long swallow. The smooth buttery liquid burned his throat, but couldn't change the facts sneering in his face. "Son of a bitch."

Charlie finished his drink in one long swig. "Yeah...son of a bitch."

Chapter 52

"Holy crap, Cowboy. Are you saying we're looking for a cop?"

"I'm not saying it. The evidence is." Hunter tapped his finger on the table.

"Are you serious?"

Hunter nodded. "I had a conversation Sunday which reminded me of something from early in the investigation that got lost in the chatter. There are a couple of factors that when taken together point in a really ugly direction."

"What's that?"

He pulled up a chair, turned it around and straddled it. "The same gun was used for both Tyler and Logan. And they were only hours apart, so it's a pretty good assumption it was the same shooter."

"Right."

"That gun was supposed to have been in the FWPD evidence lock up. Our logical conclusion is that whoever shot Tyler and Logan either had access or had a connection with access to the gun."

Sanders nodded. "Okay. Took our eye off that a bit when Hopkins was murdered."

"We've made the assumption all along that whoever killed Tyler and Logan was at least involved with killing Hopkins and is likely the shooter."

"Yeah, because of the fact that Tyler, Logan and Hopkins, in his undercover role, were all part of Dalton Foster's organization."

"Correct, but..." Hunter held up a finger. "Whoever killed

Hopkins was familiar enough with crime scenes to do a pretty decent job of faking a suicide."

Billy's shoulders slumped and his face went slack. "If it hadn't been for you catching the whole left handed thing, we might not have caught it at all, and certainly not for quite some time."

"Exactly. Now add the fact that whoever killed Hopkins thought it through enough to frame Calderon with the shoes, cell phone, bracelet and security photo."

"And who would know how to frame a person better than someone who investigates crimes for a living?" By the time Sanders had finished the statement, his voice sounded tight. "Shit. But why? Who?"

"You just summed up our to-do list." He stood up and looked at the whiteboard. "Our whole line of thinking needs to change."

"Wait. How do we even go down that path? I mean, internally. Don't we need to get approval from Sprabary? Or Internal Affairs?"

Hunter held up his hands. "Slow down, my friend. Before we start talking about IAD, we need more than a logical path." He paused for a moment and chewed on his cheek. "As for Sprabary, yeah, we need to loop him in, but I want to have something more solid first."

Sanders nodded, but looked like he might puke. "Where do we even start? There are over 1,500 officers in the FWPD. That doesn't even count the Sheriff's Department, any of the suburbs or the Feds." He frowned. "Our pool of suspects didn't exactly shrink with this revelation of yours."

"No it didn't, but... It's not as bad as you think." Hunter walked over to the whiteboard, found a blank spot and started writing bullet points. "Take the three murders and find the common links. Then we'll narrow it down pretty easily."

Sanders had regained his composure. "Okay."

"Tyler and Logan were lifelong felons, but all of their criminal history is drug related."

"Yeah, but a cop killing those two? That doesn't make any sense. Calderon killing them makes sense. Even Foster killing them makes sense. But a cop?" Sanders shook his head.

"A dirty one." Hunter turned and looked at him. "If this guy is dirty enough to kill someone, he's dirty enough to be into anything."

"I guess so." Sanders didn't sound convinced.

Hunter didn't slow down to worry about it. "So, if all three of the victims are directly tied to drugs, then the first place we need to look for our killer is someone who knows that world."

Sanders nodded. "Someone from the Narcotics team."

"No one else would know that Hopkins was undercover. Based on his file, they pulled him in from way over on the west side. He was supposedly going into the Burglary Division, so even the guys that knew him on patrol probably didn't know he was in Narcotics."

"Okay." Sanders rubbed his chin. "So how many guys are on that team?"

"Not sure." Hunter paused. "Now that you ask, we may need some help even getting that answer. Narcotics is notoriously cryptic."

"No doubt. The only Narcs I've ever met are Chambers, Nix and Carlson." He stopped. "You're not thinking of asking them, are you?"

Hunter shook his head. "No. I think it's time we go see the boss." He stepped over to the table and punched Paige McLaren's extension into the conference room phone.

Twenty minutes later, Hunter and Sanders stepped into the lieutenant's office and when he gestured to the chairs, they sat. He eyed them for a moment as he closed the door. "If the news is as bad as your expressions, I think I need to sit down."

Hunter cut his eyes to Sprabary's chair. "Might not be a bad idea."

"Shit."

Hunter walked him through their thought process step by

step. As each piece of the puzzle fell into place, Sprabary's face grew more pale. "So, you think our murderer is a cop." He rubbed his temples. "More specifically, someone from Narcotics."

"Yes sir."

"No wonder you didn't want Carlson here." Sprabary tapped his fingers on his desk, the wheels clearly churning. "We have to tread lightly here gentlemen. Especially if you don't have a name."

"That's where we need your help, sir. We need a list of everyone on Carlson's team."

Sprabary stopped tapping. "That's going to be a problem. I don't have access to his roster. Because they do so much undercover work, the names and information for his team are closely guarded. If I made a request for that information, it'd set off alarms all over, and Carlson would be in my office in a fiery second."

Neither Hunter nor Sanders commented while they watched Sprabary process. In a moment, his eyelids sagged and his shoulders slumped as if the opposing team just scored a touchdown. "I have a way. You're not going to like it. But it's the only way I know."

"We really don't have many options, sir."

Sprabary exhaled deeply and picked up the phone receiver and punched four buttons.

"Internal Affairs."

Chapter 53

"Detective Hunter, I didn't expect to see you again so soon." Benson gave a creepy smile and held out his hand.

"No offense, but I was kind of hoping to never see each other again, ever." Hunter looked for a long moment at the outstretched hand before he slowly raised his. He nodded to Billy. "This is my partner, Billy Sanders."

"Yes." Benson stretched the word out. "We've met before." He nodded toward Billy.

"Are we through with the high school reunion?" Sprabary spat the words out as he pointed to the door. "Shut the door, Benson. This conversation needs to be private."

"Most of mine are."

Sprabury ignored his comment. "We have a situation that requires your access. We have reason to believe that a cop may be involved in one or more of the murders my two detectives are investigating."

Benson's initial pleasure washed off his face. "Murder? Do you have evidence to support the accusation of a cop killing someone?"

Sprabary nodded. "Possibly three someone's, one of which was another officer."

Benson pulled out his notebook and pen. "Let's start from the beginning."

Hunter started with the Friday that Tyler and Logan were shot and walked Benson through everything they'd found to that point. It took an hour to review the ballistics match, the gun missing from lock up, Hopkins' staged suicide and the frame up of Carlos Calderon. He explained their realization that all of these would have needed to have been done either by a cop or with the help of a cop. From there, they narrowed the field to the Narcotics team because all of the players are connected to the drug trade.

When Hunter finished, he shrugged. "I know it's a bit of a fishing expedition, but every other path we've gone down has been a dead end."

Sprabary had been quiet throughout but now leaned forward in his chair. "While I understand the logic in your theory, I'm concerned that because we don't have evidence pointing to a specific person, we aren't going to be able to get warrants for the information we need."

"Don't worry about that." Benson raised his eyebrows slightly. "I'll be able to get any and all of the information we need."

That answer evoked quizzical looks from Sprabary, Hunter and Sanders.

"Let's just say that IAD's access to information isn't as restricted as yours."

"That's comforting." The sarcasm dripped from Hunter's voice as a look of disgust rolled over him.

"Detective Hunter." Benson set down his notepad. "Police departments across the country are neck deep in a vicious public relations battle. As you know, there have been a rash of high profile police-involved shootings very similar to your recent incident." He paused. "Fortunately, for you and this department, your incident was caught on video and fairly conclusive. Had it not been, the streets of Fort Worth over the past two weeks would have looked like Ferguson or Baltimore."

"What's your point?"

"My point, Detective, is that as distasteful as you might find my role, what I do is critical to maintaining the confidence of the public." He sat up taller. "We, as law enforcement officers, must be above reproach. We can never even step on that line, much less cross it. My job is to make sure no one does."

"Whatever helps you sleep at night."

Benson's cheeks cracked as he smiled. "Don't forget, you called me."

"Enough." Sprabary cut them off. "Hunter, what do you need from Benson?"

"I need the names and jackets for Carlson's entire team. We need to know their current and past assignments, along with their arrest records."

"I'll set up an internal site on our network with a folder for each officer. I'll send you a secure link and a password. You'll have access for forty eight hours and I want to be in the loop on every step of the investigation." He turned to Sprabary. "I can't stress enough that without IAD involvement, the access to and use of this information will be a major issue for you."

Sprabary nodded and then glared at Hunter and Sanders. "I can assure you the complete cooperation and transparency of my department. Can't I, gentlemen?"

"Yes sir." Hunter nodded even though his teeth hurt from grinding them. He turned back to Benson. "How soon can we have this?"

Benson looked at his watch. "Take an early lunch. I'll have it all set up by the time you get back."

"Seriously?"

"Welcome to the Information Age, Detective Hunter."

Chapter 54

"Damn, that's a lot of data." Sanders let out a low whistle as he looked at the laptop display.

"Looks like our boy Benson delivered on his promise." Hunter stood behind Billy looking over his shoulder.

"What now?"

"Process of elimination. How many folders are there?"

Sanders tapped his finger on the screen as he counted. "Fourteen, including Carlson."

Hunter pursed his lips as a sinking feeling pulsed through him. "IAD can pull a history on a lieutenant that fast based on a theory?"

"Scary, huh?"

"No shit. Gives a whole new meaning to Big Brother." Hunter shook off the thoughts. "That's for another time. We've got work to do. You take the first seven on the list. I'll take the last seven. First pass is to look for reasons to eliminate someone based on their connection or lack of connection to either Hopkins or Foster and his organization."

"So we're looking for people that didn't have connections with either?"

"Yep."

Sanders scrunched his forehead. "But won't everyone on this list have a connection to Hopkins? They're in the same unit."

Hunter shook his head. "Not necessarily. He's only been in the unit for a little over a year and he's been undercover nearly the entire time. Rule out anyone else whose been on unrelated undercover assignments for that same period." Hunter straightened up from looking at the laptop. "Think about it. You've been in Homicide for what, nine months?"

"About that."

"I bet there are guys in our squad that you've never even met beyond the first day when you made the rounds."

Sanders nodded. "Good point." He exhaled and puffed out his cheeks. "So this is what it feels like working in IAD. This ought to be fun."

For the next hour, they both had their heads buried in their laptops, clicking away and occasionally jotting notes on their pads. Time seemed to creep by for Hunter. In order to stay focused, he routinely stood and paced around the room.

Shortly before two, Hunter tossed his pen on the table. "Stick a fork in me, I'm done."

"Right behind you, partner. Give me five minutes."

"Just enough time for me to go see a man about a horse." Hunter got up to head to the door.

Sanders snickered and shook his head. "Don't take too long. I understand it's difficult for guys your age."

Hunter grab a whiteboard eraser and tossed it over his shoulder at Sanders as he stepped out.

When he returned, Sanders had just finished writing three names on the board. He read them. *Johnson, Gonzalez and Crane*. He walked over to his notepad and picked it up. "Add Barrow and Porter to that list."

"Got it." Sanders wrote the names on the board.

"Tell me about Johnson, Gonzalez and Crane." Hunter sat down.

"Okay. Just like you suggested. Both Johnson and Gonzalez have been on long term undercover assignments that have nothing to do with either Fosters' organization or Calderon's. My guess is that they've never even met Hopkins."

"And Crane?"

"A newbie. Only been with Narcotics for two months. Transferred in from the east side. Wouldn't have had any reason to cross paths with Hopkins." Sanders looked at Hunter. "How about your guys?"

"My guys might have gotten introduced along the way, but their work has been exclusively on the south side and there's no indication that they knew him before he joined the squad so there'd be no personal ties." Hunter stood, walked to the whiteboard and put check marks beside each of the names. "Five down, nine to go."

"What's next?"

"Now that we've got it down to single digits, let's call our boys over at the evidence lockup and see which of our guys have been over there."

"Won't all of them have been there at some point?"

Hunter nodded. "Most likely. We'll tighten down the parameters to eliminate as many as possible."

He picked up the phone and stabbed at the buttons with his finger.

"Sergeant Thompson."

"Sergeant? This is Detective Hunter. We met a week ago when we discovered that missing weapon."

"Yes Detective. We're still looking into that matter. Unfortunately, I don't have a resolution at this time."

"I might be able to help with that."

"Okay. How's that?"

"If I give you a list of nine names, can you tell me if they've been there in the last three months and if they've accessed boxes where the evidence is stored near our robbery case?"

"Absolutely. Shouldn't take more than about thirty minutes."

Hunter gave him the list of names, hung up and looked at Sanders. "Up for some real coffee? We've got time to step down the block."

"Maybe they can just give me an IV of caffeine."

A grande coffee later, they were back and energized after

paying homage to Starbucks and walking a few blocks in the afternoon sun. The phone rang as they were walking back into the conference room. Hunter grabbed it. "Hunter here."

"This is Sergeant Thompson. I've got your results."

"Shoot."

"Out of your nine names, there are three of them that don't meet your criteria. Keller and Carlson haven't been here in the last three months and the case Dagar accessed was in a whole different section of the facility. All the others have been there recently and they've all accessed cases reasonably close to where the gun went missing. I hope that helped."

"Better than where we were before. Now we're down to six. Thanks for your help Sergeant."

"Sounds like you're making progress." Benson's voice boomed from the doorway.

Hunter sighed when he heard Benson. "Slowly."

"I assume my information helped." He strolled to the whiteboard with the names eliminated. "So, are these our six possible contestants?" He sat down as if he belonged there. "Can you pop up their profiles and pictures on the projector? Maybe we can narrow it down more."

Hunter started to object, but checked himself and over smiled. "Why not." He connected his laptop to the projector and popped up the first possibility. "Candidate number one is Lamar Crabtree. He's a five year veteran in Narcotics and has been on several of the lower level busts of Foster resources based on intel from Hopkins. He's—"

"Wait a minute." Benson held up his hand. Hunter stopped and clamped down on his jaw. "Based on your briefing, didn't you say that both the jewelry store and the T-Mobile store said our guy was white with dark hair?"

Hunter looked at Benson and grinned.

Sanders laughed. "Yeah, considering Crabtree looks an awful lot like my cousin, I don't think he's a fit."

"Good catch." Hunter quickly scrolled through the remaining five candidates. "We've got one more we can eliminate." He pointed to the screen. "Peterson has flaming red hair."

"So we're down to four." Sanders walked to the whiteboard and wrote down the names.

"Yes we are, and I've got an idea." Hunter turned to his laptop and started clicking. "I'm printing off pictures of our remaining four. Combine them with two decoys and put them in a six person photo lineup. We'll let our clerks at the two stores do the rest of the work for us."

Benson stood, flashed a satisfied smile and turned for the door. "Let me know what they say." He looked straight at Hunter. "I want to be there when we cuff this guy."

Chapter 55

"Welcome back Detectives." The T-Mobile manager, Susan was expecting them. Hunter had called ahead to make sure the clerk they'd spoken with before was working today. "Let me get Mark."

A moment later, Mark walked over. "Hey guys."

Hunter cringed at the thought of this kid being on the witness stand during a trial. But for what they needed now, he'd do just fine. "We need you to take a look at these pictures and tell me if one of these men bought that phone and identified himself as Carlos Calderon."

Mark shrugged. "Sure." The casual manner he used in flipping through the photos unnerved Hunter. As close as they were, they had to be certain.

"This is important, so look carefully." Hunter crossed his arms to keep from popping his knuckles.

Mark nodded, and moved through the pictures more slowly, then finally looked back up at Hunter. "Nope." There wasn't a hint of disappointment in his voice.

Hunter tried to hide his surprise, but his voice gave him away. "Are you sure? Take another look."

Mark complied, but the results were the same. There was no use pushing further. Hunter thanked Susan and Mark and motioned Billy toward the door. They were in and out of the store in less than ten minutes. Hunter cranked the ignition. "Dammit."

"He was an airhead." Sanders shook his head. "He would have been a nightmare in court. Let's hit the jewelry store." He grinned. "According to Jimmy, she was a snob, but she was sharp."

Hunter turned west on Seventh Street and headed back to the Sundance Square area. "I hope so. If we strike out there, we're sunk."

After a few twists and turns on one way streets, Hunter found a parking spot near the front of the store. "We must be living right."

"Maybe it's an omen and this conversation will be more fruitful."

"Let's hope."

They stepped into the cool elegance of Haltom's Jewelers and were immediately greeted by an equally elegant blond. "Welcome to Haltom's. What are you looking for today?"

Hunter matched her smile. "Are you Ashley?"

"Why yes."

He flashed his badge. "Then we're looking for you. I'm Detective Hunter and this is my partner Detective Sanders."

"Oh." Her expression dropped as if she'd just gotten the first glance at a bad hair dye.

"I think you spoke with Detective Reyes the other day."

"Yes. What is it now?" Her attitude wasn't improving.

"We need you to take a look at the photos of these six men and tell us if one of them is the man who bought the bracelet."

He laid the sheet of photos down on the counter and she took a long moment to look at each man before she answered. "No. None of these."

"You're sure?"

"Detective, remembering names and faces is key to effective selling. Trust me. I've never seen any of these men in my life."

The ride back to the station was quiet, unless you considered the sound of Hunter's palm pounding the steering wheel every minute or so as he mumbled under his breathe.

Hunter was in full pace mode by the time they were back in the conference room. "It has to be one of those four. Who else is there?" He moved back and forth in front of the whiteboard, cutting his eyes toward it each time he passed. "Eyewitnesses are notoriously wrong. Maybe one of our guys changed his hairstyle or complexion or something when he went to the stores. How else can we tie one of those four to these cases?"

"What about the shoes?"

The comment stopped Hunter in his tracks. "Yes. The shoes. Let's check the credit cards for each of the four to see if they've bought a pair of Altra Triathlon shoes." Hunter snapped his fingers. "Speaking of which, have we gotten our report from Altra yet on all the purchases in this area?"

Sanders shook his head. "Not yet, but it was supposed to get here today. I'll send them a note right now and then run the cards for all four guys."

"Okay." Hunter looked at his watch. It was already past five. "I need to fill in Sprabary on our progress. Or lack of." Hunter headed for the door as Sanders started clicking away on his laptop.

By the time Hunter got back, the look on Sanders' face didn't make him feel any better about the ass chewing he'd just received from Sprabary. "Any luck?"

"I checked every credit card I could find for all four suspects going back three months. I had to scan pretty quickly so I guess it's possible I missed something, but I didn't find the name Altra on anything."

"What about the list from the company?"

"Expect it any minute, but I'm not holding my breath."

Hunter looked at his watch. "Damn, I promised Jessica I'd go to her symposium. It starts in a few minutes."

"Go ahead. There's nothing else we can do until we get that list."

Hunter tapped his foot, looked at the whiteboard and tried to think of any reason Billy wasn't right. He couldn't. "All right." His jaw was clenched. "What a waste of time."

As Sanders turned back to his laptop and Hunter started to pack up, Detective Benson stepped through the door. Based on his expression, he was clearly expecting good news. Before he could ask,

Hunter shook his head. "No luck. I'm done for the day." He nodded toward Sanders. "Billy's wrapping a few things up and then he's out of here as well."

Benson's face sank and he started to comment, but Billy sat up so fast that he almost fell out of his chair. "Just got it."

"Got what?" Benson and Hunter asked in near perfect unison.

"The list from the shoe company. I'm sending it to the printer now." He pointed to a printer right beside Hunter. As if on cue, the machine started whirring and clanking like it was trying to take flight.

Hunter impatiently tapped his fingers on the machine as it printed and spit out three sheets. He grabbed them and slid into a chair next to Sanders. Benson looked over their shoulders. Hunter guided his finger down the list on page one, then page two. About halfway down on page three, his finger stopped as if it had hit a brick wall. His face went flush and he felt the air suck out of his lungs.

"Oh shit."

There was a moment of absolute silence in the room. Even the background white noise from the air conditioner seemed to evaporate.

"Oh shit is right." Sanders pushed back in his chair, his face was almost gray.

Hunter grabbed the conference room phone and banged in four numbers.

"FWPD Evidence Lockup."

"I need Sergeant Thompson now."

Sergeant Thompson answered and Hunter gave him a name to check. A moment later, he was back. "Yes sir, I show him here and in that general area a little over four months ago. That box would've been right there at that time."

"Thanks." Hunter hung up and looked at the other two. "It's him." He paused and started to get up. "And I know where he's at right now."

Benson held up his hands. "Hold on, Hunter. We'd better be damn sure."

Hunter hadn't slowed down. He was packing up his stuff, but stopped and grabbed his phone, dialed and tapped his foot while he waited. "Jimmy, this is Hunter. I've got an urgent situation. Billy's emailing you a photo right now." He turned and gestured to Sanders who jumped into action. "I need you to take the photo to the T-Mobile store and to Haltom's and confirm the ID. Immediately."

"I'm moving now, Cowboy. I'll have you an answer in fifteen minutes."

Hunter hung up and looked at Sanders. "Pack up. Let's go. We can be there by the time Jimmy confirms the ID. I'll call Sprabary on the drive over."

"What about SWAT? You think we need to call Zeke?

"No. I don't want to spook him. There's going to be a lot of people around. The last thing I want is for him to see us coming."

"What about me?" Benson's eyes were wide.

"What about you?"

"I'm going with you."

Hunter frowned. "Fine, but you're backup. You follow our lead."

Benson nodded and followed suit as Hunter and Sanders gathered their belongings. As the three headed for the door, Hunter stopped at the whiteboard, picked up a marker and scrawled a single name in a lone open space.

Carlson.

Chapter 56

The beautiful Greek architecture of the front facade of the downtown Fort Worth Public Library towered over the intersection of Lamar Street and West 3rd in between N. Taylor and N. Burnett streets. The facility housed almost 250,000 square feet of collections, meeting rooms and exhibits.

It's location makes it extremely accessible to the public, unless you're trying to get there in a hurry on a Monday evening in downtown rush hour traffic. Hunter banged on his steering wheel for the third time, each after he'd tried to call Jessica and got nothing but her voicemail. "Damn it, she must have her phone turned off."

Even with his lights flashing and siren blaring, his progress was slow. He made the best of his time by calling Lieutenant Sprabary and filling him in on what they had learned.

"Okay." There was rustling in the background as Sprabary spoke and he sounded slightly out of breath. "Wait outside of the library for confirmation from Reyes. Then move in quietly. I'll meet you there, but if you get the confirmation from Reyes, you've got the green light to take him down."

They were at West 4th and Throckmorton when Reyes called.

"Hunter here. What's the word Jimmy?"

"Carlson's definitely our guy, Cowboy. Our jewelry lady, Ashley confirmed it. I'm heading to the T-Mobile store just to cover our bases, but don't wait for me."

"Thanks Jimmy." He hung up, looked at Billy in the passenger seat and then Benson in the back seat. "It's him. We have confirmation."

"Oh my God." Benson seemed to be mumbling more to himself than to Hunter. Dread oozed from his pores.

"We need to find out where they are in the building. That place is enormous."

"That shouldn't be too hard." Benson's voice chimed in from the back seat. "It's past normal operating hours for the library on a Monday night. All special events need a permit. I'm sure it's the only thing going on there tonight."

Hunter scrunched his forehead. "You know the library's operating hours off the top of your head?"

"What can I say? I'm an avid reader." Benson smiled.

At 4th Street and N. Taylor, Hunter killed the siren. It was a big building, but if it was empty, it would be very quiet. He didn't want there to be any advanced notice.

He turned on Lamar directly toward the front of the library. Without slowing down, he hopped the curb to the right of the flag poles and screeched to a stop on the sidewalk.

The security guard at the front door scrambled to his feet and started their way. All three of them were out of the car with badges held high before he made it half way.

"Fort Worth Police. Where's the anti-drug symposium?"

He looked confused for a moment, then his face lit up. "Oh, you mean the CADC event. That's in the Tandy Lecture Hall around the corner off the gallery." He paused for a moment as if contemplating how to direct them, then turned and jogged for the door. "Follow me."

He pushed through the ornate doors into a foyer with vaulted ceilings, his heels clicking on the granite floor and echoing off the walls. Moving fast for a gentlemen of his years, he weaved through several book kiosks before he turned right down a short hallway. He came to an enormous open area lit up by a massive sky light. All four walls were lined with artwork and the center of the room was filled with a flight of stairs leading to the lower level.

The guard pointed to two sets of doors. "That's the Tandy

Lecture Hall. Both sets of doors enter to the back of the room."

Hunter nodded. "Thanks. We'll take it from here."

The three detectives hustled across the expansive open area of the gallery, not slowing down until they stood outside the doors. Hunter could hear a muffled voice emanating through the thick wood.

"Gentlemen, I hope we don't need guns, but check your loads just in case." Hunter pulled out his Glock 17, popped out the magazine, gave it a visual check, slammed it back home and chambered a round. Sanders and Benson followed suit.

"Okay, he has no idea we're onto him." Hunter holstered his weapon and looked at the other two. "Use it to our advantage. We go in as if we're simply here for the event. Quietly through the doors and stand in the back. Billy, you go through the set of doors on the right. Benson, you and I will go in the set on the left. Unless something happens, we just wait for them to finish the program and we quietly escort him out at the end."

"Got it." Billy nodded.

Benson looked a little pale but nodded as well.

They moved down the hall, positioned themselves by the doors and when Hunter pointed, they quietly opened the doors and stepped in.

From the doorway, the crowd and Billy were to his right. The Tandy Lecture Hall is theater-style, with the stage at the bottom of the room and the rows of seats moving up to the back doors. Against the outside walls on each side were steps leading down from the back doors to the foot of the stage. Based on his quick glance, Hunter guessed the room held a little over a hundred people and most of the seats filled.

His stomach twisted when he saw Jessica standing at the podium facing the crowd. To her right, on stage with her sat Dr. Maxwell Arnett. To her immediate left was Lieutenant Carlson, dressed in his formal Police uniform. To his left was Dr. Liam Anderson, the head of John Peter Smith's Emergency Department.

As Jessica spoke, there was a projection screen behind her with Carlson's picture and biography displayed. His introduction.

"Ladies and gentlemen, from the Fort Worth Police Department Narcotics Division, I'm pleased to introduce Lieutenant Trevor Carlson."

Their suspect stood as the crowd politely applauded, and then he stepped to the podium. Jessica sat in her chair to the right of the podium, between Dr. Arnett and Lieutenant Carlson.

"Thank you." Carlson surveyed the audience. "I'm often asked why I chose Narcotics as the focus for my career." He paused, looked down at the podium before continuing. "That's simple. I've seen the impact, the carnage that illegal drugs leave in their wake. While all crimes create a ripple effect for the victims and their families, the waves created by burglary, assault or even murder, are more limited. Drugs, by their very nature, are insidious and addictive. They affect the behavior of the user and therefore impact the lives of their friends, family and coworkers. The money generated from drugs affect the behavior of the sellers and therefore impact the lives of their friends, family and the communities. The devastation lingers longer. It's heartbreaking.

"Watching that devastation on a daily basis takes a toll on the police officers, social workers, healthcare workers and first responders who are called in to clean up the mess. I chose this path so that I could make a difference, so that I could affect both sides of the buying and selling equation, and stop some of those ripples ."

He took a moment and scanned the faces in the front few rows as the crowd applauded.

Hunter took that opportunity to move down a few steps to take two empty seats.

When he stepped down, Carlson noticed the movement from the stage. He looked up, caught Hunter's eye, smiled and nodded. His eyes then panned left to where Benson stood. The reaction was visceral and in that moment, Hunter realized his mistake. Benson was Internal Affairs. Carlson knew it. The only reason IAD would be here would be if they were investigating an officer.

Before Hunter could take a breath, Carlson took a quick step to the right of the podium, grabbed Jessica's arm and pulled her to her feet. In one swift motion, he spun her around and put a gun to her head. There was a split second of echoed gasps, then stunned silence before the crowd erupted into chaos.

A burn swept through Hunter's stomach as he pulled his Glock 17 and took one step down before he became a salmon swimming upstream against the flow of panicked people fleeing up the steps toward the back of the hall. From the corner of his eye, Billy was having the exact same problem on the opposite side.

Time warped to a crawl as he fought his way through the crowd, not caring who he pushed or shoved in his efforts. He yelled for people to move but couldn't hear himself over the screams of the audience.

With every person he elbowed past, he looked up to the stage. Carlson had Jessica from behind in a death grip, his left forearm under her chin and his service revolver held to her temple with his right hand. Her first reaction had naturally been complete shock but now she gripped his forearm with both hands and struggled to pull away.

Dr. Anderson had vacated the stage behind Carlson, but Maxwell Arnett, while ghost-faced, was still on stage standing just in front of Carlson to his right. As Hunter moved in closer, Arnett was directly in front of him.

The seconds stretched into hours in Hunter's mind before most of the crowd had rushed past him and he found himself about three rows up, at stage level.

"That's far enough, Detective." Carlson's voice was ragged and his eyes were wide. Even from fifteen feet away, a sheen of sweat glistened on his face. "Unless you want to be sprayed with brain matter, don't take another step."

Hunter stopped, his heart raced so fast, it was hard to catch his breath. The pulse pounding in his ears made it hard to hear what

Carlson said. He gulped for air and held it to calm himself. His mind flashed to the sight of Brandon Jenkins standing in the headlights in front of him.

He shook away the thought. "Carlson, let her go. She's an innocent. You know, one of the people you've pledged to protect."

"I had no choice. Foster is going to murder my family."

There's the motive. "I hear you Carlson. But before we can help you, you've got to let her go." As Hunter spoke, his focus narrowed in on Carlson and Jessica. Everything else blacked out. He looked down the site of his pistol at a spot in the center of Carlson's forehead.

"You don't understand. I can't just sit around and play by the book anymore. The *rules* are making us lose the fucking war, detective. Our only victories are taking down the occasional foot soldier. It's a waste of time. Ten more pop up behind them for every guy we put away. Guys like Foster always walk away clean. I had to do something."

Hunter's eyes were locked in. "We can talk about the reasons when we get back to the station. But this is over, Carlson. There's only two ways out of here and one of those is in the ME's van. You don't want that."

"You think the other option's better?" Spit flew from his mouth as he screamed at Hunter. "I won't last ten minutes in prison. I'd rather you put a bullet in my brain now."

"We can keep you safe. But not if there's any more blood —"

Carlson rolled his eyes. "*Safe?* That's a joke."

Hunter felt more than saw Billy's movements to his right, and Benson's breathing quickened.

Hunter cut his eyes to the left and saw that Arnett still stood on stage. Just holding a water bottle staring at the pair.

Jessica's eyes widened, the pupils so dilated her brown eyes looked black.

"Stand down, Detective." Carlson barked, and tightened his grip on her neck.

"Not gonna happen." Hunter's vision tightened in on that one inch spot on Carlson's forehead. Everything else in the room faded to gray. There was no sound, just his pulse pumping in his ears.

In a blink, something flew through the air to Hunter's left. Carlson jerked to his right as the water bottle arched toward him. Jessica dropped like a sack of flour. Hunter pulled the trigger.

The hole appeared instantly in the middle of Carlson's forehead with a cloud of red mist behind his head. His already-dead corpse still stood on the attached two legs. His eyes turned distant as Jessica slammed to the stage.

The water bottle hit Carlson in the chest and his body crumpled into a pile behind Jessica.

Time paused...one breath, then two. Hunter blinked. Then everything warped back to full speed.

Sanders climbed the stage in two giant strides. He kicked Carlson's gun away, pulled Jessica off the floor with one arm and carried her to the back of the stage, all the while never taking his aim off Carlson.

Hunter, weapon still raised, slowly made his way up to the stage.

Except for flicking the water bottle, Maxwell Arnett never moved.

Hunter forced a deep breath, more to steady his own heartbeat. "Nice move, Mr. Arnett. Your actions likely saved my niece's life."

"You're welcome, Detective Hunter." A sheen of sweat had formed on his brow. "It's too bad yours didn't do the same for my nephew."

Chapter 57

Detective Bonner James Hopkins, age 29, was finally laid to rest Tuesday morning with a full honors Police funeral. Hunter stood at attention in the morning sun wearing his dress blue uniform with a strip of black tape stretched across the middle of his badge signifying the loss of a fellow officer. It was the first time he'd worn his full uniform in nine years, the last time the Fort Worth Police Department honored an officer killed in the line of duty.

Over a thousand law enforcement officers from multiple agencies across North Texas stood strong together on the manicured lawn of Greenwood Cemetery as Hopkin's flag-draped casket was carried from the hearse to the gravesite. Chills raced through Hunter at the silence, and the gravity. Because most of the late detective's squad mates worked undercover, they couldn't attend the service to be pallbearers. So today, the honor guard consisted of detectives from other squads including Sanders, who represented Homicide. His stoic face and austere stature matched the others around him.

Since Hopkins' Commanding Officer was unavailable for the service, Lieutenant Sprabary stepped in, presenting the crisply folded flag to Hopkin's father, who nodded with tear-filled eyes. Hunter's stomach twisted. Taps blared through the air in the mournful tone all policemen dreaded. Hopkin's father winced with each shot from the seven sharpshooters, three rounds into the morning silence.

As beautiful as it was, Hunter couldn't help but think how inadequate it seemed. Not only had Hopkins sacrificed his life for the department, that life was snuffed out by the one person he should have been able to trust more than anyone else. For that, he got a thousand salutes and his Dad received a folded flag for the mantel.

Though the funeral was over, Hunter's job wasn't. When a Lieutenant from the FWPD admits to three murders and is gunned down by a fellow officer while he's holding a hostage, there were a lot of questions to answer. Above all, the mandatory paperwork had to be filled out. Sure to suffocate their department for weeks.

Hunter and Sanders spent the rest of the day quietly going through Trevor Carlson's life with a fine-tooth comb. Every phone record, bank statement and credit card statement for the past year lay across the conference table. The technology team located two personal email accounts he'd used for hidden communications.

Then came the dubious task of searching his home, car and storage unit. Because Hunter had pulled the trigger, he wouldn't join Sanders and Reyes when they interviewed Carlson's wife.

When he finished the last of the required paperwork, he leaned back from his laptop, stretched and turned to Sanders. "Didn't we promise the gang we'd meet them for a late afternoon drink?"

"It's about that time, isn't it?"

Movement at the conference room door caught Hunter's attention and he looked up to see Benson standing there. Before Benson could speak, Hunter smiled. "You're just in time." Before he continued, he looked at Sanders. "God, I never thought I'd be saying these words to an IAD guy, but..." He turned back to Benson. "Billy and I were about to go have a beer with the team. It's kind of a tradition when we crack a big case. Since you were part of the take down, care to join us?"

Benson smiled like the awkward kid in school who finally got picked for the team. "When and where?"

"Thirty minutes at the new location of the Flying Saucer, where 8.0 used to be."

A half hour later, Hunter and Sanders walked in to find Benson happily chatting up Stacy and Jessica, while Jimmy Reyes watched with a smile. After hello hugs from the ladies, they placed their orders with the waitress.

Once Hunter had a cold beer in his hand, he raised it to the team. "This one was tougher than usual. I couldn't have gotten through it without each of you. Thanks for your usual great job." He looked down and cleared his throat. "And your above and beyond support."

After a few minutes of idle chatter, Jessica looked to Hunter. "So tell me. How does a guy that far up, the expert on the drug problem, become a crazed nut bag who murders three people? Not to mention..." She paused, momentarily gripping her glass tighter and biting her bottom lip.

Stacy reached over and held her hand.

Jessica cleared her throat. "Hold a gun to my head?"

"It was a case of good intentions gone bad. Carlson had watched Foster and his type slip through the system so many times that he just snapped. But moving in on Foster himself only backfired on him."

Billy picked up the narrative. "Foster has stayed one step ahead of law enforcement throughout his career, and somehow got wind that Carlson was gunning for him and turned the tables."

Hunter nodded. "He hit Carlson where he knew he was most vulnerable, his family. Foster kidnapped Carlson's wife and daughter."

"And Carlson was too scared to get help." Benson frowned.

"Wouldn't you be? With a guy like Foster and his reputation?" Sanders added.

"Once Foster had his family, he owned Carlson." Hunter continued. "Foster had decided a while back that living harmoniously with his competitor, Calderon, just wasn't cutting it anymore. He wanted to expand. Unfortunately, about the time he was planning to make his move, the tainted batch of Ecstasy hit the streets."

Sanders nodded. "But like all good entrepreneurs, he took the opportunity to turn limes into margaritas. With Carlson's family under his control, he forced him to clean up the people in his organization who he blamed for the issue."

"Dear God." Stacy's eyes widened. "So Foster forced Carlson to give up Hopkins."

Hunter nodded, and took a drink. "Not just give him up. Take him out.." Hunter frowned. "Hopkins discovered that it was Foster cleaning house, so he went to his boss with that information. Like any good undercover cop would. But Carlson used it as an opportunity to buy his way out from under Foster. He promised to eliminate his own guy, and put Calderon out of business by framing him for the murder, if Foster would let his family go."

Sanders smiled. "The good news is that, apparently when he heard about Carlson's death, Foster cut his family loose."

Hunter frowned. "Yeah, they were unceremoniously left in a downtown parking lot last night. When they managed to find their way home, they were welcomed by a bunch of police officers with the news that her husband was dead. Not just dead, but...well, you know."

Sanders nodded. "We found enough evidence in our follow up to lock Foster away for the rest of his natural life. Chambers and Nix were more than happy to take lead on that. They're rounding up him and his associates as we speak."

Silence speared through the group. Hunter took another sip of his beer, trying to swallow the shit-storm they uncovered with Carlson's death. Stacy broke the silence. "But why Brandon Jenkins? They went out of their way to set him up."

Hunter paused long enough for Sanders to jump in and answer the question. "That was Foster's idea. Brandon had always been an anti-drug crusader in the neighborhood. With the deaths from the tainted Ecstasy, he'd grown even more vocal. Thereby, a danger and threat to Foster's organization. Or at the very least a huge pain in the ass. So he killed two birds with one stone. The original plan was to frame Brandon for both the Tyler and Logan murders."

"Unfortunately, that didn't exactly work out." Hunter blinked several times as he sipped again.

"Which brings us to last evening." Benson raised his glass to Hunter. "That was nice work."

Jessica smiled. "No kidding. I never knew you were that good a shot."

Stacy almost spit her beer out laughing. "Are you serious? He can barely hit the target at the range."

"What?" Jessica's eyes were wide. "You mean you shot a gun inches from my head, and you're not a good shot? Are you crazy?"

Hunter shrugged. "Never a doubt from my vantage point."

Jessica threw a wadded up napkin at him. "Wait until I tell Grandpa."

After the laughter died down, Benson looked at Hunter. "You know we still need to do our after action interview."

Hunter put down his beer a tad hard. "I thought since you saw the whole thing, we could skip that part."

Benson shrugged. "Rules are rules."

Hunter sighed and tipped his glass to the team. "Then it's a good thing I've already got an appointment with Dr. Murray."

Chapter 58

Hunter had begged off of spending the evening with Stacy. As he was climbing into his Explorer, he mumbled something about wanting to be alone. Instead of going directly home, he stopped back by the station and, like he had every day since it happened, he turned on his laptop and pulled up the video file.

He hit play and watched the shaky black and white images move across the screen. Maybe it was because the case was over or because for the first time in two weeks, despite what happened with Carlson, he'd actually slept like a baby the night before, but this time he wasn't watching like a self-flagellating zombie.

After plugging his laptop into the conference room's 50" HD wall-mounted display, he hit play again. His stomach twisted as the almost life-size images popped up on the screen. Brandon Jenkins reached into his pocket, pulled the metal object out, and then jerked back twice from the impact of his rounds. Hunter flinched. Every time.

He hit play no less than ten times. It never got easier to watch, but on the last few plays, he realized that he was staring at the same spot, the gun.

Why am I drawn to that spot? What's wrong?

He reached for his laptop and started poking around with the settings. Not a true techie, he rarely used the video function. After a few tries, he found a way to isolate and enlarge a portion of the image. He zoomed in on Jenkins' hand that held the gun and hit play again. This time in slow motion.

His eyes strained against the blurred image caused by the

magnification, but as he watched the hand come out of the jacket, he stopped breathing.

Oh my God.

The gun was turned all wrong. His hand held the barrel, not the grip. His finger was nowhere near the trigger. There was no way Jenkins could have fired the weapon in that position.

He wasn't trying to shoot me. He was trying to throw it away.

* * * *

The evening was pleasantly warm. The heat of the day receded as the sun dipped behind the expansive trees, changing the sky from blue, to pink, to purple. Hunter had parked by the curb in front of the small house for the last twenty minutes. He hadn't turned off the engine or even moved his hands off the steering wheel.

The air conditioner compressor churned on. He took a deep breath and killed the engine.

His feet trudged up the sidewalk, the doorway further away than he expected, but he finally found himself standing at the door. With one last inhale, he knocked twice. When the door opened, he swallowed."Mrs. Jenkins, I'm Detective Jake Hunter with the Fort Worth Police Department. May I come in?"

Afterword

As I've done with all three of my Jake Hunter novels, I started with a broad theme in mind. I wanted to highlight the impact of drugs in our society. But instead of just telling a story about drug dealers, overdoses and shoot-outs, I wanted to view the topic from different angles. I chose the title *Unseen Carnage* because much of the damage done by drugs is often left invisible by the public.

In early 2014, while I was busy releasing my first two novels, I researched how America's War on Drugs has devastated the inner city minority and lower income communities. I read *The New Jim Crow: Mass Incarceration in the Age of Colorblindness* by Michelle Alexander. I watched the documentary *The House I Live In* directed by Eugene Jureki. And I listened to the Ted Talk on Mass Incarceration by Byron Stevenson.

The topic fascinated me, and while I don't buy into the concept that the War on Drugs is some deep-seated white racist conspiracy to oppress minorities, I do think the statistical evidence proving we've accomplished as much harm as good is overwhelming. That was a viewpoint that I thought could be well served in a fictional format.

However, I didn't just want to tell a single story. After all, whether the results were good or bad, there was a reason that the War on Drugs was launched. I also wanted to address the devastating impact drugs have had on our society as a whole, especially on the indirect victims such as friends and family members.

In October of 2014, while I was still early into the book, a high school friend experienced this tragedy first hand. He and his wife lost their beautiful twenty-one-year-old daughter when she had a fatal reaction from Ecstasy. One day, she was a bright shining star with a wonderful smile and a promising future. The next day, her parents made funeral arrangements for their only child.

While the memorial service was a lovely celebration of her life, the undercurrent of pain was palpable. Watching a parent bury a child is unnatural and yet it happens every day in our country. I hope I never have to witness that again.

Many victims of drugs end up in jail, and many more end up in the cemetery. But there is also a third group of victims. They are all of the people who are on the front lines in the war trying to save others. Doctors, nurses, social workers, fire fighters and especially law enforcement.

Consider when every day, sometimes every minute, you are faced with cleaning up the mess, trying to save a life, or making a split second decision to end a life, the toll taken is unimaginable. Over the last year, we have seen daily headlines where law enforcement has been put in the situation of making that split-second decision. Most of the time, the decisions they make are appropriate. Sometimes they aren't. Either way, the individual who makes the decision will carry that burden for the rest of their life. A very high price to pay.

As with my other novels, I'm not professing a solution. I'm merely pushing for awareness and involvement. Below are a number of organizations whose missions are to help the victims. Please get to know them and be a part of the solution.

The I Know Jessica Project
Facebook: IKnowJessica
Website: www.iknowjessica.com

Foundation for a Drug-Free World
Website: www.drugfreeworld.org

Dallas Area Drug Prevention Partnership
Website: www.drugfreedallas.org

Courageous Hearts
Website: www.courageoushearts.org

Acknowledgements

Each book seems to be a new and very different journey from the last. This was certainly the case with Unseen Carnage.

As I continue to learn the process, I've realized that one of the most elusive aspects is the initial idea itself. In this case, the seed of the idea actually came from a critique of my first book The Victim. The topic of how well intentioned laws can destroy lives was a passion for one of my critique readers, Robyn Short. Once she got a feel for my writing style, she suggested writing a novel about the impact of the War on Drugs. That thought germinated and expanded over time in the background until it took shape. I thank her for that initial seed of an idea.

On the opposite, and even more devastating side of the drug impact spectrum, are the victims of drug use. My friends Alan and Debbie Hunter lost their only daughter Jessica to a fatal reaction to Ecstasy. They have dedicated their lives to raising awareness of the tragic effect of drugs. They graciously allowed me to name a key character in the novel after their daughter. They also read my first draft and provided input on their experience. I thank them for all their help and I pray that their loss will serve to help others.

Although the volume of my questions has reduced somewhat, I continue to leverage the talents of the Greater Fort Worth Writers group. Susan Sheehey has once again played the role of chief critic and editor. I can't imagine a Jake Hunter novel without her input. The rest of the gang have continued to support, encourage and teach by example.

Finally, for the folks who once again, have suffered as I chase the next idea or go to the next writer's meeting. My wife Greta, who is always my first editor and sounding board, now also gets to review cover art, marketing ideas and schedules. My two wonderful daughters, Caitlin and Aubrey, continue to put up with their dad constantly daydreaming about plots and characters and dragging his laptop everywhere. I love you dearly. You are why I'm on this earth.